About

Hebru Young is a UK based author with a passion for storytelling, character development and attention to fine detail.

SUCCESS, OPULENCE AND POWER

Hebru Young

SUCCESS, OPULENCE AND POWER

Vanguard Press

VANGUARD PAPERBACK

A CIP catalogue record for this title is
available from the British Library.

ISBN 978-1-80016-039-2

*Vanguard Press is an imprint of
Pegasus Elliot MacKenzie Publishers Ltd.*
www.pegasuspublishers.com

First Published in 2021

**Vanguard Press
Sheraton House Castle Park
Cambridge England**

Printed & Bound in Great Britain

Dedication

First and foremost, I thank God.

Secondly, I would like to dedicate this to my wife, my children and the extended family… and to Margie. This book wouldn't have seen the light of day without your support.

Love you all.

This is a work of fiction. The characters, names, dialogue, and situations have been fictitiously created by the author for the sole purpose of entertainment. A mix of actual and fictional locations have been used in the book to provide a feel of authenticity. Any similarities to people, alive or dead, and all events and dialogue are coincidental. All product branding was created by the author and the copyright for these brands belong to the author.

Chapter 1

Meet Eddie Dominguez
Where: The Nations High Court, The United Nations of Europe and Americas — Washington, DC
When: 1105 hours, Tuesday, October 1, 2041
Currency: UNEA credits

"Calling docket number 1177896, *United Nations of Europe and Americas v. Edward R. Dominguez*. All rise for the presiding Nations High Judge Thomas H. Davidson."

Now just how did I end up here? Someone chirped. Snitches, they're the scum of the earth. The enforcers, politicians, lawyers, judges—all shady, just like me. What makes them think they have the right to sit there and judge me?

In the courtroom, I could see the court officials through the Vexa True D-i installed in my cell. The Vexa True D-i is a super-advanced hologram projector. It was rigged with some sort of synthetic mist emitter, true-definition imagery or True D-i as it is often referred to. It also had a satellite receiver. The mist from the emitter captured the light that was project by the Vexa True D-i. The mist would contort and respond to the light and then form the required imagery. This meant that you didn't need a solid background. The synthetic mist acted as a flexible background, so to speak. With this, I could see everyone in the court and they could see me.

With the advance capabilities of the True D-i, we were seeing flat screen TVs gradually becoming a thing of the past.

As consumers, we had reached a point where super-fast networks were a must. So naturally, network providers had to ramp up their innovation. The end result was advance satellite micro-receivers that were included in most portable gadgets. The tiny receivers are powerful enough to receive signals from lower levels of multistory buildings. Vexas could produce high-quality 3-D images over a fast network making it difficult to differentiate the real from the fake. Three years ago, this kind of technology was only available to the Nations Law Enforcing Unit (NLEU). Enforcers had been using them for secure communications and interrogations. But now Vexas were being used everywhere—universities, movie theatres, you name it.

We prisoners were no longer allowed in the courtroom; it was too risky. One of the reasons for the security measure was to ensure that no attempts were made to spring prisoners out. The courts had to put this rule in place after the Carlsdale incident. During a court hearing in 2012, the head of the Carlsdale crime family was sprung out of court by his nineteen heavily armed goons. This was the event that triggered the immediate beefing up of security protocols.

With access to all this advanced technology, not only did remote trials become possible, they eventually became standard practice for trials of major crimes. There was another reason why they kept us out of the courtroom. Members of the judicial system weren't exactly fond of the idea of being in close proximity to alleged criminals. They had developed a certain level of repulsion for people like me, people they felt didn't emanate a particular level of social class. The way that they saw it, people like me stank up the courtroom and just didn't belong in there. Boy, were they all hypocrites?

During court proceedings, we had to remain in our cells and were patched in via the satellite network connection. My image was transmitted from the cell and then projected right next to my defence attorney. The digital replica of the courtroom and everyone in it was projected to my cell. I could see and hear everything that was going on like I was actually there. A chair was placed in Vexa-Position, the specific position in my cell for when the cell's Vexa powered on and the trial commenced.

It was all really impressive technology, but I wasn't a huge fan. When it comes to tech, I'm quite old-school—I preferred legacy stuff. A lot of the new tech is based on technologies that made it far too easy for the government to keep tabs on society—much easier than it used to be. With the push of a button, a significant amount of personal information could be made available to anyone with the appropriate level of clearance: your blood type; the ingredients used in baking a cake; the fact that the cake is for your four-year-old's birthday; the kind of movies you watch; a digital model of your exact DNA structure. All this information was available to the government.

I wasn't comfortable with this level of surveillance, hence my preference for legacy technology. Old-school tech was virtually untraceable and had a sort of vintage and classy feel to it. Old-school communication devices run on obsolete retired networks that were now privately operated by the crime syndicates that required them. The high demand for such technology made it expensive, illegal, and hard to come by. My organization owned a number of these old devices as well as the networks that they were connected to. We used the old tech to exchange dialogue or data that we didn't want to fall into the wrong hands.

Judge Davidson was in the third year of his term as high judge; he had attended the University of Pennsylvania and graduated law school in 2022, shortly before the UNEA merger. In those days, Penn Law offered top-notch legal training that other leading law schools didn't. Shortly after finishing law school, Davidson worked in the US attorney's office as an assistant prosecutor and then worked his way up to US prosecutor. This meant that he had jurisdiction in the

United States only.

After seven years in the US attorney's office, he became a US judge in September of 2029, and by 2038 he was sworn into the NHC as Nation's high judge. My lawyer had done his research and yeah, this guy was cut from different cloth. One could tell by the way he carried himself. Nonetheless, he was still shady—one doesn't make it up the ranks in the short space of time he did without bending the rules or stepping on a few toes along the way. There had been rumours of bribes, and although no one could prove this or even had the guts to do so, the truth was obvious. Aside from his salary, there were all the other sources of income, the main one being regular dividends from Zhang Heng stocks. Zhang Heng Motor Industries was responsible for all the automobiles that were exported out of the United Orient Nations.

The judge also owned holiday homes across the African Union (AU) as well as log cabins in the Independent Swiss Territory (IST). These exclusive, luxurious properties were rented out to VIPs. I stayed at one of his log cabins during my visit to the IST. At the time, I didn't think they were anything to write home about.

It was difficult to ascertain all the sources of Davidson's wealth, and the fact that he was from a wealthy family made it even more difficult to find the cracks in his finances.

The judge was quite ambitious; he was planning on

running for office as a member of the UNEA Council. This office ran parallel to the executive office, the office of the UNEA president. His plan was to climb up another level of his already illustrious career ladder, using my trial to boost his political popularity and media presence. I am the number one bad guy in the Nations, and my case is high profile, perhaps one of the highest that the Nations court had seen in a while. My trial is the best way to gain the global exposure he needs for his election.

After the bailiff announced his entrance, his honour Judge Davidson took his seat and gave me a look of disgust. One would think that I ran away with his wife, sent his three kids to boarding school, and had his dog put down. This guy did not like me. He glances down at his interactive desk and taps in the secure code that gives him access to a digital file containing my case documents. After flicking through a few of the digi-docs, his Honour looks up at me—again with disgust—before proceeding to read the charges.

"Edward Dominguez, you have been charged with cyber-crimes that include record tampering, identity cultivation, and online racketeering. You have also been charged with distribution of narcotics, distribution of military-grade firearms, kidnapping, conspiracy to assassinate a government official, and murder in the first degree. How do you plead to these charges?" the good old judge asks in what he probably feels is his sternest and most intimidating voice. Hell yeah, I pleaded not guilty. I have a ten-thousand-UNEA-credit-per-hour lawyer who is more than capable of handling everything that the prosecution team was planning to dish out. The way I see it though, I will be lucky if I didn't do at least twenty years in prison for all this. It seemed like they had been building cases against me for a while, and now this bunch of shadies wanted to lock me up for life and throw away the key. The best outcome here is maybe fifteen years—there was no way I was going to beat all these charges.

Persuading any of the jury members to deliver a not-guilty vote was out of the question—the NHC had them on twenty-four-hour lockdown. All twelve jury members were assigned a team of enforcers for security for the duration of the trial. Enforcers weren't like the cops I knew when I was coming up. Policing had evolved significantly since the Great Merger. It wasn't officially called that, but people often referred to the unification of Europe, the United Kingdom, Canada, the United States, and all of South America as the Great Merger. After the Brexit catastrophe in 2016, England, Scotland, Wales, and Northern Ireland had no choice but to be a part of the new union.

The merger took place in December 2022, and it was decided at that point that there was to be a single law enforcement agency for the UNEA. Enforcers were made up of cross-trained military guys from all parts of the collective nations. Normal cops had to get army, navy, and air force training. Either that or retire. To make matters even more complicated, enforcers within the higher ranks had to obtain a degree in international law. A lot of the older cops just didn't make the cut; it was easier to cross-train younger cadets or people who were already enlisted in the military. So, the UNEA for the most part ended up with soldiers enforcing the law and policing the streets. To ensure that these guys were almost incorruptible, the government made sure that they were very well paid.

Enforcers were also assigned to all the witnesses that were going to testify in my case, so this made it impossible for my team to get close to any of them. All this, plus the fact that I had found a new best friend in Judge Davidson, meant that this case was not going to be a walk in the park. Not to mention all the evidence that will be presented by the prosecution. The odds of beating the charges weren't in my favour, not in the slightest.

I knew that I was doomed—the charges the good judge had just read out were monumental. Yes, I knew this, but it didn't stop me from getting up out of my not-so-comfy cell chair and replying with confidence, "Not guilty, Your Honour."

I am Eddie Dominguez, friends call me Dom. To everyone else, I am Soap.

Chapter 2

Puerto Plata
Where: Puerto Plata
When: 1720 hours, Thursday, March 9, 1995
Currency: Dominican peso

Guillermo owned a small restaurant in the city of Puerto Plata, the ninth largest city in the Dominican Republic. He was married to Anna, and they had a daughter named Isabel. He and his family lived a very humble life, one that was far from that which he envisioned as a youth. He grew up in a poor family and had no choice but to work hard since childhood. His father was a fisherman who supplied an assortment of seafood to the local restaurants. Guillermo learned the fishing trade from his father, and he became very good at it. It was his years of fishing experience that allowed him to make the natural transition from fisherman to restaurant owner.

Guillermo woke up every morning and drove to the north coast, towing his sixteen-foot Otis Sealiner on the back of his pickup truck. The Sealiner was an old 1985 model. It wasn't the prettiest thing, but the old boat got the job done. He would fish for three hours, between 5 a.m. and 8 a.m., pulling in a variety of fish, lobster, shrimp, and crabs. When he didn't have enough for the day, he would stock up from the local market. Eventually, he didn't have to do the fishing any more. He trained his staff to do the task, showing them the best techniques, and told them when it was best to set out to sea. Since he no longer had to go out to sea, all he had to do was supervise the daily operations at the restaurant.

Guillermo really wasn't happy with his current standard of living. He always dreamt of being wealthy but didn't know how to accomplish this. Proceeds from the restaurant only generated enough money to pay his staff and just about enough to make sure that the restaurant had an adequate number of supplies. After deducting business expenses, there was barely enough money left for him and his family to live on. The economy in Puerto Plata was partly based on tourism and agriculture. However, the bulk of the economy was centred around export. The economic stability of the region relied heavily on Puerto Plata's seaport, and the rich people in the region had direct involvement in all aspects of port activities.

Puerto Plata was not exempt from the corruption that plagued similar cities around the world. The majority of its government officials earned their living collecting bribes and misappropriating government funds. Most of the illegitimate funds were derived from siphoning tax proceeds from port operations. The proceeds were then channelled into personal investments. Eventually, all the embezzled money was transferred into personal offshore accounts where they were virtually untraceable. Guillermo was willing to do whatever it took to become wealthy, but he didn't have the connections that would give him the necessary access to Puerto Plata's club for the elite.

Guillermo did, however, have a friend that happened to be a low-ranking officer of the port authority. The officer's job involved inspecting cargo ships that arrived from overseas. His other tasks included performing administrative duties. His port officer friend would frequent the restaurant for Guillermo's acclaimed asopao de camarones, which was a tasty shrimp and rice pottage. One evening, the officer made his usual stop at the restaurant and headed to the spot where Guillermo always sat. It was in a corner towards the back of the restaurant, near the kitchen entrance. They shook hands, exchanged pleasantries, and then sat down on handcrafted, red-cushioned, wooden chairs. The square table was covered with a red-and-white plaid tablecloth with a white lace trim.

Guillermo called the waiter over and requested an ice-cold American-brewed Cerveza Americana for the officer. The officer loved American beer. Guillermo, on the other hand, ordered an El Toro Mexicano for himself—he preferred Mexican beer. They both drank and talked as they waited for the officer's pottage. Whenever he visited the restaurant, the officer ordered the same meal, so no one ever asked what to serve him. The officer praised Guillermo for his hospitality.

"My friend, you are a good man. I have known you for a long time now, I come here almost every day, and you hardly let me pay for anything," said the officer.

"It's no big deal—what are friends for?" Guillermo replied.

Owning a restaurant in Puerto Plata was not an easy feat. The food inspectors, the tax officers, and the port authority regularly visited restaurants in the surrounding area for food inspection, auditing of financial records, and validation of licenses. Restaurant owners who supplied their own fish had to pay a seafood distribution license validation fee on a regular basis. This was the most expensive fee for a self-supplying seafood restaurant, since validation checks were carried out monthly.

The inspectors and officers were only after one thing: bribes. The license fees would be waived once the supplier or restaurant owner paid the bribe. These bribes were paid in cash, and the cash went straight into the officers' pockets. Once the bribes had been paid, the licenses would be endorsed with a cheap rubber stamp. Guillermo knew that by feeding his port officer friend on the house, he would never have to worry about the validation fees. It was also less expensive than constantly having to pay the bribes.

As far as Guillermo was concerned, this wasn't a friendship. He didn't enjoy the officer's company, he saw the whole thing as a business arrangement. The officer, on the other hand, was an opportunist who enjoyed the free food and occasional booze. He was fully aware that Guillermo equally benefited from their arrangement. The officer knew that Guillermo would be able to avoid paying the bribes by simply dropping the officer's name when other port officials showed up. In fact, most officers were aware of the arrangement, so they didn't bother doing the checks at Guillermo's place. This was standard practice in the region. All the officers frequented the shops, butcheries, and markets for regular checks. Establishments that had desirable commodities would offer these instead of the bribes, if the officers felt that it was a suitable option.

The waiter finally walked over with tray in hand, and Guillermo shouted at him. "What took so long, can you not see that my good friend is hungry, yet you keep him waiting?" The restaurant employees knew that Guillermo was only putting on a show for the officer, so they didn't take it personal.

"Why don't you join me?" The officer invited Guillermo to partake in the meal; this was customary in the region.

Guillermo replied, "I'm okay, thank you. I already had some food, all I need now is my El Toro and my cashews." While the men ate and drank the officer talked about his job and all the pressures that came with it, and Guillermo listened attentively. People that frequented the restaurant always had something to talk about. Sometimes the information that he gained from conversations was useful and other times, not so much. Guillermo's mindset was to use vital information for personal gain but disregard anything that was unimportant.

By the time the officer had finished his shrimp and rice pottage, Guillermo could tell that he was ready for another Cerveza, so he beckoned the waiter over by signalling with a drinking gesture. The officer was in more of a talking mood than usual on that day, and he started talking about his plans for the future.

"Guillermo, one isn't getting younger, and time waits for no one. This job of mine pays, but it doesn't pay enough, if you know what I mean." Guillermo acknowledged this with a nod.

The waiter arrived again with tray in hand and set the Cerveza in front of the officer. The officer took a gulp, put the bottle down, and continued. "You see my friend, given my age, at this point in my career I can only be promoted one, maybe two more times, and even at that point I still won't become a senior officer. By the time I retire I won't have enough money to provide a decent future for my children. You see, in the port authority, only the senior officers make the big money."

Again, being an attentive listener, Guillermo merely responded with a nod. The officer paused and took another gulp from the cold bottle that had formed some condensation due to the hot Dominican weather. The officer put the drink back down and glanced through the restaurant window. With the view from the restaurant, he could see the sun was about to set and people were relaxing and having a good time. There was music playing, people sat on benches drinking, chatting, and singing. This was what the atmosphere was like every evening in that part of Puerto Plata.

It had become apparent that the conversation was about to get serious as the officer turned his head back towards Guillermo. He took another gulp from the almost empty bottle. "My friend," the officer leaned forward and said in a low voice, almost whispering, "I need to make moves; I am moving to America."

Guillermo leaned forward and mimicked the officer's tone, "For people like you and me, it is impossible to get visas to America."

The officer stared at Guillermo with a mischievous look on his face, as though he knew the world's biggest secret, and no one else knew about it. He sipped what was left of the Cerveza, and Guillermo signalled the waiter to bring over another bottle.

The officer pretended to protest, "Guillermo, this is too much. The food, the drinks, please allow me to give you some money for this."

Guillermo insisted, "For you, it's on the house—your money is no good here."

Just as the waiter arrived with the third bottle of Cerveza, the officer continued the conversation. "In my line of work, we meet all kinds of people: some good, some bad, some useful, some useless. I met a useful person a while back, and this person will be key in helping me make my moves." The officer told Guillermo about a special cargo ship that often docked at the port. This ship's main purpose was to transport goods to and from Miami. The officer's whisper got even quieter as he explained how the ship was used to illegally transport people from Puerto Plata to Miami.

Information about the ship's illegal activities was available to the officer, because he was friends with a member of the ship's crew, a man named Jean-Luc Pierre. This cargo ship was not under the officer's jurisdiction, so Jean-Luc had to introduce the officer to other port officers, crew members, and the ship's captain. Following the introduction, the officer referred trusted clients on a regular basis. These clients were people that were interested in migrating to America and had enough money to do so. In return for the people the officer brought in, Jean-Luc's crew would pay him a finder's fee.

This operation was allowed to continue because there was so much corruption in government. The high-ranking officials were too busy misappropriating government funds to be concerned with such trivial matters. Some were even awarded a share of the proceeds from the dodgy venture. A proportion of the money collected from the illegal travellers would be used to bribe port officials in America. For a set fee, the travellers were allowed to enter the United States covertly. This ship and others like it were responsible for roughly three percent of the illegal immigrants residing in the United States. With such a vast number of illegal migrants, one could conclude that the cargo ship was pulling in millions of dollars annually.

"So you see, my friend, once I have enough money, the plan is to use the ship's travel service to move my entire family to America. I tell you this only because you're a friend."

Guillermo leaned forward. "My good friend, I hope that you are successful with the moves that you intend on making."

The officer wasn't telling Guillermo all this because they were friends; he told him in case there was a chance that Guillermo might be able to bring in potential travellers. The officer downed the rest of his beer, got up, and shook Guillermo's hand. "Guillermo, you are too good to me. My regards to your family, and I will see you soon." Guillermo smiled, got up from his chair, and they both headed towards the exit.

Chapter 3

The Defence Team
Where: DC Corrections Division, The United Nations of Europe and Americas — Washington, DC
When: 1135 hours, Tuesday, October 1, 2041
Currency: UNEA credits

Getting His Honour to grant bail was going to be close to impossible, but that didn't stop my lawyer from asking.

"Your Honour, Edward Dominguez is a respectable member of society. He is a family man and has been a law-abiding citizen his entire life. Mr. Dominguez owns several reputable businesses across the Nations, and these businesses provide a source of income to many. He is known to support a number of charities; he has never been connected to illegal activities; and he has never been charged with, or convicted of, any crimes. Your Honour, these outrageous charges have caused a significant amount of damage to my client's image and reputation. This debacle has had a significant impact on his family life, destabilizing what was once a happy home. We plead with Your Honour that my client be allowed to be with his family during these trying times.

We request my client be granted bail, Your Honour," my lawyer pleaded.

My lawyer sounded convincing. I was even starting to believe that I was a saint, and that this whole thing was a big misunderstanding. The prosecution, however, wanted to draw blood. You could see it in their eyes—they weren't having any of it. The lead prosecutor jumped out of his seat to object.

"Your Honour, we have evidence that proves the defendant has access to a substantial amount of offshore funds. He also owns a number of real estate investments outside of the UNEA. For these reasons, we believe that he is a flight risk. We request that the court deny bail due to the serious nature of the crimes with which the defendant has been charged, Your Honour."

My lawyer was really good but, considering the damning argument that the prosecution had just made, it now seemed they were going to give him a run for his money.

Joseph Abrams was sharp. I put him on retainer about eighteen years ago, but before throwing all that money his way, I did a bit of research on him. This guy finished law school at the top of his class at the age of twenty-five and passed the bar at twenty-six. He initially worked for a couple of law firms but ended up setting up his own firm shortly after I put him on retainer. His previous firms had no intention of making Joe partner, so naturally, he decided to leave. He acquired a number of clients during his tenure at these firms, clients that he didn't hesitate to take with him when he left.

Members of the Assembly also used Joe's services, which guaranteed him all the clients he needed to pay for the costs associated with running his firm and still have a surplus. Over time, Joe and I became close friends; he also became friends with members of the Assembly. He would bring his family over for Sunday lunch; his wife and my wife developed a good friendship and kept in touch with each other.

Joe's co-counsel was an intern fresh out of law school, a kid named Fredric Johnson. This kid was bright, and Joe saw a lot of himself in the young intern. He believed that with good mentoring the youngster would turn out to be a fine lawyer; he was grooming the kid with the intention of making him a partner. Of course, Fredric would have to work hard and pay his dues.

"Objection, Your Honour," Joe barked. "As stated previously, my client owns several businesses within the UNEA; jumping bail and fleeing the UNEA would be of no benefit to him. There would be severe disruption to the services of several establishments that rely on his day-to-day involvement and decision making. Moreover, the idea of fleeing would be preposterous, considering that my client has worked hard to establish a good life for himself and his family right here in the UNEA. Not only that, but fleeing the UNEA would send the wrong message to his clients and business partners. He would appear guilty, and people would cease to do business with him. Your Honour, jumping bail would make no sense at all, and it just isn't in my client's best interest."

"Mr. Abrams, there is no need to be overly dramatic. You do realize this is only the arraignment, right?" replied the judge.

"Apologies, Your Honour, I admit that maybe I'm being a bit overdramatic at this point of the proceedings. I'm simply concerned about the prosecution's extreme hostility in regards to the bail request. At the end of the day, it is a man's life we are talking about here, and I want him to be treated fairly, in line with the provisions of the law," Joe responded.

"We will have a thirty-minute recess, after which I will give my decision on the issue of bail. Court is now in recess," said the judge.

I didn't expect this; the judge actually needed time to think about whether or not to grant bail. Perhaps Joe knew what he was doing all along, perhaps he had his strategy planned out before the arraignment. Prior to the hearing, he told me that not all hope was lost, and that we might get lucky with bail. I couldn't see how this had happened, considering how fierce the prosecution was.

The Vexa True D-i was powered down by one of the prison enforcers. Speaking through the intercom, the enforcer said it was okay for me to disengage from my Vexa positioning. Shortly after this, I had an incoming call on the prison's comms device. The ID read *Joseph Abrams*.

"What's up, Joe?"

"Dom, how are you holding up?"

"Not bad. You didn't do too bad in there, you know. The prosecution hates you as much as they do me. Also, you forced the good judge to have to think about bail—nice work!"

"Ha-ha, that's why you pay me the big bucks, good friend. Look Dom, we are not going down without a fight. I am going to pour my all into this trial."

"Do I need to worry about anyone one else listening to our conversation over this comms line?"

"Nope, not at all—the calls aren't recorded. That would be highly unconstitutional, the courts would be subject to all kinds of inquisitions, and a lot of old cases would get thrown out. So, even if they were listening, our conversation would be inadmissible evidence."

"Good—Alex and Chris. How far have they gotten gathering jury info?"

"Nothing at this point. I'm afraid we don't even know who these people are, and the court has them under watch twenty-four-seven. I'll be honest with you, Dom, messing with the jury is not an option here."

"What then?"

"Well, we will have to wait until the prosecution presents its evidence. Then we will know what we are up against and deal with it accordingly. Once I have all the information, I will be in a position to start preparing my argument."

"Okay."

"We just have to pray that bail is granted. This will give you an opportunity to meet with people, make the necessary plans, move some money around... You know, the opportunity to sort out all the things that need sorting out."

"Okay."

"I better start making my way back to the courtroom, we'll talk later. Hang in there, Dom."

"Thanks, speak to you soon, Joe."

Joe was shrewd, but I could tell the case seemed to have him on edge a bit. Not sure if this was because of genuine friendship and loyalty, or if it was the possibility of his practice suffering a financial blow if I ended up spending the rest of my life in prison. Joe has done exceptionally well being on my payroll, and me behind bars wouldn't be in his best interest.

I was worried about how things would transpire. I wasn't sure how my family would cope if I had to do time. I wasn't sure what would happen to the empire I had worked so hard to build. I had plausible reasons to completely lose my cool, but somehow, I was able to keep my nerves under control.

The buzzer sounded, alerting me that the Vexa was about to start transmitting—court recess was almost over. I sat back down in the Vexa chair. A few minutes later, the judge emerged from the side door that led to his chambers, and again everyone was asked to rise.

As the judge approached his desk, I couldn't tell what was going to happen next, gauging by the look on his face alone. He looked as angry as he did before he left the room. After the good judge sat down, everyone else in the courtroom sat down as well. I also sat back down on my jailhouse throne. There was what felt like a million minutes of silence, and the tension was palpable. No one knew what the judge's decision was going to be. Joe needed me out on bail, as this would make the trial a lot easier to manage. We would be able to talk more freely in private, and I would be able to attend meetings with key individuals to smooth things over and to make sure that business would continue to run efficiently.

The prosecution, on the other hand, wanted me to remain in custody for the duration of the trial for those same reasons. They didn't want me to salvage any of my business relations. Denying me bail would also give them an upper hand in that I would not be able to make public appearances and influence members of the community to my advantage.

Even though they had a solid case, the prosecutors knew that my being restricted to the confines of prison made their jobs a whole lot easier.

The judge finally decided to start speaking again. "I have listened to the prosecution and the defence; both sides have made compelling arguments regarding bail. Although this case is being referred to by the media as a high-profile case, not a single decision in my court will be made as a result of classifications made by the press or anyone else. We are members of a respectable judicial system, and we have to act in a responsible and professional manner. For this reason, I will do everything within my power to ensure that justice is what takes precedence during these proceedings, from start to finish. After careful deliberation, I have decided that, because Mr. Dominguez has never been convicted of any crimes and fleeing the UNEA realistically would not be in his best interest, bail will be granted."

"But Your Honour!" the lead prosecutor responded in shock.

"I have made my decision. Bail is set at thirty million credits. Mr. Dominguez, you are not to step foot outside of the UNEA. A tracking bracelet will be placed on your wrist, which should not be tampered with or removed. These are the terms of your bail. Any violation of these terms nullifies your bail, you will be fined five million credits, and you will be returned to jail. Court adjourned," the judge concluded.

I stood up and replied, "Thank you, Your Honour." I couldn't believe what I had just heard. I panned over to Joe, and he looked almost as shocked as I did. I'm sure that deep inside he must have had his doubts about getting bail. The look on the prosecutors' faces almost brought a grin to mine, but I kept my cool.

Chapter 4

I Want In
Where: Puerto Plata
When: 1725 hours, Friday, April 14, 1995
Currency: Dominican peso

Guillermo couldn't stop thinking about his conversation with the officer—migrating to America with his family would mean better opportunities. He had heard stories about people who travelled to America and made a decent life for themselves. He believed that the Americans had it way too easy. As far as he was concerned, they had life handed to them on a platter, and they didn't know how to make the best of the opportunities available to them. He also believed, that, if given the opportunity to go to America, he would become wealthy in a matter of years. With the information he received from the officer, he was going to find a way to get himself and his family to America, one way or another. He didn't have much information about the logistics of the special cargo ship, but he was already devising a plan to come up with the travel fare. It had been weeks since his discussion with the officer, and though the officer had visited the restaurant frequently, Guillermo hadn't mentioned his travel interest.

El Pez Grande restaurant had a very busy day serving lunch and drinks to local workers. El Pez Grande was the name of Guillermo's restaurant. It was the bistro of choice for people in the area. Busy days kept Guillermo in a good mood; busy days meant more money in the cash register. It was Friday and the restaurant had more than enough supplies of seafood, drinks, and snacks. He increased the restaurant's supply in preparation for the weekend, for it was then that the restaurant served the highest number of customers.

Most of the men in Puerto Plata spent their Friday and Saturday evenings at the local restaurants eating and drinking, but mostly drinking. The weekend was when people had the time to relax and enjoy the ambience of the local eateries. It wasn't exactly five-star, but El Pez Grande was one of the best restaurants in the area. It served fresh seafood and played the best music, and the customers loved it.

Most of the customers who frequented the restaurant on weekends came to meet young ladies. A number of them were married men with children. Some of the girls who turned up at the weekend were university graduates who were just out having a nice time. The guys didn't seem to have a problem with spending their hard-earned cash on entertaining these young women. Money that could have been put towards feeding their families, towards school and clothes for their children.

El Pez Grande was a decent-sized restaurant and could seat at least forty customers. There were times when extra tables and chairs had to be set up outside the restaurant, but this was only during the busiest nights when the restaurant was at full capacity. Guillermo would request the restaurant lights to be dimmed around eight o'clock, and the music came on around the same time. Eight o'clock was the time that most customers finished their main course. It was around this time they all ordered beers, wines, and spirits. Some would order nuts and pretzels to go with their drinks.

Guillermo had a backup generator that would run whenever there was a power outage. The generator would come on automatically during a power cut to prevent interruptions to the music and ceiling fans. Power cuts were a regular occurrence due to the city's unstable electricity infrastructure.

At about 5:25 that afternoon, Guillermo's officer friend waltzed into the restaurant in the manner that he usually did. Anyone that didn't know better would think he owned the place. "Guillermo, my friend!" the officer bellowed with much excitement.

"Hello!" Guillermo responded with a matching tone. The officer seemed to be in a good mood. They both walked to the back to sit down in their usual spot, and the waiter brought drinks.

"So, my good friend, you seem to be in a very good mood. I take it today has been a good day?" Guillermo said to the officer.

"Yes, it has, it has been a rewarding day indeed. Business has been a bit slow lately, but today I was able to complete a travel deal" the officer responded.

"A travel deal?" Guillermo asked.

It was obvious the officer had found another travelling customer for the cargo ship, and chances were, he had already collected his finder's fee.

"Yes, a travel deal," the officer responded. "Remember I spoke to you about the special cargo ship?" the officer said.

"Ah yes, but of course. It's a good thing that you brought this up. I have a few questions about it, but not to worry, we will get into that after you've had your meal," Guillermo insisted.

"Oh, so you have questions for me, eh?" the officer asked with a smirk on his face.

Guillermo had caught the officer's attention. His mind was already clocking at full speed, trying to work out what Guillermo was thinking. He was hoping that this meant even more money in his pockets.

"So, like I was saying, I completed a deal today. I introduced a man and his wife to the ship's crew. That ship left harbour this morning, and I made two hundred dollars from the deal," exclaimed the officer.

Two hundred dollars wasn't a great deal of money. However, when you took the exchange rate into account, it worked out as seven thousand Dominican pesos. This amount of money would go a long way in the Dominican Republic.

"Wow, you did really well today then," Guillermo responded.

"Yes, I did. It's not really a steady income, because most of the people that are trying to travel to America can't afford it right away and generally have to save towards it. So, as you can imagine, it takes time for me to get the money. This then means that there will be times when business will be slow for me," explained the officer.

"Well, here's to a good day of business." Guillermo lifted his bottle of El Toro Mexicano and they both clinked bottles. As they put their bottles back down, the officer insisted on paying for their drinks.

"It has been a successful day for me, Guillermo. You have to let me buy you a drink today," said the officer.

"As I always say to you, your money is no good here," Guillermo responded.

"Today I insist, it will make me happy if you allow me to do this," insisted the officer.

The officer didn't mind paying for the drinks. After all, there was a good chance that Guillermo was about to bring some business his way. So, to him paying for the drinks would be a small investment. The waiter made his way back with the officer's meal on a tray.

"Wow, that was quick," the officer said with surprise.

"My good friend, in this restaurant my guys know

that we have to provide the best service. Especially for you," said Guillermo.

The pottage was steaming hot, so the officer had to let it cool down while they continued talking. It was quite a hot day, hotter than usual. The two sat directly under an old-fashioned ceiling fan. Guillermo could see that the officer had been sweating through his uniform, so he stood up, reached for the fan switch, and cranked it up a notch.

"That's much better, isn't it?" Guillermo asked.

"That's perfect. All the hustle and bustle under the hot Dominican sun really has me sweating today," the officer responded.

"Yeah, I'll be glad when the sun goes down and everything cools down a bit," said Guillermo.

"So how are Anna and Isabel doing, all is well with them I suppose?" asked the officer.

"Anna is doing well. She is the glue that holds the family together; she is always in church praying for the family. Little Isabel is doing well, she has started play school now, and she is so bright," Guillermo responded proudly.

"Like her father, eh?" the officer said.

The officer did not want to beat around the bush any longer.

"So Guillermo, what's on your mind?" the officer asked.

"You haven't even had your meal yet—it can wait," Guillermo said.

"No, it's fine, please carry on," the officer insisted.

"Very well then. How much would it cost if someone was interested in travelling to America on the magic ship?" Guillermo asked.

"It costs $3,800, and I can make the necessary arrangements as soon as the person is ready," the officer replied, trying not to sound too excited.

"Well, my friend, that person is me. You have inspired me with your plans to move to America, and I wouldn't mind the opportunity of moving my family there as well. As you know, the opportunities here in Puerto Plata are limited, and like you, I am willing to do whatever is best for my family," Guillermo said.

This news really had the officer's mind racing. If Guillermo could come up with the money, it would mean a three-hundred-dollar commission. This would get the officer closer to achieving his own personal travel goals.

"Guillermo, you have no idea how happy this makes me. You and I share the same dream—this is big news. Waiter, more beers please!" the officer shouts.

The officer and Guillermo spent the rest of the evening discussing plans for the trip. They talked about the education, career, and business opportunities in America and how their families would benefit from them.

On any other Friday, Guillermo would not leave the restaurant until closing time, usually around 1 a.m. However, today was different. Shortly after his conversation with the officer, he left the restaurant. He jumped in his truck and headed home. He lived on the outskirts of Puerto Plata where some of the other business owners lived. It was not the most prestigious neighbourhood, but it was clean and safe enough for his family. When he got home, he found that his wife was still awake, watching TV in the living room.

"Oh, hello, Anna. I didn't expect you to still be awake," Guillermo says with a smile.

"I didn't expect you home so early. Is everything okay, do you want something to eat?" Anna responded.

"No thank you, I had some food at the restaurant earlier," Guillermo said.

Anna was in her early thirties, just a few years younger than Guillermo. From time to time, she helped out at the restaurant, but her main focus was looking after Isabel and making sure that the house affairs were in order. Anna was raised in a Catholic family, so she had high moral values. She was soft spoken and had a great deal of respect and admiration for her husband. She held firmly to the belief that Guillermo was a good man, and she trusted that he had the family's best interest at heart. Guillermo also respected his wife and would do whatever it took to make sure that she was happy.

"Anna, my love, we have to talk."

"What's wrong, Guillermo?"

"Oh no, nothing is wrong. It's just something that I have been thinking about for a while now. I didn't say anything before, because I didn't have all the information. I had to think things over before speaking to you about it," Guillermo responded.

"Oh, I see. So, what is it?" Anna asked.

"So, what do you think about the three of us moving to America?" Guillermo said.

"America?! I think moving to America is a dream, almost impossible considering we are not in a position to get travel visas," Anna responded sceptically.

"What if I told you that I know a way to make that dream come true?" Guillermo said.

"Okay, Guillermo, I need to prepare myself for this. I am going to the kitchen to make myself a drink. Would you like one as well?"

"No, I'm okay, thanks," Guillermo responded with a smile.

Anna was a bit of a tea connoisseur, but because they lived in such a hot country, Guillermo couldn't understand why she loved drinking it so much. She would make the tea from local herbs and add a bit of lemon and honey. Guillermo would try some from time to time, but he didn't like it as much as she did. Anna came back to the living room with a smile on her face, turned off the TV, and perched on the old, dark-green sofa next to her husband.

"I left some tea in the tea pot, just in case you change your mind," Anna said.

"Why do you have that grin on your face?" Guillermo asked.

"I'm looking forward to hearing what you have planned, I'm just a bit excited, that's all," replied Anna.

"You even turned off the TV and everything," Guillermo said with a quiet laugh.

"Come on, Guillermo, just tell me! I can no longer handle the suspense."

"Okay, all right. Gosh, you are really excited about this, aren't you?"

"Absolutely."

"Well, you know the officer?"

"Officer?" asked Anna.

"Yeah, you know, the officer. The guy from the port authorities," Guillermo said.

"Oh, him," Anna replied.

"Yes, him, ha-ha. He has some connections with people that work on a cargo ship. With help from the officer and the guys on the ship, we will be able to travel to Miami," Guillermo explained.

"How are they going to be able to help us?" Anna asked.

"Well, here's the thing. It will cost $3,800 for each of us—half price for Isabel," Guillermo continued.

"Wow, that's a lot of money! The guys from the cargo ship, they will help us get visas?" Anna asked.

"Not exactly. The money that we are paying them will cover travel costs and bribe money for port authorities in Miami," Guillermo explains.

"I don't know, Guillermo. What happens if something goes wrong in Miami and we get arrested?

Even worse, what happens if something bad happens to the ship? We could all die," Anna responded sceptically.

"Come on, Anna, we are not going to die. These ships do hundreds of trips, and they are well looked after because of the amount of money at stake if anything was to go wrong with the ships. You know that I don't really like breaking the law either, but I look at our lives now, and I don't really see many good opportunities for people like us in this country. The restaurant barely keeps us afloat, and when you think about the kind of life that we want our daughter to have, it is impossible to achieve that on our current income. Listen, my love, I have thought about this long and hard. If these guys can get us to Miami, we will have an opportunity to build a good life there. Right now, though, Puerto Plata has nothing to offer us," Guillermo said convincingly.

"Well, Guillermo, I trust that you will only do what is best for us, and I know that this decision couldn't have been an easy one. So, I support your decision—let's do it," Anna said.

"Really, you mean that?" Guillermo said with excitement.

"Absolutely. I mean, we don't have the money, but I am sure that you have already thought about that," said Anna.

"Wow, I thought it would take a lot more to convince you," said Guillermo.

"God forgive us for breaking the law, but it's like you said, we don't have good opportunities in Puerto

Plata. I trust your decision. Besides, we have friends and family in America, and we should be able to reach out to them for support," Anna said.

"Anna, you are the best, and yes, I have thought about the money. We obviously will have to sell the restaurant, the truck, the boat, and this house. All the money we get will go towards the trip and spending money for when we get to Miami," said Guillermo.

The couple spent the rest of the night talking about their plans and everything that needed to be done. It was a life-changing decision, but one that would pay off in the long run.

Chapter 5

Bail out
Where: DC Corrections Division, The United Nations of Europe and Americas, Washington, DC
When: 1215 hours, Tuesday, October 1, 2041
Currency: UNEA credits

I was perplexed at the outcome of the bail hearing, and just when I was starting to wonder when I would be released from custody, the comms rang. It was Joe again.

"Hey Joe, what just happened?"

"I know, right! We are in a better position now," Joe responded.

"A better position indeed. Boy, that was incredible. For a second there, I didn't think I was getting bail. The prosecutors are out for blood."

"Yeah, Dom. They are going to be hard work, but like I said, we are in a better position now. You won't be getting out till the monitoring enforcer tags you with a bracelet. Once that's done, you will be relocated to the exit block and processed for release," Joe said.

"I see, so how much longer do you think?" I asked.

"Another couple of hours," Joe replied

"Okay, please make sure the jet is ready. I'll need to leave DC as soon as I get released. We fly straight to Milwaukee the very minute I get out of here. It's been almost forty-eight hours, and I'm sure Laura and the kids will be worried sick by now. As you probably guessed, there are a few things that we will need to discuss on the flight back," I said.

"Okay, no problem," Joe replied.

"We'll need to touch down in Albany Thursday afternoon. I won't go into too much detail now, but we'll talk about it on the plane," I said.

"No problem, Dom. I'll make sure everything is in place by the time you're released."

"Good. See you in a couple of hours," I said, and then hung up with Joe.

Laura and I had been married for twenty-three years. We had two children, Jonathan and Carla. Jonny was in his final year of high school, and Carlie was in her second year at Yale. Laura and I met in our late twenties and got married shortly after, even though it was against her father's wishes. She was brought up in a Christian family, and I was more or less Catholic. People viewed Christianity and Catholicism as the same thing, but both had opposing views on certain scriptures. In all honesty, my religious beliefs had become a little shaky over the years. The main reason for this was the way so-called Christians treated nonbelievers. Their behaviour was downright hypocritical and a stark contrast to biblical teachings. My lacklustre

Catholicism did not impress Laura's father. He also had his reservations about how I came into so much wealth at such a young age. Laura's mother loved me. She loved that I was always courteous, and that I treated her daughter with the utmost love and respect.

The arrest happened at my office in Milwaukee, and it had been all over the news and social media. Four enforcers came in to read me my rights, and the other four waited outside, to control the press—I wondered how the press found out so quickly. The enforcers put me on a government plane and flew me to DC. I had only spoken to Laura once since the arrest. She would have been worried sick every minute I spent in lockup, and the kids would be worried as well. The charges brought against me wouldn't have been crimes that my family would associate me with. As far as they were concerned, I am a good husband, a good father, and a successful businessman. They would have been under the impression that my business affairs were all clean. Laura would probably be thinking that I was being set up. My only worry at this point was how my family was coping through all this. I would have a lot of explaining to do once I got home.

I only had a couple of days to calm things down at home before having to leave again to meet with the Assembly. I will need to instruct them on how business is to be conducted during the trial. So that no one was the wiser, Assembly meetings were held at various locations, and the location was never disclosed in advance to members. Members would be dropped off at the venue at the required time. The venues included hotel conference halls and exclusive restaurants. We even used holiday cabins from time to time. Sometimes meetings were arranged with individual members. No one ever knew for sure if meetings would include all members. Each location would be swept for bugs before the meeting started. Once the meeting started, everyone spoke in a code that I developed. It was made up of corporate jargon, so that when we spoke it sounded like we were discussing legitimate business, and sometimes we actually were. The Assembly was made up of thirteen members, with me being the head. Five directors oversee operations in Canada, the United States, and South America. The other five were in charge of Europe. Russia was excluded and so was Ukraine—we had no jurisdiction in those countries. The directors in the Americas reported to Alex, and the ones in Europe reported to Chris.

I had already decided that the location for the Assembly's next meeting would be in Albany, a general meeting that would include every member. As soon as I get out of the holding cell, the plan is to get Joe to contact Alex and Chris to set up the meeting.

The hierarchical structure of my organization was set up like a Fortune 500 company with me as president. I, Alexander Lewis, and Christopher Abbadelli grew up in the same neighbourhood. They both serve as vice presidents and CSOs, overseeing a number of directors.

They were second in command and senior members of the Assembly. The two had senior regional managers reporting directly to them.

The company and all its branches carried out illegal activities. However, all the branches had a legit front. On the surface, things appeared legitimate, with all branches generating a reasonable amount of legal revenue. However, it was the criminal activities that generated the most funds. The funds were then laundered through multiple investments around the world.

In my organization, employees who were involved in the underhanded parts of the business were handsomely paid. Lower-level employees from the legit side of the business wouldn't be privy to the shadier parts of the business. Such employees would be on a regular pay packet. Only a select few from mid-level staff were trusted with specific pieces of information about the shady side of the business. Key employees and members of the Assembly were assigned financial advisors. This was to ensure that everyone's finances were managed in a way that wouldn't raise red flags whenever the authorities ran audits. Employees who didn't heed financial advice were considered a risk and would more than likely be relieved of duty—permanently.

After waiting an hour and a half, the cell intercom came on. It was one of the cell enforcers. "Mr. Dominguez, your bail has been processed. It's time to transfer you to the exit block. Please approach the door and stand behind the red line, extending your left arm towards the monitoring enforcer. A biometric GPS tracker will be fitted on your wrist, and shortly after you will be asked to exit your cell." My cell door opened, and on the other side was the monitoring enforcer. I'm not entirely sure why the red line had been placed there—it's not as if it would stop an inmate from attacking the guy.

The tracker was equipped with three layers of security. Once fitted, the biometric band would analyse my DNA and cross-reference it with the counterpart that was stored on the UNEA's database. It did this, every ten seconds, to ensure that I was the person actually wearing the bracelet at any given time. The band also included a sensor that monitored my pulse, again to ensure that I was wearing the bracelet at all times. The GPS would track my exact location, and this was the part that would cause real problems for me. In the coming weeks, I would need to attend meetings with business associates, and the last thing that I needed was the authorities monitoring my movements. "Mr. Dominguez, it will take a couple of minutes for this to synchronize. When it beeps, we're done here." These guys were robots, showing no emotion, and like the inmates, they were unpredictable. The tracking bracelet beeped, and I was asked to remain in my cell for a few more minutes.

While I was waiting, the door opened, and another

enforcer appeared. In his hand was an air-tight vacuum storage bag. The bag contained my personal items, including my Army-style overcoat by Tranchard & Co. London, bespoke navy-blue Bellucci suit, Barzetti shoes, canary diamond cufflinks, an upgraded Avant Mécanique gold watch that had belonged to my dad before he died, and my wedding ring. My personal communicator had been left on a side table at the office when they arrested me. It was a good thing none of the enforcers noticed this at the time. I wouldn't have had anything incriminating on it. However, I'm still glad that they didn't find it, because it's difficult to know what they could conjure up to use as evidence.

Shortly after, I rid myself of my horrible yellow prison attire and put on my own clothes. I was starting to feel like myself again. The intercom came on. It was the cell enforcer again. "Mr. Dominguez, it's time for you to vacate your cell. Please step into the hallway, turn left, and follow the yellow luminous light all the way to the exit block. When you arrive at the exit block, an enforcer will direct you to one of the waiting rooms."

I could already smell the fresh air, and couldn't wait to get out of this hellhole. As I walked along, I could see the other inmates in their cells, people from all walks of life. Some looked like they didn't belong in there, and others looked like complete psychopaths that deserved to be in there forever. I had to keep to the left side of the corridor between a red line on the floor and the concrete white windowless wall. There were LED prompts that flashed from the floor and walls that read "Stay inside the red line." This must have been for times when groups of prisoners needed to be escorted from one end of the facilities to another. This would keep the prisoners separated from staff or something. There were also the yellow flashing arrows that pointed to the exit block.

As I approached the corridor junction, in front of me was a projected signpost that pointed right to the infirmary and left to the exit block. As I turned left, I could see an enforcer booth in the distance. Before I reached the booth, I was instructed through the intercom to step into waiting room E314. Not more than ten minutes later, a woman's voice came through the intercom in room E314. This was the only female voice that I'd heard during my visit to the corrections facilities. "Mr. Dominguez, it is time for you to vacate DC Corrections. Please exit the waiting room and go straight to door number eight. Wait for the buzzer, and the door will open automatically. On the other side of the door, you will find a walkway. Proceed through the walkway. At the end of it you will see a gate. The gate will open automatically as you approach. At that point, you'll be free to go."

Music to my ears, I was a few minutes from freedom, sort of. I could not understand what was going on with the whole "Mr. Dominguez" thing. I was under the impression that once you became a prisoner, you automatically lost your name and you became a number.

By the time I reached the fifteen-foot electric barbed wire gate, it swung open automatically, just like the voice on the intercom said it would. On the other side of the gate was a black stretch limo with Joe standing near the rear door next to the chauffeur. There was an SUV right behind the limo for my security team. As I approached the limo, Joe and I exchanged a grin and a nod. However, we knew this was far from over and the battle had only just begun.

"Hey, Dom!"

"Hi Joe, we good to go?"

"Indeed. We are heading straight to DCA, our guys will be waiting at the hangar. We take off at 4:35 p.m. I know you're desperate for a nice hot shower and a decent meal. The flight crew have been instructed to have everything in order," Joe said.

"Good, let's get going," I responded.

We sat in the back of the limo, and I reached for a club soda and dropped a slice of lime into it. I had developed a taste for club soda and lime over the years. Joe knew this and suspected that I would need a drink, and he made sure it was available for the ride to the airport. We had to use a different limo service this time. For some reason our usual limo service wasn't available in DC. I didn't trust the limo or the chauffeur, because for all we knew the driver could have been undercover, and the limo could have been bugged.

We didn't talk about business or about the trial the entire way to the airport. We talked about family, vacations, Thanksgiving dinners, the children, and sports. I was a huge baseball fan and supported the Milwaukee Miners. There hadn't been a major-league baseball team in Wisconsin for over a decade until 2030. The previous team had been sold to Tennessee years ago. Joe was a Seagulls fan, and even though his team was mediocre, he was die-hard. He would always say, "We're going all the way this year, Dom, we're going all the way." So we talked about the rival teams and argued about which team had the best players. In all honesty, we were both hopeless fanatics. We knew every intricate detail of the sport right down to individual players and their stats.

We finally arrived at DCA. The limo stopped, the chauffeur opened our doors, and as we stepped out, our luggage was moved from the trunk onto the plane. I headed straight into the Gulf Streak. This one was mine, and it was paid for. The private jet is one of three that I own. It comes with suede seats, mahogany trim, and all the bells and whistles gadget-wise. I bought them, not to be a show-off, but because it was the most convenient way to travel. We were up in the air in no time, and my plan was to have a quick shower before eating. After that, Joe and I would get down to business.

Chapter 6

La Ambición
Where: Puerto Plata
When: 0720 hours, Sunday, August 13, 1995
Currency: Dominican peso

On the morning of August 13, 1995, the special cargo ship would be departing the Puerto Plata port to head for Miami. This information had been provided to Guillermo by his friend the port officer, so he could make the necessary preparations for the journey. Guillermo had been busy trying to come up with the travelling fees. He had already sold the house, the Otis Sealiner, and his pickup truck. The only thing left was the restaurant. It was difficult to find a buyer at short notice.

In the end, Guillermo found a solution to this problem. He sold sixty percent of the restaurant to one of his competitors. Sixty percent was all that the competitor could afford. The remaining forty percent was sold to El Pez Grande employees. It was a good deal for all parties involved. Guillermo walked away with around six hundred thousand Dominican pesos, which was around fourteen thousand US dollars. The restaurant owner had gotten rid of the competition and gained sixty percent of a new business. As far as the six employees were concerned, their forty percent stake in the restaurant guaranteed a regular income significantly higher than the salary Guillermo had paid them.

After selling everything, Guillermo was able to generate about twenty-five thousand US dollars. In the weeks leading up to the journey, he and his family needed a place to stay. They had to move in with relatives immediately after finalizing the deal on the house.

***

Guillermo was already awake when the alarm went off at four a.m. on the day of the journey. His anxiety level was the reason for the sleep deprivation, and understandably so. Shortly after he told Anna about his plans for America, they had discovered that she was pregnant. They were both excited about the baby. However, there was a bit of worry about how they would cope with a new-born in foreign territory in the coming months.

Even though there was good reason to worry, they were happy all the same. The excitement of moving to America overshadowed their fears. Guillermo woke Anna up, and she got herself and Isabel ready. He had previously arranged for a taxi that would take them to the port, where they were to meet up with his friend the port officer. By 5:30 a.m. the taxi had arrived. He loaded up all their luggage, three regular suitcases. The instruction from the port officer was for them to travel light. They headed for the port and arrived around 6:50 a.m.

The officer was already at the harbour, standing next to another individual. Guillermo stepped out of the taxi and waved to the officer, the officer, waved back. He paid the cab fare and unloaded their luggage. He, Anna, and Isabel started to walk towards the harbour where the ship was docked. It was a huge white ship with a black lower deck. It had the words "*La Ambición*" sprawled across the lower deck in large white letters. He noticed that there were several lifeboats attached to the side of the ship. The lifeboats were fastened with ropes that could be used to release them if there was an immediate need to abandon ship. On board the ship, he could see a number of uniformed men dressed in dark blue and armed with submachine guns. The armed men were navy officers. It was standard for cargo ships to travel with naval security personnel. The men took turns patrolling the ship's perimeter and regularly checked in on their walkie-talkies.

They finally arrived where the port officer and the other individual were waiting. The officer had a ridiculous grin on his face: the three-hundred-dollar finder's fee would be the reason for this. The officer introduced Guillermo to the man who stood next to him.

"Guillermo, this is Jean-Luc, a very good friend of mine." the officer said.

"It's a pleasure to meet you," Guillermo responded, and the two shook hands.

Jean-Luc was shrewd and heartless. He had made a great deal of money over the years by illegally transporting immigrants from South America to the United States. He was the point of contact for the ship's illegal operations. All proceeds were shared with his crew members, and even the ship's captain received his share. The largest share of the money went to the crooked US port officials.

Something to add to Jean-Luc's list of dubious undertakings was that he was also an informant. He would snitch out his competition to the US port authorities. It worked out perfectly for both sides. For Jean-Luc it got rid of the competition, and for the port authority it meant regular busts. The busts showed the press and members of the public that the US Port Authority had the illegal immigration issue under control. It also meant that Jean-Luc and his crew had a monopoly in that line of business, with hardly any competition in their way. He was also involved in importing illegal goods into the US. These were mostly contraband cigars, knockoff shoes and handbags. He did whatever it took to keep money rolling in.

Not more than five seconds into the initial introduction, Jean-Luc asked for the travel fees. He was going to do most of the talking from this point on.

Guillermo's friend the port officer was not to get involved at this stage. His job was to make the introduction and collect his finder's fee once the payment had been made.

"I take it you've been informed of the travel fees?" Jean-Luc asked.

"Yes, I have the $9,500 in hand." replied Guillermo.

"The fee is ten thousand dollars. Unfortunately, the prices have gone up, and I have already included a discount," Jean-Luc said.

Guillermo turned to his officer friend in astonishment. The officer also looked surprised. Guillermo knew that he would have to cough up the extra money if he wanted to board the ship, however, he felt the need to argue his case.

"I was told $3,500 each for me and my wife, and two thousand dollars for my daughter. It is unfair that I am only finding out about this on the day that we are supposed to be traveling. You don't expect us to just have an extra five hundred dollars to spare?"

"I understand your situation, Guillermo, but the truth is that the Americans are getting greedy, they have started asking for more money. To be honest, those Yankees are the ones that really dictate how much we charge our customers," replied Jean-Luc.

Jean-Luc was lying; there had been no price increase, and the Americans didn't decide how much the ship was charging people. The fact was he had a knack for sizing people up, and he could always tell who would be willing to pay extra. This time Jean-Luc was right about Guillermo. He knew that a man travelling with a wife and child would have made the arrangements to ensure that the necessary finances were in place.

Guillermo turned his back to Jean-Luc and the officer, reached into his backpack, and rifled through some of the items. He had managed to count out the requested five hundred dollars from a stash of hundred-dollar bills in his backpack. He added this to the original $9,500.

"As you wish, Mr. Jean-Luc. Here is ten thousand dollars."

"Thank you, you have made the right decision. Please wait here, one of our security personnel will come down to escort you on deck," said Jean-Luc.

As Guillermo waited, Jean-Luc directed the officer towards the opposite side of the dock, away from where Guillermo and his family stood. They stopped about thirty yards from the anxious family. The men talked for a couple of minutes before Jean-Luc counted out some of the money and handed it to the officer. Without wasting any time, the officer shoved the money into his left trouser pocket, and they both started back towards Guillermo. He had always been able to read situations, but Guillermo could not understand what had just happened or what was going to happen next. The ordeal with the price increase and Jean-Luc walking away with the officer made him feel uneasy. However, he kept on a brave face and didn't show any signs of worry.

"My good friend, I guess this is where we say goodbye. I am really happy for you, and I wish you and your family the best," the officer said.

"Thank you so much for making this possible. You are the reason my family and I are going on this wonderful journey. If you had never told me about this ship, everything that is happening now would not be possible. So thank you, my good friend," said Guillermo.

"Goodbye, my friend, maybe we'll meet again in the future," said the officer.

The men shook hands, and the officer took his hat off to bid Guillermo's wife farewell. Anna reluctantly smiled and nodded in acknowledgement. She did not like the officer; she never had. The officer wasn't happy for Guillermo and couldn't care less what happened to his family. He had collected his finder's fee, and this was all that mattered to him. Guillermo knew this, but he humoured the officer like he always did during the officer's visits to the restaurant.

After saying their goodbyes, Guillermo noticed an armed guard walking in their direction. Jean-Luc had spoken to someone on his walkie-talkie, but Guillermo did not understand what had been said. However, it made perfect sense now. Once he had secured the payment, Jean-Luc gave the order for one of the guards to come down and escort the family on board the ship.

As the armed guard led the family on board, the officer shook Jean-Luc's hand and then left the dock. Jean-Luc pulled out a small notebook from his back pocket, scribbled down a couple of lines, ripped out the page, and handed it to the guard.

"Guillermo, please follow the guard, he will take you on board and show you to your temporary living quarters," Jean-Luc said.

"Thank you, Mr. Jean-Luc."

The armed guard was wearing sunglasses, which made it difficult to read him. On the outside, Guillermo showed a calm demeanour. On the inside, he was nervous about the predicament that he now found himself in. He did not expect armed guards, although it made sense to have security on board to protect the cargo and crew. Guillermo could tell that Anna was worried, he could see it on her face. But Isabel was very excited; as far as she was concerned it was all one big adventure.

At the main entrance, Guillermo and his family were searched for weapons. The US port officers didn't want any surprises. After the search, they walked across the main deck towards the hull. There they saw even more armed guards, most of them wearing dark sunglasses. Guillermo took note of everything he saw. Everyone appeared to be busy, people pushing trolleys and driving forklifts. The trolleys contained trays with sealed meats and fruit, while the forklifts hauled unmarked wooden crates. The crates usually contained coffee, nuts, bananas, sugarcane, cigars, cocoa, leather goods, and probably illegal narcotics. He took a mental note of the nearby exits in case a there was a sudden need to escape with his family on one of the lifeboats.

"This is your living quarters. You are not to leave this area without the permission of a guard, and your door is to remain shut until a guard unlocks it. There will be consequences if you fail to comply with these rules. We have to inspect your luggage, then it will be returned to you shortly," the guard said in a stern voice.

"Okay, thanks." Guillermo replied.

Guillermo was even more worried than he was before the armed guard arrived at the dock. The guard's tone was very unfriendly.

Guillermo felt they were being treated like prisoners, not paying customers. The so-called living quarters were more like a tiny jail cell. As they stepped in, there was a man lying down on a single bed, reading a magazine. The man appeared to be in his mid-thirties. As the family inspected the living quarters, the guard disappeared, and the door locked behind them.

"Hi, my name is Carlos," said the young man, who seemed happy that other people had joined him in the living quarters.

"Hello, Carlos," Guillermo responded reluctantly. "I am Guillermo. I take it you are a travelling passenger, or do you work on the ship?"

"No, I am a passenger. I sold everything I had, and now here I am, ready to embark on this wonderful journey," Carlos replied.

Carlos seemed like a nice person, but Guillermo had his suspicions. He didn't know the man and was not willing to divulge too much information about himself or his family.

"This is my family, and I guess you can say that we are after the same thing you are," Guillermo said.

"Great, it's a pleasure to meet you. Welcome aboard," replied Carlos.

The living quarters were a very tight space that now housed three adults and a child. The room had three additional beds, so at least everyone had a bed to sleep on. The walls had massive screws that had formed circular rust stains around the edges. It wasn't exactly clear what the screws were holding in place on the other side of the wall. Accompanying the rust stains was what appeared to have once been a white wall that had now almost completely turned light brown. The room was musty and in need of a complete revamp.

There were no connecting toilets or bathroom, and Guillermo started to wonder if he had made a mistake by putting his family in this situation. That thought only lasted a few minutes, as he decided to make the best of the situation. He could see that Anna still looked worried, so he reassured her that it would be over in a few days.

Chapter 7

The Strategy
Where: Pennsylvania airspace, the United Nations of Europe and Americas
When: 1542 hours, Tuesday, October 1, 2041
Currency: UNEA credits

After a much-needed shower, I went to the dining section of the jet and saw that food had been served. I couldn't wait to unveil what was hidden underneath the stainless-steel plate covers. I hadn't eaten anything in prison the entire time that I had been detained, and I was starving. As I sat down at the table with Joe, one of the flight attendants came over and began to remove the plate covers. The starter was garlic bread bruschetta, served with Sicilian olive oil. Spaghetti alla Puttanesca was the main dish, with strawberry vin santo atop mascarpone trifle for dessert. Among the assortment of drinks were a couple of bottles of club soda. I saw the flight attendant had served some lime to go with the soda. Once the he had finished serving, I gave him the nod, and he left us to enjoy our meal.

"All refreshed?" Joe asked.

"Yeah, who's the new guy, Joe?" I said.

"Who, the flight attendant? Don't worry about him, we put him through the six-week vetting process, you know how that goes," Joe replied.

"Good, I'm sure that I don't need to explain why we need to be even more vigilant from now on," I said.

I am meticulous when it comes to secrecy, and considering everything that had just transpired, it made sense to be a bit paranoid. Joe was right though. Everyone that we employed, especially those that worked in close proximity to me, had to undergo a rigorous vetting process. This included various forms of education and criminal background checks. We acquired as much information as possible. We knew everyone's family, and if they had no family, we knew their friends; and if they didn't have any friends, we knew about their pets. We rarely employed people that had no family ties. It's difficult to persuade people to cooperate by threatening to harm their loved ones if they don't have any. Of course, such a drastic measure was used only as a final resort.

The houses, offices, cars, boats, helicopters, and planes were regularly swept for bugs. The sweeps were performed using the most advanced signal sniffers that money could buy. I was sure that no one would be listening to the conversation Joe and I were about to have. I picked up a bruschetta, dipped it in the olive oil, and took a bite. It was delicious.

"So, do we have a real chance of winning this trial?" I asked.

"I have to be honest with you, Dom, this isn't going to be easy. We have been very careful over the years, which is how we've managed to keep you clean and made it difficult for anyone to pin charges on you. Whatever they've got on you, it must be solid. We will have to wait till I get the list of evidence from the prosecution before I can put a strategy in place. With that said, I will fight hard for you and do everything I can to win." replied Joe.

"Okay, let's talk worst-case scenario. If I'm found guilty and sentenced to prison, will I lose everything?" I asked.

"We will need to clarify with Julian after your meeting with the Assembly. I believe everything has been organized in a way that ensures that Laura and the kids are set up for life. UNEA law requires that in order to seize assets, the courts must be able to prove that those assets were acquired by illegal means. As far as I know, Julian has always made sure that company accounts appear legit. I am pretty sure all the assets are safe. It is not the financial crimes that we need to focus on, but the other charges will definitely require our full effort," replied Joe.

Julian Seawall is my chief accountant, and boy, was he a magician—the way he cooked the books was magic. I was still struggling to come to terms with the arrest though. I couldn't figure out who had chirped.

"This is really messed up, Joe. I am sure someone from the inside is talking. Have you spoken to Alex and

Chris?" I asked.

"Yes." Joe replied.

"Do they have anything yet? Have they started the internal inquiry?" I asked.

"No. I think it's going to take some time to get everything in place," Joe responded.

"Not good enough, Joe, this is not good enough. I am the head of this organization, it's my neck on the line here. They need to understand there is too much at stake. What's taking so long?"

"I completely understand your frustration, Dom, but the CSOs know what to do, and everything is being handled."

"We really need to find out who is behind this," I said.

"I know. The way I see it, there is more than one person involved. The organization is structured in such a way that no one can single-handedly bring you down. The people behind this will have to be from both sides of the Nations to be able to pull this off," said Joe.

"We need to find out if any of our employees have shown inconsistencies in their work patterns. I think that there is a good chance that they might be responsible for this," I said.

"You're right, Dom—we should flag this with the CSOs."

Alex and Chris also served as the organization's CSOs, which meant they were in charge of all aspects of security. They not only had to do everything in their power to protect company information, it was also their job to acquire any information that was considered beneficial to the company. So, any information relating to my trial was high priority. Alex and Chris would need to get our guys on the hunt for every bit of information about everyone involved in the trial.

"What do Alex and Chris have lined up so far?" I asked.

"I had a secure conference call with them this morning, and their strategy is to do surveillance on members of the Assembly. They'll be keeping an eye on all other senior employees as well. It is unlikely that anyone outside these ranks would have been close enough to you to gain any information that would harm you. However, we can't rule anyone out, so we should get the CSOs on the case. They would need to immediately set up surveillance on anyone suspicious. We shouldn't take any chances. Once all the evidence has been presented, we can start narrowing things down to a more specific group of individuals," Joe replied.

Joe was making sense, but we wouldn't be able to do too much until the prosecution presented their evidence. I just needed to be patient. I had finished my bruschetta and started with the spaghetti. I spoke to Joe between every mouthful.

"What about the tracker? We need to get it off. I know that leaving it on doesn't really affect my movements within the Nations, but I don't want enforcers knowing my every move. The tracker doesn't allow them to track my voice or anything, but I don't want to give them the opportunity to connect any dots. Also, I will need to leave the UNEA during the trial, and the last thing that I need is to get caught doing this," I said.

"Nothing is set in stone, but Alex knows someone that might be able to sort out the tracker problem. He mentioned this during our conference call, and yes, the line was secure. I'm no techno wizard, but I think if Alex's guy is able to get the bracelet off, it will be expensive," Joe replied.

"I think we both know that money is not an issue, especially when it comes to something like this. As far as the murder charge goes, we should have no problem beating that, because I didn't do it. I have never killed a man in my life—we have people to handle that kind of stuff. The main charge that bothers me is the conspiracy to assassinate a government official, that charge carries a life sentence. If I'm found guilty, do we know which of the prisons I will end up in?" I asked.

"Yeah, I believe the murder charge was just tossed in there to stir things up. They know they don't have any proof of that, and even if they did it will be difficult for them to win murder by proxy. I believe the hitters used by Alex and Chris cannot be linked back to them, or to you for that matter. The thing with the government official, there was never any concrete plan to carry out the assassination. You said you called the whole thing off, pending when you had a better plan. With that said, if the prosecution has managed to get their hands on a written note, a voice recording, or anything like that, then we have a problem. The drug charges won't go far, too many high-ranking officials have been bribed to cover things up. If you go down, everyone else goes down. As far as prisons go, I'm sure this is something Alex and Chris have thought about. They have contacts in every prison across the Nations. I will bring up the matter after our meeting in Albany," replied Joe.

Joe already knew exactly what we were going to do if the ride got bumpy along the way, and we weren't able to find our chirper. We would need to deal with things the old-fashioned way, erase a few bodies. He hardly touched his food, he just moved the spaghetti around his plate. He did throw back a couple of swigs of cognac though. I guess he needed to take the edge off. It had been an interesting couple of days for us both. After I was done eating, I poured some Gładka Królewska into my glass, the best vodka Poland had to offer. I added a couple of lemon slices and chased it with a bit of club soda.

"You haven't eaten a thing, Joe, this is good Italian food."

"I not really hungry. You're drinking the hard stuff today, huh?" Joe said.

"Yup. Like you, I need to take the edge off," I replied.

"How did you know?" Joe asked.

"We've known each other for a long time, my

friend. You barely touched your food, and we both know you love food. So, how's Sandra doing?" I asked.

"She's great, things are a bit manic at home, but she's coping," Joe replied.

"And the boys?" I asked.

"They're great. Joseph Jr. is playing well, and Paul plans on trying out for the team next year," Joe said.

"I'm sure that makes you happy. My Jonny hates baseball, can you believe that?" I said.

Joe's wife and kids often came to the house for dinner, and Laura and Sandra played tennis at the country club on Thursdays. My guess is they won't be playing any tennis this week, considering everything that has happened. All I could think about was what I was going to say to the family when I got home. I will be able to handle the situation, but it's not something I was looking forward to doing. I was going to have to figure out a way to put everyone's mind at ease. We are a high-profile family, and because of the trial, our image had taken a hit. Family life was never going to be the same. Even if we won the trial, things would never be the same. The only thing we could do was implement damage control. We had just the right guy to put things in motion to reduce the impact of the damage and restore people's trust in me, as well as the Edom Group brand.

"I don't need to ask if damage control is already in play. Right?" I said.

"Yup, we've got the team working on this," Joe

replied.

“As far as the legit side of the business goes, I will be able to fix things with some of our clients. High-profile businessmen are often involved in scandals and legal trouble. I’m sure I will be able to convince them we have our integrity intact. Some clients would definitely not want to be associated with Edom Group during or after the trial, but we’ll be able to live with that,” I said.

“Okay. I’m sure that the press will be at the house in the morning. Before leaving for Albany, it will be a good idea for you to give a brief statement and then hand over to our PR guy,” Joe replied.

“Yeah, sure. I already know what to say,” I responded

The pilot announced we would be landing in Milwaukee shortly. Joe and I left the dining area with our drinks in hand and headed to our seats. We strapped on our seat belts and carried on talking strategy. For the most part, Joe and the guys seemed to have everything under control and rightfully so: I pay them handsomely to do just that. The plane landed, and as it made its way to the private hangar, I could see the convoy. Chris and Alex would be there waiting to give me an initial briefing.

Chapter 8

Meet Laura Dominguez
Where: The Dominguez residence, The United Nations of Europe and Americas, Milwaukee, Wisconsin
When: 1950 hours, Tuesday, October 1, 2041
Currency: UNEA credits

This thing with Edward, I can't believe that it's come to this. I have always had my suspicions. I mean, no one gains this amount of wealth without having to have cut a few corners. One would also need serious political connections: getting this far without that is pretty much impossible. I always knew in the back of my mind that there had to be something. Nevertheless, what the media is saying is far from what I could have ever imagined. Although there is a chance, they may be blowing this out of proportion—it is the media after all.

I met Edward in 2018 at a restaurant called 'The Big Fish', the best bar and grill in Milwaukee. I was having dinner with a couple of girlfriends one evening, when I noticed a distinguished gentleman walk in. The man was well dressed, poised, and appeared to be familiar with the staff. He was ushered to a table in a corner not too far from where we were sitting. As he sat down, one of the waiters approached his table, blocking the man from my view. The waiter removed the sign that read "Reserved" from the table and spoke to him for a few seconds. After that the waiter walked away, and the gentleman was back in my view. I kept talking to my friends but would glance over at him every now and then. He was reading a copy of the *Milwaukee Economist*. Eventually, he closed the pages, folded up the newspaper, and placed it on the table. The waiter returned to the table, set down a drink and a tray of hors d'oeuvres. As the waiter walked away, the gentleman and I locked eyes. I quickly turned away and tried not to look in his direction again. I kept talking to my friends, pretending not to be interested in the man. A few moments later, I noticed from the corner of my eye that he had gotten up from his seat and was walking towards our table. He had a bottle of champagne in his right hand, which he presented to me and said, "Good evening, ladies, my name is Edward. Apologies for interrupting."

I wasn't sure where the bottle came from, I hadn't seen any of the waiters bring it to him. He was very polite as he apologized. "Please don't be offended by this gesture. I felt that if I didn't approach you in this manner, I probably would never get the opportunity to meet you again. I don't want to take up any more of your time, so please accept this bottle of champagne for you, and your friends, to go with your meal. It would be an absolute delight if we could have a quick chat later, perhaps after your meal. If not, here is my card. You can use this to get in touch with me some other time, if you're not in the mood for a chat this evening. Again, I apologize for being so forward. Enjoy your meal."

I didn't utter a word, I just smiled. As he walked away, my friends started to whisper and giggle like a bunch of schoolgirls. They kept teasing me. I tried to pretend like it wasn't a big deal, but no one was buying that—I had just been hit on by a good-looking and eloquent hunk of a man. My friends knew me well enough to know that I wasn't going to let this one get away. The bottle he handed me was premium Vieux Vignoble, very expensive champagne. The card, which read "Edom Group," had his name and personal number on it. I had never heard of the company before.

The girls were going to order dessert and would leave immediately after to give me some private time with my new admirer. I was still busy pretending that it wasn't a big deal, but the girls could see right through me. Before they finished their dessert, a man rushed into the restaurant and handed a cell phone to Edward. He glanced at it, spoke a few words, and then slipped the phone into his lower-left jacket pocket. Edward glanced over to me, gestured with prayer hands, and whispered, "Sorry." Then he hurried out of the restaurant with the man who came in to ruin what was probably going to be a wonderful evening. It was a good thing I had his business card—I was definitely going to give him a call. I didn't call him that night though; that would have seemed desperate. His business card had one of those bar codes on it. I scanned it and downloaded his contact details onto my phone and put the card and phone in my purse.

I didn't call him for two whole weeks, but when I finally called, I couldn't get hold of him. I had to leave a voice message. Edward called me back an hour after he got my message. For some reason, I got excited and a bit nervous at the same time. I didn't give anything away during our conversation though. I just played it cool.

"Hello. Hi, is this Laura?"

"Yes, hi, Edward. You seem to be quite a busy man."

Most people called him Eddie and his friends called him Dom. I've always called him Edward because that's the name he gave when he introduced himself to me and my friends.

"Sorry I couldn't pick up earlier, I was in a meeting. I am so glad that you decided to call me. To be honest, I didn't think that you were going to. I apologize for leaving abruptly the other night," Edward said.

"No need to apologize. There was no guarantee that I was going to speak to you that night anyway," I replied.

"Well, I apologize anyway. How have you been?"

"I've been okay. It's the same old—work, work, and more work."

"Listen, I would really like to get to know you and

hear more about your work. Any chance we could meet up for lunch, or dinner perhaps?" Edward said.

"I don't know Edward. judging by how you left the restaurant the other night and just your whole vibe, I don't think you'll have the time for me."

"For you, I would make the time," Edward replied.

"Hmm, you are quite the charmer," I said.

"Well, is my charm working?"

"Ha-ha. On a different note, I looked up Edom Group. You own the company. It doesn't say that on your business card?" I asked.

"I didn't think there was a need for that. Not everyone needs to know that I own the company."

"That's fair enough. You arc quite an accomplished man though. I can only imagine that you dedicate a lot of time to running such a huge company. I just don't think you'll have time for romance. That is what you are proposing, isn't it?"

"Gosh, straight to the point, huh?" Edward said.

"What's the point of playing games, we are both adults, and we need to be upfront about what we want out of this, don't we? By the way, I need you to understand that your money doesn't impress me. I have my own money. I'm only interested in being treated with respect," I replied.

"Hey, I have a sister, and a mother that raised me the right way. All I have ever known about how to treat ladies is to be respectful. Now regarding not having time for you, I understand why you would think that. I'm not always busy, though. One of the perks of being company chief is that I can delegate most of the work to other people. I will make time for you. So, what about it?" Edward asked.

"Okay, Edward. Don't mess me around, I mean it."

"I won't, I promise. Do you want to meet up soon? You pick the place."

"Okay, how about dinner at the Big Fish Friday evening?" I suggested.

"That sounds good. For the sake of transparency though, you should know that I own that place. Actually, there are three others with the same name. One in New York, one in Miami, and another in Los Angeles. All three are part of Edom Group," Edward replied.

"Oh, I did not know that. It all makes sense now that I think about it. You seemed to be getting special treatment from what I observed. The reserved table, the level of service from the staff, and the bottle of champagne. There was also the fact that you didn't pay for anything before you rushed out of the restaurant with your friend," I said.

"Yeah, that wasn't my friend, it was my chauffeur. He came into the restaurant to hand me my cell phone. I left it in the car, and he came in to inform me that it had been ringing. I had to leave urgently for an impromptu meeting. This doesn't happen often, so don't worry," Edward said.

"Okay. I have to go now, but see you on Friday?" I

said.

"Yes, I wouldn't miss it for the world. I am really looking forward to it," Edward replied.

"Yeah, me too. See you soon, bye!"

***

Edward and I met up for dinner, and the rest, as they say, is history. We've been married for twenty-three years, and we have two wonderful children. When the story about Edward broke, the kids were quite upset and didn't understand what was going on. Jonny, Carlie, and I had a three-way comms conversation. Apparently, some of their fellow students had been asking them questions about the situation, and they didn't know how to deal with it. I reassured them that everything was going to be okay. I told Jonny that we would discuss it when he got home from school. Carlie was flying home from Connecticut this weekend, so I told her that we would catch up when she got home.

The house comms had been going off all afternoon, and after eight or so calls I decided to stop accepting incoming connections. Edward's mother, called my personal comms to find out what was going on. She asked if I wanted her to stop by, but I insisted that she didn't have to. She lived in the annex about fifty yards from the main house, and she could have easily popped round. I said it was probably best to come over after Edward and I have had the chance to discuss what was going on. I told her that I would send someone over with the golf cart to bring her to the main house. Edward's mother and I had a wonderful relationship, so asking her not to come by at that moment wouldn't have offended her.

Edward called me to let me know he had already landed in Milwaukee and was on his way home. I was anxious and finding it difficult to relax. I even had to take the day off from work. I decided to go into the study. Through the massive arched window, I would be able to see the limo as soon as it drove through the gates of the main entrance. There was the drinks cart in the far corner of the room. I poured myself a glass of cognac to take the edge off. I paced back and forth, occasionally stopping at the window in anticipation. I asked the virtual assistant to direct all calls to the messaging system. I needed it to be quiet so I could hear my own thoughts.

Eventually, the electric gates opened, and the limo drove through. It seemed to take forever for the car to pull up the drive. As the car got closer, I left the study and headed back to the living room. I wasn't sure how our conversation was going to go down. I was worried. Edward, though—it took a lot to rattle him. I was sure that he would be calm about the whole thing. If he had any worries at all, he wouldn't let me see it. He never wanted me to worry about anything, and he would always downplay stressful situations. Sometimes he would dismiss them altogether. I could see the front door from where I stood. The door swung open and Edward emerged.

"Hi, honey," Edward said.

"Edward, what in heaven's name is going on? I have been worried sick!" I said.

"It's all a big misunderstanding, and I can explain," Edward replied.

"A big misunderstanding—are you kidding me!" I said.

"Honey, please calm down," Edward said.

"Calm down—are you, serious right now? With everything that's happened, you want me to calm down? I'm no fool, Edward, so please don't be dismissive like you always are and just be honest with me. I'm not naive, I know the amount of money you make and everything else that you've accomplished doesn't come without cutting corners. But these charges, Edward, this is a lot for me to handle."

"Okay, honey," Edward said calmly.

"So, are we going to discuss this?" I asked.

"How are the kids, are they home?" Edward asked.

"Jonny is here, but Carlie will be on the first flight from Connecticut Saturday morning. I have spoken to them, and they just want to know what's going on. It's all over the news, and people are asking them questions," I replied.

"Okay, let's sit down and talk about this," said Edward.

***

Edward was more forthcoming than he had ever been, explaining that not all the charges were true. He said the kidnapping, murder, and assassination conspiracy charges were false, and that the High Court was desperate to pin something on him that would stick. As for the narcotics charge, Edward explained that it wasn't as bad as it sounded. He said that Edom Group's pharmaceutical division was involved in the distribution of prescription drugs that weren't approved by the NFDA. The NFDA wanted to tax everything sold in the Nations. Edom Pharmaceuticals branding and purposely mislabelling illegal drugs in an effort to mislead the NFDA hadn't gone down well.

I'm not even sure how Edward and his people had managed to pull this off to begin with. Surely it would have been extremely difficult to keep this under wraps—I mean, this stuff was on pharmacy shelves all over the Nations. Edward came clean, about the other charges as well. He said he was very sorry for everything he had put me through and wished he could do things differently. What was I to do? I loved him. He was a great husband and father, and I wasn't going to leave him in a time of trouble. I've always had my suspicions, and I could have left him long ago. I didn't leave then, and I'm not leaving now.

"Edward, you should have trusted me enough to tell me things, you know," I said.

"I know, honey. Things had gotten complicated with business over the years, and I just didn't want to involve you in any of it. Also, I wasn't exactly proud of everything that was going on," Edward replied.

"What happens if you somehow manage to beat all the charges, are you going to put a stop to all the illegal stuff?" I asked.

"It's not that straightforward, Laura. For the illegal stuff, I just can't stop. I will have to hand that side of the business over to someone else, and that takes time. But yes, I will put a stop to it soon. I don't want to ever put my family through this again," Edward replied.

I trusted Edward would take care of everything. He always had a way of figuring things out, he was very good at that. The anxiety had subsided a bit now. Edward and I spoke at length about how we were going to move forward. He would be holding a press conference, during which he would declare his innocence.

Chapter 9

Port of Miami
Where: Port of Miami
When: 1330 hours, Wednesday, August 16, 1995
Currency: US Dollar

La Ambición docked at the port of Miami on the afternoon of Wednesday, August 16, 1995. One of the security officers came to Guillermo's living quarters to tell them they had arrived in Miami and the ship had docked. They were told the US port authorities would need to board the vessel to do routine checks. Guillermo, his family, and the man that was sharing the living quarters with them were instructed to follow the armed officer.

They were escorted to the part of the ship where all the containers were stored. Within the stacks was a marked container located amongst many others like it. The huge orange container had the numbers 4377 etched on the front, the back, and the sides. It was showing signs of age with visible patches of rust that had developed from prolonged exposure to sea water. Across the top of the container were several ventilation holes that were barely noticeable at first glance. The tiny holes would allow airflow and tiny rays of light into the container. In the middle of the top of the container was a silent fan that was connected to a large truck battery. The battery was tucked away safely in a wooden box attached to the back corner of the container. This temporarily housed the illegal migrants and would be exempt from the checks carried out by the US port officials.

Jean-Luc and the ship's captain had an arrangement with their contacts at the Miami port that involved moving the marked container to a specific terminal. Once the checks had been carried out and the containers had been off-loaded, the immigrants would remain in the container until sunset. Once port activities had died down and most employees had gone home for the day, one of the officials would unlock the container, allowing the immigrants to make an exit. Once released, the immigrants would be escorted to a nearby van and then dropped off at a specified location in the city.

There was always a possibility for things to go wrong. For example, if any of the port officials involved in the scam weren't able to make it into work, the entire operation could fall apart. The marked container could be checked by an officer not involved in the scam. The immigrants would be discovered, and the entire operation would be exposed. Even changes to shift patterns or assignments could cause problems. The plan would fail if someone responsible for manning the security cameras was suddenly given a different assignment by a shift supervisor who wasn't part of the racket. If anyone noticed that people were being moved from a container and into a van, it would be catastrophic.

When the container was opened to let them in, Guillermo was shocked to find there were at least twenty other people in there. Anna was quite anxious, and the pregnancy didn't make the situation any more bearable. It had been a long trip, and everyone was exhausted. Guillermo, his family, and the man from their living quarters went into the container as instructed. Jean-Luc switched the fan on and warned the passengers to remain quiet. The container doors were shut and locked from the outside.

About ten minutes later, voices could be heard from outside the container. The Captain and Jean-Luc had been showing the US port officers around the ship. By the tone of their voices, it didn't sound as though the US officers that had boarded the ship on this day were aware of any arrangements made by the ship's crew. They sounded very stern and professional. Everyone with Guillermo heard the sound of containers being locked and unlocked, and the sounds were getting closer and closer.

It didn't seem as though their container would be exempt from the search. The port officers didn't sound as corrupt as Jean-Luc had implied. They questioned the Captain and Jean-Luc in a manner that would lead anyone to believe they had never met. For the illegal passengers, this only made a stressful situation more so. Half an hour later the initial checks were completed. Further checks would be done once the containers were offloaded. All the US personnel exited the vessel, and the illegal passengers could no longer hear the voices. Anna was growing more and more anxious.

"Anna, everything will be okay, we will be okay. We have made it this far, there is nothing to worry about," Guillermo said.

"How do you know that? How do we know that the doors of this container won't be kicked open by the Americans at any moment?" Anna said.

"Please my love, try to relax, we do not want to scare Isabel. Just pray silently, okay? You have your rosary beads, don't you?" Guillermo asked.

"Yes, I do. Isabel, don't you worry, my dear, everything will be okay, and we will be in our new home soon," said Anna.

An hour later everyone in the container heard loud clanging noises coming from the doors. The tension heightened, as no one was sure what was going to happen next. After a few more loud noises, the container doors flew open, and to everyone's relief it was Jean-Luc.

He assured everyone that things were going according to plan. He informed them that within the next couple of hours the container was going to be lifted off the ship and lowered down into the dockyard. He explained the container would be lifted by its four corners, and they would feel some movement but nothing too dangerous. He stated how important it was for everyone to remain quiet while this was going on. Everyone nodded in agreement. The doors were again locked from the outside, and the people waited.

"You see, Anna, everything is okay, we will be fine. Are you okay, Isabel?" Guillermo asked.

"Yes, Papa," replied Isabel.

To Isabel this was still all one big adventure. Guillermo had thought about everything that could go wrong. Back home, he'd seen on the news and read in the papers about how illegal immigrants were sometimes sold into forced labour or prostitution. There was also the possibility of getting arrested and their child being sent to social services. He wasn't oblivious to the possible outcomes, and this made him anxious. However, he managed to keep his composure.

About two hours after Jean-Luc's announcement, there was more clanging and jangling. The noise was much louder than the first time. This was followed by a series of loud thuds from the four upper corners of the container. The passengers braced themselves and remained silent. No one wanted to be responsible for jeopardizing the plan. Eventually, the container started to move.

The passengers grasped onto loops made of rope that had been placed around the container. Isabel couldn't reach the ropes, so she held on to Guillermo. The passengers felt the container rise, turn 180 degrees, then stop. They were suspended in mid-air for fifteen minutes before they started moving again. The container gradually descended. As it settled on the ground, the passengers breathed sighs of relief. More noises came from outside the container—squeaking, screeching, thudding. The thuds were produced by the giant claws releasing the container. The giant orange box was finally resting on US soil.

The passengers had another three hours to wait. The silent fan and air vents made sense now. It would have been disastrous being stuck in a dark, hot container scorched by the Floridian heat with no airflow. The wait seemed to last an eternity, and again the passengers could hear voices outside. Some of the passengers brought snacks for the journey and shared with those that didn't. So far, the container experience hadn't been too bad. Guillermo was feeling more confident than he had just hours ago.

Everything had happened exactly the way Jean-Luc said it would. He could smell the Floridian air, the coastal breeze, and it was only a matter of time before they rendezvoused with Guillermo's cousin Raphael.

They would be staying at Raphael's for one month, which would allow them time to sort out a place of their own. Raphael had a contact in the local forging racket. The plan was for Raphael to use his contact to acquire fake IDs and work permits for Guillermo's family. This would make it possible to get jobs as well as enrol Isabel in school. All this would cost a significant amount of money. After paying the travel fees, Guillermo still had approximately fifteen thousand dollars.

It was around 8 p.m., and it was completely dark inside the container. Suddenly, more clanging noises came from the doors. When the doors flew open, all the passengers could see initially were bright beams from two flashlights. Loud voices emanated from the direction of the beams. "Okay, everybody on your feet—let's go, let's go, let's go." The command was repeated in Spanish by another voice.

When everyone stepped out of the container, they were asked to form a line. These men did not sound friendly. Guillermo's confidence diminished, he felt that things could still fall apart. The two, armed US officials, sounded aggressive. It briefly crossed Guillermo's mind that there was a possibility these men could be unaware of Jean-Luc's arrangement. Guillermo tried to get a glimpse of the officers' names, but they were not wearing name tags. He felt this was a good sign. If this had been a legal bust, it wouldn't be necessary for the officers to conceal their identity.

One of the men walked towards the back of the line, while the other one remained in front. Everyone was given instructions to follow the officer at the front and not to break formation. The passengers were informed there would be no toilet breaks after they left the docks. Whoever needed to use the toilet needed to say so now. Guillermo and a few others put their hands up. The officer pointed in the direction of a few portable toilets nearby.

Once they had finished, the officer in front instructed everyone to follow him. After walking for five minutes, they stopped at the east section of the docks. Attached to a nearby barbed-wired fence was a gate with a green sign that read 'Emergency Exit Only'. The crew had someone manning the security cameras, and they gave the signal that they were approaching the gate. The camera panned in the opposite direction, away from the gate. A minute later, the travellers were directed outside the gate, towards three white vans. Once they were in the clear, the camera resumed its normal cycle.

Guillermo and his family were assigned to the same van, but the man from their living quarters was placed in a separate van. All three vans pulled away from the docks in different directions. The driver of Guillermo's van turned the radio down and said, "Welcome to America," in Spanish. This was music to his ears; he could finally relax and be happy that the trip had been successful. The driver told everyone where he would be taking them and said there would be pay phones available so they could get in touch with their contacts in Miami. He warned them that, although the van had clean license plates, there was always a possibility of getting pulled over by the police. He explained that if this were to happen, there would be nothing he could do about it. Arrests leading to deportation would be inevitable. This sent Guillermo into panic mode again, but he didn't let it show because he knew it would make Anna anxious.

The driver made it all the way to Thirty-Sixth Street with no problems. He told the passengers they had reached their destination, and that they could now exit the vehicle and off-load their luggage. Guillermo and his family were ecstatic. He turned to Anna and could see that she was tired, but she looked happy nonetheless. Isabel looked tired as well. He collected their luggage from the back of the van and said goodbye to the driver.

"Anna, my love, we did it!" Guillermo said in excitement.

"Yes, we did, we should call Raphael quickly. I am very tired and hungry. Isabel needs to eat something too." Anna said.

"Yes, there is a pay phone just over there. I will call Raphael now. We can get some food at the restaurant across the road while we wait." said Guillermo.

Guillermo made the call. Raphael told him to look out for a green, four-door Dauntless with plate number GIP-07A.

Raphael pulled into the restaurant parking lot in his hideous monstrosity of a car. It had massive chrome spoke rims, a white leather interior, and all kinds of tasteless ornaments on the dash. Guillermo spotted the car and told Anna and Isabel it was time to go. They came out of the restaurant, and both men hugged and shouted greetings. Guillermo introduced Anna and

Isabel to Raphael, and he hugged them both. Raphael grabbed their luggage and after putting them in the trunk, they drove off.

Chapter 10

The Assembly
Where: The Royal Scepter, The United Nations of Europe and Americas, Albany, New York
When: 1300 hours, Thursday, October 3, 2041
Currency: UNEA credits

Before our flight to Albany, we did the press conference and things couldn't have gone more smoothly. Joe and I prepared my address, and the plan was to be short and simple. My spokesperson would take over the press conference once I had given my speech.

I opened by stating that all the allegations against me were false and that the intention of the Nations prosecution team was to assassinate my character. I further explained that Edom Group had been approached by the authorities, requesting access to our client database for reasons they refused to disclose. We had declined this request, explaining that there was no legal precedent, and Edom Group was bound by a nondisclosure agreement. Edom Group's refusal to cooperate had garnered a barrage of harassment by various branches of government. There had been unwarranted office visits, unnecessary surveillance, and insurmountable audits. I concluded by saying their actions against us were a personal vendetta on the part of the prosecution as well as the judge.

These were all lies, of course, a ploy to restore my clean image. The request for Edom Group's client list never happened, neither were there any office visits or unusual audits.

Sewing doubt in the minds of the media and the general public would improve my chances of making things right with my clients. It also put the spotlight on the prosecutor and judge, which would motivate them to run a clean trial. The press had no way of proving any of this anyway—information about the government's operations was classified, and all they could do was deny my accusations. Joe confirmed Section 10-6(B) of the UNEA Law Enforcement & Investigatory Act prevents the government from divulging such information to the public. The evidence and findings derived from investigations, on the other hand, are made available to the public upon request.

I told the press I appreciated all the work they were doing, and I trusted they would use sound judgment and carry out responsible journalism when reporting my case. I asked the press to respect my privacy and that of my family. I closed my speech by introducing and handing over to my PR spokesperson.

There would be loads of fluff strategically scattered all over social media. There would be ads praising my personal contributions to schools and charities. There would also be publicity around the work Edom Group does with students and interns across the Nations. All this to show the public how much of a nice guy I was and how much involvement Edom Group had in the community.

Later that afternoon we landed in Albany. We arrived at the Royal Scepter where I, Joe, Alex, and Chris would meet with the Assembly. After the meeting, everyone would be dismissed, and there would be a second meeting between me, the CSOs, and the tech guru. Alex had made the necessary arrangements to get the tech guy to Albany to sort out the tracking bracelet conundrum. Joe would not be attending the second meeting.

The Royal Scepter was a luxurious hotel where you would find only the elite of the elite. Sheiks, emirs, and AU dignitaries. Members of various royal families from across the globe also frequented the hotel. The owner and I are close friends, and he made sure one of the presidential suites was always reserved for me. I owned a couple of properties in Albany, but I often opted to stay at the hotel suite. Sometimes after meetings, clients would visit Edom Group's headquarters, which was only a couple of miles from the hotel.

I never held internal meetings at the Royal Scepter, but this time it was necessary. The building was the most secure of any location we'd ever used. Everyone was informed about the meeting at the last minute, and they were all flown in via hired private jets. My friend, the hotel owner, Geoffrey Livingston, got his people to prepare the suite and the conference room before I arrived. The CSOs sent the sweep team ahead of our arrival to carry out rigorous checks. Once the checks had been done, a security team was dispatched to the location. A couple of guys were posted at the suite entrance, another four at all entrances to the conference room, and two inside the conference room. There were a few other guys dressed inconspicuously that were dotted around the venue, keeping an eye on everything and everyone. In total, there were fifteen trained men carrying concealed weapons. This didn't include the four men that formed my personal security detail, who were also armed and highly trained. Call it paranoia, but you don't get to my position without gaining an enemy or two. No one has ever made an attempt on my life, but one can never be too careful.

Only the lawyer and the CSOs knew when and where the meetings were going to take place. Not even the tech guy knew where he was going. Alex showed up at the guy's apartment, told him to put on a suit and come with him. Alex told the guy that his services were required and he would be paid five hundred thousand credits for the consult. Alex informed me that he had spoken with the tech guy on the way to Albany, and the guy had the perfect solution for the bracelet problem. This was music to my ears: it meant that I would be able to travel without anyone knowing my movements.

Slipping out of the UNEA was now a possibility. It

was highly likely that I would be tailed by plainclothes enforcers for the duration of the trial, but this didn't matter. They could only follow me on land and at sea—no one would be able to trail me in the air. Air traffic laws required a specific amount of distance between aircrafts flying within a given airspace, and this distance wasn't sufficient for tailing another aircraft. Tracking my private jet would be impossible because we would instruct the pilot to switch of trackable comms, and flight transmitters when necessary.

Geoffrey was waiting in the lobby near hotel reception, where we exchanged pleasantries briefly and agreed to meet for a drink later that evening. I asked if everyone had arrived, and he confirmed that everyone was waiting in the conference room. He had my luggage sent to my suite, then my team and I headed to the conference room. The tech guy was to wait in the lobby until the end of the first meeting. Alex instructed security to keep an eye on him.

As I walked into the room, I saw a lot of worried faces. Looking the way they did, made it difficult to identify our potential chirper. This was the main reason for the meeting, to find out if anyone would express tell-tale signs of guilt. I was convinced that one of the directors was responsible for all of this. I couldn't order a hit on every single person in the room. The best I could do was to feel everyone out. I had no intentions of spooking anyone by making rash comments. As I sat down at the head of the table, Chris leaned over my shoulder to inform me that everyone's comms had been taken away and that I could speak freely. By freely he meant no one outside of the walls would hear us, but despite this we would still need to speak in code.

Since I had no intention of spooking our chirper, the plan was to mislead the directors into believing that we suspected someone outside the organization was responsible for everything that had happened. I was also going to lay out our business plans for the duration of the trial. The parts of the company affected were our pharmaceutical and armoury and ammunitions divisions. Edom Pharmaceuticals specialized in drugs and food supplements, while ProteriTek specialized in ammunitions, body and vehicular armour.

I greeted the Assembly and then started my opening speech. "Hello everyone, it has been an interesting couple of days to say the least, and I am sure you all have questions. We will get to that soon enough. I'm not going into too much detail about how much of a hit the company has taken as a result of recent events. Our main concern right now is how we move forward. As you are aware, the areas of focus are pharmaceuticals and armoury. Someone has given false information, leading to the conclusion by the government that we are involved in dealing illegal narcotics and firearms.

As you all know, we run a reputable organization and have done so for several years. The CSOs have conducted an internal investigation and have come to the conclusion that this false information did not originate from inside the company. The CSOs have narrowed it down to two suspects, and I can confirm they are rival companies. The only way to get back at the rival companies is a hostile takeover, so the CSOs will work with Seawall & Associates to go over the costs. We have taken a financial blow in these two areas of the business, and we will struggle to keep these divisions afloat.

With that said, I would like to ask you to stop production for the two divisions in every branch across the Nations. I would also like you to get your individual teams to carry out an internal audit, ensuring that no digi-docs have gone missing or been incorrectly filed. We also need take an inventory of profits and losses to see what the numbers look like so the CSOs and I can make relevant decisions regarding where we focus resources and funds."

So, what did all this mean in plain English? A hostile takeover meant killing the people that chirped. The military weapons and narcotic sales needed to stop temporarily, and the two divisions that served as the front would struggle to stay afloat. Each division needed to go through invoices, tax documents, payroll information—everything—to make sure all parts of the organization looked legit.

"I ask everyone here to exercise patience during the trial—your lives will no longer be private. You might find that you and members of your household may suddenly be under surveillance because of your affiliation to me. This more than anything will be annoying and perhaps embarrassing. Some of the surveillance will be covert, but seeing as you have nothing to hide, I suggest you just ignore this," I continued.

What this really meant was that the directors needed to be careful from this point on, as their every move was being monitored. The prosecutors wouldn't shy away from presenting new evidence that guaranteed not only my conviction, but the conviction of the directors and CSOs.

Working in a crime syndicate, everyone is aware of what they signed up for. They knew this day might come, and everyone was prepared for it—at least they should have been. Only one of the directors had concerns about the things I said, and that made me uncomfortable.

"With that said, do any of you have any questions?" I asked.

"But Dom, the Portland office has been exceeding our targets, surely our region shouldn't have to sacrifice its bonus?" Jason Byrne, one of the directors asked.

"I completely understand, Jason, but we are a collective, and bonuses have always been based on performance of the group as a whole. We'll all take a hit in order to keep the group profitable for the foreseeable future. I am not saying bonuses will be gone forever, but there will be no bonuses for at least six months. I hope that makes sense to you," I said.

"Yes, Dom," Jason replied.

"Okay, that is all for now, but we will reconvene at a later date. I assume everyone knows what to do from this point, periodic information will be cascaded to you by the CSOs. See you all again soon," I concluded, without giving anyone else the chance to speak.

Jason Byrne clearly wasn't the sharpest tool in the box. He had to go—it's this type of attitude that worried me. Someone like this would cooperate with the authorities when the chips were down. He will be terminated. Whenever I decided that someone had to leave the organization, they would be terminated or retired. Terminated meant they had to die. When someone was retired, they were no longer expected to participate in illegal business and would receive a retirement package. Members of the Assembly were handsomely compensated during and after service.

The directors had managers who reported to them. The managers were responsible for managing the supervisors. The supervisors were responsible for overseeing street-level activities and had direct contact with street workers. None of the managers were part of the Assembly, and only a limited number of managers knew about the shady part of the business. One of these managers would be promoted to take Jason's place.

Everyone waited until I left the room before making their exit. It was time to head up to my suite. My security detail, the CSOs, and I made our way back to the lobby and headed for the elevator. As we walked past the lobby, I asked Chris how much we were paying Jason.

"He gets ten million credits per annum before bonuses," Chris replied.

"Okay, so he is getting nearly as much as our more experienced directors then," I said.

"Yes, Dom, he is," Chris replied.

"I see," I said, as I went over what Jason said in my head.

We both stopped talking as we got in the elevator. The operator didn't need to ask which floor, he pressed the button for the eleventh floor, the penthouse. We exited the elevator and entered the suite, while the security detail waited outside the door.

"Dom, I take it you want us to get rid of him?" Alex asked.

"Can you imagine the nerve of that guy—I mean, is he on drugs? Clearly something's up with him. He is well paid, and he complains about not getting a bonus for a few months? We can't risk having someone like this around—he'll give us up at the first opportunity. I'll need to talk to him first to find out if he has been chirping, and if he has, find out what he's been saying."

We would need to take Jason out in the cleanest way possible, because his death would raise alarms if the appropriate precautions weren't put into place. It was a shame, really, and it broke my heart that he said what he did in that meeting. Many years ago, my dad had a conversation with me about running a business.

He said that one needed to pay close attention to the things that employees talked about. He believed, since employees could make or break a business, having insight into employee morale could prove invaluable. The words of an employee would give one a clear understanding of how they felt about their role within a business, and this had a direct correlation to their level of loyalty to that business. I felt that the comment by Jason showed that he only cared about himself, and if that was the case, then he would be capable of betraying me.

Chapter 11

Progression
Where: Guillermo's Cabana, North Walnut Grove, Miami
When: 1630 hours, Wednesday, January 15, 2010
Currency: US dollar

"Hi, Pops."

"Hi, son. You're late again."

"I know. Sorry about that."

"Let me guess, you've been hanging out with Christopher and Alexander again."

"Yes, sir."

"Son, I keep telling you, you are way too smart to be hanging around with those boys. They are nothing but trouble. What do you see in them anyway?"

"Well…"

"Don't even bother answering, I don't want to know. How was school today?"

"We had an algebra test today. I got an A."

"See what I mean, smart. You really need to focus on your studies, this is how you become successful in life. You do well in school, and you will end up with the best job. You can earn your money the right way, and you don't have to worry about cops or gangsters coming after you. You also don't have to worry about someone trying to kill you because of something that you or your friends have done. Anyway, put your bag in the back and help me clear up these dishes."

It had been fifteen years since Guillermo's arrival in Miami. Anna had given birth to a baby boy shortly after they arrived. They had named him Edwardo. Young Edwardo was vibrant and inquisitive, unlike his older sister, Isabel. She was more of an introvert and only interested in her studies. She was studying at the community college in Miami to become a nurse. After years of hard work, Guillermo was able to open a Dominican restaurant similar to the one that he had left behind in Puerto Plata. It even had similar décor. Since Guillermo couldn't afford to hire people to work in the restaurant, everyone in the family had to chip in. Anna did most of the cooking while Guillermo dealt with the customers. After school hours, Edwardo helped with the cleaning up and dishes. Isabel chipped in whenever she didn't have lectures or assignments. From time to time, the kids got some pocket money for helping out.

Edwardo was a smart kid who loved making money. He was also a dreamer like his father. He hoped to become rich one day. He used his pocket money to buy things at a discounted price and then sell them to students in school. He sold everything: jeans, caps, baseball cards, T-shirts, sneakers. He had the entrepreneurial spirit, just like his dad. At the age of fifteen, he had amassed over a thousand dollars. He understood the value of money and liked having cash in his pockets.

Edwardo picked up the dishes and headed for the kitchen, dropping his school bag near the kitchen entrance. Anna kept the kitchen, her pride and joy, in pristine condition. She and Guillermo had done all the refurbishment themselves. The kitchen walls were covered with blue-and-white mosaic tiles, and they spent a significant amount of money on crockery, cutlery, and commercial kitchen equipment. The menu had all sorts of Dominican cuisine that kept the customers coming back. Every inch of the restaurant was spotless, and this pleased the customers as well as health inspectors. As Edwardo walked into the kitchen, he found Anna chopping vegetables on her marble cutting board. He walked over and gave her a hug and a kiss on the cheek.

"Hi Mom, do you want help with that?" Edwardo asked.

"No, that's fine Edwardo, just do the dishes. There are more in the sink, there are a few pots in there as well," Anna replied.

Anna rarely allowed anyone to help her with the cooking, believing she was the only one who could perfectly execute her collection of recipes. Edwardo walked over to the giant double sink, perfect for washing in one side and rinsing in the other. Anna didn't like dishwashers. As far as she was concerned, they didn't do the job well enough. All the dishes were washed and rinsed in hot water, so Edwardo had to wear a pair of thick rubber gloves to complete the task.

"How was your day, son?" Anna asked.

"I was just saying to Pops, I got an A on my algebra test," Edwardo replied.

"Well done, son, I am so proud of you. You know that, right?" said Anna.

"I know Mom, but Pops gives me such a hard time about everything," replied Edwardo.

"Come on, everything?" Anna said.

"Okay, maybe not everything ..." said Edwardo.

"Listen son, your father, he wants what's best for you. That is why he brought us to this country, and that is why we work so hard, so that you and Isabel can have a very good life," Anna said.

"I know Mom, Pops is great. I wouldn't change him for the world," Edwardo replied.

"Well, I'm glad that you feel that way. The reason he gives you a hard time about those boys is because their parents aren't as strict as we are. Kids need guidance and discipline, otherwise they just end up getting into trouble. Your father doesn't think that the boys' parents are giving them enough discipline," said Anna.

"I understand, Mom. I only hang out with them in school, and sometimes outside the restaurant. You can see us out there. You can see that we don't do anything that would get us in trouble," Edwardo said.

"I hear you boy, just be careful with them. When you're done with the dishes, go see if we have any customers and if your dad needs help with anything else," said Anna.

"Okay, Mom," replied Edwardo.

The restaurant wasn't doing too bad, however, running a restaurant in that part of Miami wasn't an easy feat. The Cuban Cartel Sin Nombre had a stake in all the local businesses in North Walnut Grove. Every business that didn't lend its services to the cartel had to pay protection fees—it was as simple as that. If you failed to offer your services or didn't pay the protection fees, bad things generally happened. Your business would be vandalized, and the vandalism often extended to your home. Sometimes physical assaults were carried out, not just to the business owners—their families were also in danger of being hurt.

As a business owner, you either laundered drug money or provided a storehouse for the drugs in your place of business. Protection fees were an extortionate thirty percent of your earnings. By the time a business had paid its bills, fees, and taxes, there would be no profit. A business would be in danger of folding, which meant the owners would eventually accept cartel involvement to stay afloat. The alternative was to find another way to generate undocumented earnings through the business and try hiding it from the Cartel.

One of the benefits of working for the cartel was the two thousand dollars they paid the business owners for storing the drugs. They got that amount for every drop-off, and this was happening at least once a month. It was a win-win.

The authorities and rival cartels didn't know where the drugs were kept, and the business owners had extra money for themselves. Guillermo's business could not afford the protection fees, so he had to operate as a storehouse. He kept a low profile though—no fancy house, cars, clothes, or jewellery. He reinvested most of the earnings from the cartel into his business. This meant he could operate the restaurant efficiently and at a decent standard of quality. Anna chose not to ask questions about that side of the business—she didn't want to know the details. Guillermo felt this was probably best in case things went wrong and law enforcement got involved. She would have plausible deniability.

The drop-off for the drugs often took place after business hours. The cartel switched their drug courier and delivery time regularly. Upon delivery, the courier would go over the inventory of cocaine and heroin with Guillermo. Each package was labelled uniquely, allowing Guillermo to identify which drugs belonged to whom. Once the delivery had been made, the dealers within the restaurant's district would turn up at their assigned times to collect their share of the drugs. There was no exchange of money, because the dealers worked directly for the cartel and received a certain amount for the drugs they sold. There was no wholesale, which allowed the cartel to maximize profits. This was how they could afford to pay businesses to store and distribute the drugs. This system worked to perfection.

The restaurant closed at nine o'clock from Sunday to Thursday and eleven o'clock on Fridays and Saturdays. Anna and Isabel had already gone home for the day. Guillermo was expecting a delivery for ten o'clock that night, an hour after closing time. Edwardo had stayed behind to give him a hand, because it had been a busy night and Guillermo needed him to help tidy up. It was already 9:20 pm, and Edwardo was still in the middle of tidying up when Guillermo asked him to wrap-up and go home. He didn't want Edwardo hanging around when the drug courier arrived. Although it was dark outside, the house was around the corner, so Edwardo would make it home safely in less than a minute.

"You've done a very good job here today, son, it's time for you to go home. Please take the leftover rice pottage home and put it in the fridge," Guillermo said.

"Sure Pops, see you when you get home," replied Edwardo.

Edwardo went home, and shortly after there was a knock at the back door of the restaurant. The door led to the alleyway where deliveries for drinks and food supplies would be received. Guillermo asked who it was, and the voice on the other side of the door responded, "It's daydreamer." The courier had shown up earlier than expected. He loaded a few boxes onto his trolley and rolled the trolley through the kitchen.

Guillermo set up a table and a couple of chairs in the kitchen where the two started to count and weigh the individual bricks of cocaine and heroin. There were twenty-two bricks in total. Once all the drugs were accounted for, the dealers would collect their consignment at various intervals over the coming week. The courier informed Guillermo there was someone new representing the Pelican district, a guy they called Zorro Loco. He was going to be collecting his consignment the following evening.

Just as they were about to wrap up their meeting, a loud knock sounded from the front entrance. Guillermo headed down the hall. He hadn't lowered the shutters yet, so he had a clear view of who was knocking. It was Edwardo.

Looking frustrated, he opened the door. "Why have you come back, Edwardo? It's too late to be out of the house."

Edwardo noticed that his dad seemed irritated, and he apologized as he walked in. "Sorry Pops, but I forgot to take my school bag earlier."

Guillermo told him that he was talking with an old friend, and that he needed to collect his bag and head back home. As Edwardo picked up his school bag that he had left near the kitchen entrance, he could see the courier sat at the table in the kitchen. Since the courier didn't know who was at the door, he had quickly hidden the bricks in a nearby cupboard. The boxes that had contained the drugs were now empty and scattered on the floor.

"Thanks Pops, so I'll see you soon?" Edwardo asked. His father walked with him towards the front entrance, patted Edwardo on the back and told him he'd be home soon.

The restaurant had two hidden miniature cellars underneath the storeroom. The cellars had trapdoors disguised as floorboards. Guillermo had refashioned the floorboards himself. The previous owner had used the cellars to store alcohol. They were both six by eight feet, just enough room for an average-sized adult to maneouver around. There were eight steep steps leading down to each cellar. Guillermo always placed two wheeled, metallic racks over the retractable floorboards. The racks would shelve some kitchen utensils, spices and boxes of vegetables. To the untrained eye, the floorboards matched all the other floorboards in the storeroom perfectly. The wheeled racks also formed an extra layer of disguise.

Guillermo kept a safe containing some cash and documents in one of the cellars. He would always split the drug delivery in two, stashing them in each cellar. Once the drugs had been secured, he let the courier out the back door and locked it.

Around 8:30 pm the following evening, Guillermo was sitting at the far end of the restaurant. He was working on the restaurant's sales figures when a man walked in. He couldn't see the man's face clearly, so he stopped what he was doing, got up, and walked towards the stranger. There was something familiar about the man. As Guillermo got closer, the man said, "I can't believe it! When they told me about this place, I never imagined that the owner would be you."

Guillermo got close enough to see who it was. "Wait a minute, you are Zorro Loco? This is unbelievable, it's been what, fourteen, fifteen years? Come in, have a seat." It was Guillermo's officer friend from Puerto Plata, he had managed to find his way to America. Zorro Loco explained how he didn't have a choice but to get involved in Miami's drug industry, and how he was doing it all for his family—his new family. The so-called dream of moving his original family to the United States never came to fruition. He didn't go into too much detail, but the short of it was that he abandoned his family in Puerto Plata and started a new one when he got to Miami. He said if given the choice, he wouldn't be involved in the drug business. Guillermo didn't believe anything he was saying.

The men sat down and had a couple of beers as they reminisced about old times. As usual, Guillermo didn't have much to say to him. He mostly listened with the occasional nod and a fake smile. It was getting late, so Guillermo told Zorro he had to close for the day. He asked Zorro to give him a couple of minutes to get the bricks he had come for. When he entered the storeroom, he made sure Zorro hadn't followed him.

A couple of minutes later he re-emerged with three

bricks. He handed the drugs to Zorro, who stuck a pocketknife in each package and then to his tongue to test the quality. As Zorro tested the drugs, Guillermo objected. "Come on, you should trust me. I have never given you a reason not to."

Zorro replied, "My friend, in the drug business, I trust no one."

Zorro left the restaurant in good spirits, but Guillermo wasn't happy with the encounter. He had never liked Zorro. He tolerated the man when they were in Puerto Plata, but now he felt that having to deal with him again, would be hard work. *Well, he won't have free meals and drinks here, that's for sure,* he thought to himself. The restaurant was doing well, the kids were taken care of financially, and Guillermo had a significant amount of money saved. As far as he was concerned, he had found the success that he'd always dreamed of.

Chapter 12

Project Neon
Where: The Royal Scepter, The United Nations of Europe and Americas, Albany, New York
When: 1345 hours, Thursday, October 3, 2041
Currency: UNEA credits

I was already thinking about the meetings with business partners outside the UNEA. If they were to take place, I would have to take care of the bracelet problem. I hoped Alex's tech guy would prove his worth.

"Dom, the tech guy is waiting downstairs, shall we have him sent up?"

"Yes, Alex, please do that."

If the guy manages to sort out the bracelet issue, we would need to get rid of him. I couldn't allow any loose ends. The last thing I needed was for him to somehow get himself arrested and be placed in a vulnerable position. There's no guarantee he wouldn't testify to tampering with the tracking bracelet if the enforcers applied the right amount of pressure. Once he completed the job, I would give the order to take him out and then have Alex make it look drug-related or something of that nature.

"Dom, this is the guy I was telling you about," said Alex.

"Hey kid, I hear you'll be able to help me with this fancy piece of jewellery on my wrist," I said.

"Oh God, you are Eddie Dominguez, head of Edom Group—oh my God!" said the tech guy.

"Yes, I am. Calm down, kid."

"I am so sorry, sir, oh my God!" He said, in excitement.

"It's all right, kid. Tell me what you can do about the bracelet," I said.

"Umm, is it all right if I have a look?" he asked.

"Sure, go ahead," I replied.

"Hmm, this is a model SP3-C14L series 2.5, equipped with 1.5 Terabyte Haze Hexcryption. For the layman, this is difficult to hack," he said.

"But for you?" I asked.

"Piece of cake, sir. I will bypass the HexC protocols and carry out a reverse-ping, which will probably result in hitting a hot fence. Getting past the hot fence will be tricky, but I can do it. Once I do, I will have access to the monitoring platform. Once I'm in the platform, I can manipulate location reads to give off false location info," he replied.

"Okay, what does this mean in English?" I asked.

"We don't need to remove the bracelet. You see this nano-jack—right here on the side of the bezel? I can hook up to it, connect to the remote monitoring system, and make it think you are at location A, when actually you are in location B," he explained.

"You can do that?" I asked.

"Indeed, sir. I can also redefine the location index in a way that allows you to choose the locations that you would prefer to display," he replied.

"That is just perfect. Make it happen," I said.

The kid did everything he said he would do, he even gave me a demo to prove that it had worked. When I looked up my current location, the system said I was at the office in Milwaukee. This was amazing. The best part was that no alarms had been triggered—we would have known right away if this had been the case. Within minutes enforcers would have stormed the hotel and taken me back into custody.

"Mr. Dominguez, there is something else I think you might be interested in. Do you mind if I show you?" he asked reluctantly.

"Sure, what is it?" I said.

He loaded up a screen on his comms device.

"This is something that my friend and I have been working on, we call it Project Neon. You see this right here? This is the blueprint for a singular nanite, the first of its kind. It is designed to alter a subject's state of mind. Combine this nanite with thousands like it, and you can do things like repair brain cells and manipulate psycho-neural performance.

This requires a significant amount of input from medical practitioners for us to accurately develop the code. Of course, there is also all the red tape that goes with a project like this. For now, though, we know for a fact that we can execute a program that can alter the state of specific brain cells. With this, we can manipulate the parts of the brain responsible for producing dopamine, serotonin, endorphins, and oxytocin. One of the best things about this is the nanites can be remotely controlled via a comms network, allowing remote shutdown. This means that the nanites can be switched off from anywhere in the world and released through bodily fluids of one's choosing." he explained.

"Wait, are you telling me that you have designed a micro-robot that is capable of getting people high?" I asked.

"Umm yeah, pretty much," he responded.

"And you can switch it off, and it can be released through blood, tears, sweat, or urine?" I asked.

"That's right, if someone didn't want the nanites detected in their system for whatever reason, they can be gotten rid of easily," he said.

"Hmm, this is impressive stuff," I said.

"Not only that, the nanites can be programmed to instruct the brain, to produce specified amounts of various chemicals. This will make it possible to control the intensity of any given experience," he explained.

"Okay kid, you now have my attention. What about side effects?" I asked.

"As with anything mind-altering, there will always be associated risks. Take for instance someone who suffers from psychogenic seizures, excess brain stimulation can trigger such seizures. Unique experiences may trigger paranoia or panic attacks, and people with heart problems may run the risk of suffering from heart failure as a result," he said.

"Kid, I think you might be onto something here. Have you been speaking to anyone else about this?" I asked.

"No, the only person that knows about the project is my friend. Well, and you too, now," he replied.

"Okay, you have given me something to think about. Give me some time to digest all this information, and we will let you know whether we will be investing in this. I take it that's why you have shown me this—you need someone to put the funding behind the project?" I asked.

"That's right, Mr. Dominguez, we have to fine-tune things with the robotics and coding parts of the project to be able to do this. As you've probably guessed, I will be responsible for writing the code. My friend Justin will be responsible for building the nanites. So far, I've been able to develop a considerable amount of the code. Justin's nanites, on the other hand, require expensive materials and high-end equipment. Up to this point, we've been working out of my parents' garage. We are going to need a decent secured facility to deliver the project properly. We will eventually need to involve other people, experts in the pharmaceutical field," he said.

"Okay, not to worry, we will come back to you with an answer soon. You will get the five hundred thousand credits that Alex offered for your services today. I will approve an extra one million credits to split with your friend as a retainer for Project Neon. For now, don't tell your friend where the funds came from until we've given you the go-ahead. Just tell him that you have someone who wishes to remain a silent investor for now. This means neither of you speaks a word about the project to anyone. And oh, I'm sure that I don't need to emphasise that you were never here today," I said.

"Oh absolutely Mr. Dominguez, I would never jeopardize your trust in any way," he replied.

"Good, we'll be in touch. What's your name, kid?" I asked.

"It's Matt sir, Matthew Harrington. Thank you, sir, thanks a lot!"

This was probably the best meeting I'd had in a while—this kid was definitely onto something big. If everything panned out with this project, Edom Group would make trillions. I didn't know much about nanites, but from what Matt explained, I could think of many ways to monetize this. We wouldn't need to look far to find people who would offer their expertise for Project Neon. Edom Pharmaceuticals has several qualified people who would be perfect for the project. I wasn't only interested in the end product; I wanted the patent.

"Goodness, Alex, where did you find this kid?" I said, trying to contain my excitement.

"Ha-ha. We've used his resources in the past. Believe it or not, I found him on social media where he advertised himself as a freelance data analyst. At the time, we were just looking for someone to analyse some of our data against our competitors, only to discover he had other talents. I was able to get him to hack into a number of databases to retrieve information we didn't have access to at the time," Alex explained.

"Well, we need to spend a lot more time on social media to see if there are other people like him. This kid is amazing. I think we can get our guys from pharmaceuticals in on this. My only question is, can we trust him?" I asked.

"I've never had a problem with him, none of the stuff that he's done for us has ever leaked. You know what's funny though, until today he didn't even know I was connected to Edom Group. Now that he does, I'll make sure I reiterate the importance of confidentiality. If you decide you want to bring him into the fold, it would be a straightforward affair, as we've already run checks on him. His friend, however, is a whole other matter. We would have to put him through the vetting process. Matt's track record with us as a hacker works out perfectly—it means he will bend the rules whenever he is required to," Alex said.

"Boy, is he lucky. I was going to ask you to get rid of him. However, I think he'll be of good use to us. Run further checks on him, check out his friend as well. If everything pans out, take them through the checking process. Make sure he gets the 1.5 million credits today," I said.

"Sure thing, Dom. So, Joe mentioned that you asked about worst-case scenarios and you wanted to know about our contacts in the prisons. We have most of the wardens in the major prisons in our pockets. We also have incarcerated high-ranking gang members on retainer. We pay a set number of credits onto their books every month for situations like this. This gesture ensures that our people are protected if they ever have to do time," Alex said.

"That sounds great," I said.

The trial was going to cost Edom Group a significant amount of money, and Project Neon was the way to not only recover, but it would propel the company to greater heights. We needed to figure out ways to keep generating revenue in the meantime. This was the focus of the discussion between me and the CSOs this afternoon. In the current market, there was no better place to invest than in the AU. The AU was still one of the best places to source raw materials. Erratanite had become one of the most sought-after commodities, and mining it was becoming rampant in the AU. This meant market prices had declined slightly, making it cheaper to buy. With the emergence of erratanite-related products, now would be the best time to invest. It is a lightweight, submetallic mineral found in certain parts of the AU. Due to its light weight and durability, it had become the top choice for manufacturers of ships, boats, and planes.

"So, now that this tracking bracelet is no longer an issue, we will need to arrange a trip to Nasarawa," I said.

"Wow, Nigeria?" said Chris.

"Yes, Chris. We can make a killing from erratanite. We can use it in some of the tech that goes into our armoury products. What's even better is we can also act as a broker between the AU and the IST. These territories currently don't have a trade agreement for buying or distributing erratanite. The Swiss are very thorough, and they haven't been able to come to an agreement with the Africans regarding the health and safety issues. We need to take advantage of this while we can," I said.

"Do you have a date in mind, Dom?" Alex asked.

"Nothing set in stone. I need to stick around, until the prosecution team, has laid out all the evidence they have on me. This will allow us to maneouver a lot easier, and we should know before the end of the month. I will be speaking to Dahiru to work out the logistics," I said.

Dahiru Wali specialized in mining. His company was the only one licensed to mine erratanite in the Nasarawa region of Nigeria. This monopoly gained him a few enemies in the region. He had studied metallurgy and mineralogy at the Nasarawa Institute of Science. This made him an expert in the field, knowing exactly where to find high deposits of erratanite in the Nasarawa region.

Dahiru and I crossed paths in Tokyo back in

2021—he sat next to me during the men's tennis finals. What was fascinating about how we met was neither of us were huge tennis fans. So, meeting him that day was simply being in the right place at the right time. He was at the event with a girlfriend who wanted to see the match, and I had just met with a business partner, who had chosen a venue near the stadium as the meeting point. I was looking to set up a profitable business to act as a front for my drug dealing.

Zhang Heng, a young Chinese entrepreneur, was looking for investors for a project he had been working on. By the end of the meeting, we agreed to the terms of my investment. At the time, we were both in our mid-twenties and very ambitious. Our ambition led to him owning majority of the shares in the automobile company named after him, and to me being the head of Edom Group. After the meeting, Heng handed me a ticket for the match. Since my flight wasn't till later that evening, I figured watching the match would be a good way to kill time.

Dahiru initiated the dialogue, wanting to know if I followed tennis, and I explained that I was given a free ticket to attend the event, but I wasn't a fan. He thought this was ironic, because he didn't really follow the sport either. I ordered drinks, and we discussed each other's business ventures and exchanged business cards. As fate would have it, we did quite a bit of business in the years that followed.

Chapter 13

Treachery
Where: Guillermo's Cabana, North Walnut Grove, Miami
When: 1630 hours, Wednesday, January 18, 2012
Currency: US dollar

Guillermo's son would be graduating in the summer of 2012. Edwardo asked if he could have a car as his graduation present. Guillermo shut down the idea initially. He felt that ethnic minorities were constantly getting pulled over and harassed by Miami police officers, and he didn't want his son to have to deal with that at a young age. Eventually, Edwardo convinced Guillermo that it would be a good way to learn about cars, because he had an interest in automotive engineering. It was in this field of study that he planned on enrolling, once he had decided which university he was going to attend. Edwardo made a valid point, and Guillermo could not deny the advantages of Edwardo being able to work on his own car engine as part of his studies. Isabel had graduated a couple of years prior, so he no longer had to pay for her tuition. This and the fact that he had some money saved meant he was in a good position to pay Edwardo's tuition.

Regarding the car though, he told Edwardo that he would only be contributing half of the money. He knew that Edwardo had some money saved. He told him he would have to dip into his personal savings to come up with the other half. Edwardo had no objections to this. Like his father, he had been very prudent with his money. So much so that he could have bought his car of choice three times over. All through high school, the young man had been wheeling and dealing so much that he commanded the respect of his peers. He even loaned money to other students and charged them a small amount of interest. He was a true entrepreneur. The car he was looking to buy was a 1965 Rhinox, a beastly muscle car that had a V8 5.0 litre engine. The plan was to buy one that needed restoration, and he was going to restore the engine, body, and interior.

"So, Pops, thanks for agreeing to help me pay for the car, I am really looking forward to it. I'm not going to be graduating for another few months, is it okay if I get the car sooner? Can we shop around this weekend?" Edwardo asked.

"Okay, sure. Isabel has the weekend off. I'm sure your Mom and Isabel can hold down the fort, while you and I visit a couple of car dealerships," said Guillermo.

"That's great, so exciting," Edwardo said.

"You deserve it, son. You work really hard, and I am proud of you," said Guillermo.

"Gee, thanks, Pops," Edwardo said.

The drug business had been booming, and Guillermo had been raking in a lot of money. There was a downside to this though. All this drew too much attention and the cartel rivals wanted a piece of the action. The leader of the Carlsdale family, Devin "The Duke" Carlsdale, had been imprisoned, but this hadn't affected their ambition. The Duke, along with his two younger brothers, ran the crime family, and they were determined to take control from the Sin Nombre Cartel. The Carlsdales had successfully taken over some territories and formed strongholds covering thirty percent of Miami—districts that had once belonged to the cartel. For the last seven years, the Duke managed to run the entire operation from behind bars and was still able to deal blows to the cartel.

Guillermo hadn't planned on remaining in Miami forever. His plan was to eventually sell his home, relinquish ownership of the restaurant to the cartel, and move to Milwaukee. This was what he had planned, retiring from the cartel lifestyle. He had been thinking about the nicer cities to live in, and Milwaukee was the place that seemed to be the most suitable to him.

The Carlsdales fight for territory could lead to overthrowing the cartel completely. Bloodshed was an inevitability, so Guillermo's retirement plan wasn't completely far-fetched.

Edwardo would be attending one of the local universities, because Guillermo didn't want him studying far from home. Edwardo would graduate in another three to four years, and after that Guillermo would move the entire family to Milwaukee. They were a close-knit family, so the idea of leaving Miami wasn't going to be a problem for any of them.

"So, do you need me to do anything here today, Pops?" Edwardo asked.

"Yes, the tables need to be wiped down and the floors… wait, turn the TV volume up!" Guillermo said.

"...today, during the parole hearing of crime boss Devin 'The Duke' Carlsdale, nineteen heavily armed men covered in full body armour made a forceful entry into the court building, successfully breaking out the criminal mastermind from federal custody. It is believed that the escape was staged because the chances that Carlsdale would be granted parole seemed highly unlikely. Standing by is our correspondent Karen Summers, reporting live from the federal courthouse in Florida."

"We are reporting live, and as you can see; we are about five yards from the court entrance where the armed men entered the building. The men also exited the building the same way. We spoke to one of the court bailiffs, who has confirmed to us that there was nothing that could have been done to prevent the escape, as they were outnumbered and completely outgunned."

"Karen, are you able to tell us if there were any injuries or fatalities?"

"Pat, the court bailiff we spoke to informed us that another officer had suffered a concussion after

receiving a blow to the head from the butt of an assault rifle belonging to one of the assailants. He has been transported to the hospital by paramedics, but we've been informed that the officer will be okay."

"Are you able to tell us anything else about the people that were present when it all happened?"

"Pat, what we have been told is that although there weren't any casualties during what seems to be a well-planned jailbreak, the people that witnessed the event are shaken up. This has never happened in the history of this courthouse, and it must have been devastating to have to experience something like this."

"Karen, I can only assume that no one could get a good look at any of the assailants during the attack."

"You guessed right, Pat, the gunmen were all wearing masks. There were several black, unmarked vans that dispersed in separate directions within a few minutes of the infiltration. Not only were the vans untraceable, they all just seemed to vanish into thin air shortly after the attack."

"Okay, thanks, Karen. Our hearts go out to the people that witnessed this horrible event. We will bring you updates as soon as we have more information about the courthouse attack. Pat Waters for CSCG News."

"This is not good," Guillermo said as the look of worry overcame his face.

"What's wrong, Pops? Nobody died from this," Edwardo said.

"I know, son," Guillermo said.

"Is this going to be bad for business?" Edwardo asked.

"What do you mean by that, son?" asked Guillermo.

"Come on Pops, I'm not stupid, you know. The late-night meetings with 'your friends,' the hidden cellars in the storeroom, the fact that no one from the cartel ever bothers us. It's fine, I know everything you do is not out of choice. I know that you are only looking out for all of us," Edwardo said.

"You know about the hidden cellar—you didn't look inside, did you?" Guillermo asked.

"Nah, it's none of my business. If you felt I needed to know what was in there, I'm sure you would have told me by now," Edwardo replied.

"How did you get so smart, boy?" said Guillermo.

"I learned from my smart dad, I guess," replied Eddie with a smile.

"Okay, here's the thing—the Duke escaping from prison might affect the business from the security side of things. Escaping from prison, disappearing, and then successfully staying below the radar all cost money… and because of this, the Carlsdale family might want to take over even more of the cartel's territories. The cartel might increase the number of soldiers that currently protect North Walnut Grove and all their other territories. However, if this doesn't work and the Carlsdales succeed, it will definitely affect the amount of money we make. If they take over North Walnut

Grove, who knows what kind of arrangement the Duke will have with the business owners here? There might not even be much of an arrangement; it might just be the case of working for them just to stay alive," Guillermo said.

"Do we have enough money to leave all this behind and move to Milwaukee now? You've been planning on moving there for years. I don't need to attend college in Miami, or even Florida, for that matter," Edwardo said.

"It is okay, son, it hasn't come to that yet. Listen, this is not the life that I planned for you, so forget about all of this and focus on your studies. You hear me?" said Guillermo.

"Sure thing, Pops, I understand," Edwardo said.

"Good. Look, I am expecting someone to do a collection from the restaurant tomorrow evening. So, I need to make sure that I'm the only person left in the restaurant after nine o'clock." said Guillermo.

"Okay, Pops," Edwardo replied.

Edwardo knew all about his father's side business with the cartel. His friends Christopher and Alexander's parents were also business owners who had ties to the cartel. Unlike Guillermo, Christopher and Alexander's parents didn't do a good job of shielding their dodgy dealings from their children. The two boys often bragged about their parents' connection with the cartel and the amount of money they were making. Even after Edwardo figured out that his father's business was also connected to the cartel, he never spoke a word of it to the boys. He simply told them he didn't know anything and that he never asked his dad any questions.

Around closing time, Guillermo sat in his usual spot towards the back of the restaurant, sorting out the sale figures for the day, while Edwardo was busy tidying up the kitchen. Suddenly, Zorro Loco walked in with another guy, and Edwardo heard their voices. He decided to walk over to the door that led back to the restaurant and peeked through the small circular window in the door. He saw the two men. He knew who Zorro was, because he had seen him on a couple of occasions. However, he didn't recognize the man with him. Edwardo also knew that Zorro was involved in the drug trade in his district—Christopher and Alexander talked about him from time to time. They heard rumours about how ruthless Zorro was and how he was responsible for the deaths of a couple of drug addicts that had lived in the district.

"Hey, my friend, what's going on? Your collection day is tomorrow, is everything okay?" Guillermo asked Zorro.

"Yes, everything is fine, we just dropped by to say hello, you know. No big deal," Zorro replied.

"I see. Welcome, please have a seat. Would you gentlemen like something to drink?" Guillermo asked.

"Yeah sure, why not, thanks. A couple of beers, please," replied Zorro.

Guillermo sensed something was off—he could tell by Zorro's demeanour that he was up to something. The fact that Zorro turned up with a stranger also raised a few flags. He had a feeling, things would go south. He went into the kitchen and quietly told Edwardo to hide in the cellar on the right side of the storeroom. He told him to remain quiet and not to come out until the coast was clear. He rolled the metal rack over the cellar Edwardo was hiding in but rolled away the rack from the cellar containing some of the drugs. He grabbed a couple of beers from the fridge and walked back to the table where Zorro and the stranger were sitting. He put the beers on the table.

"So, how's business?" Guillermo asked.

"Business is going well, as a matter of fact, business is about to be very good," Zorro replied.

"Oh really, that's good to hear," said Guillermo.

"Guillermo, are you here by yourself?" Zorro asked.

"Yes, I sent the family home early today. Why do you ask?" said Guillermo.

"Well, it's probably best that you are here by yourself, we wouldn't want to drag anyone else into this," said Zorro.

"Wait, what do you mean, what's going on?" Guillermo asked with a sudden look of worry.

"Where are the drugs, Guillermo? We want all of it," said Zorro.

Zorro retrieved a fifty-calibre pistol from a holster tucked underneath his jacket, and the other man drew a firearm as well. Zorro planned on taking the drugs and selling them to a dealer he knew in Tampa. The cartel didn't have strong ties there so he would be able to off-load the drugs without raising any suspicions from the cartel.

"Okay, the drugs are in the storeroom in the back, I will get them for you," Guillermo replied nervously.

"Get up, show us!" said the gentleman that came in with Zorro.

"Okay, okay, just take it easy," Guillermo said.

As he was leading the two men to the storeroom, he told Zorro that what he was doing wasn't sensible. Being sensible was the last thing on Zorro's mind. The only thing he cared about was making a lot of money, and Guillermo and his drugs were the key.

"So, you've known me for this long, and you are willing to do this to me?" asked Guillermo.

"Hey, it's a cold world, my friend, you do what you have to do to get ahead in this life. If it means killing someone you know, then so be it. Don't take this personal, Guillermo, it's just the nature of business," said Zorro.

"What I don't understand is that you know that I am protected by the cartel. Do you really think that you will get away with this?" Guillermo asked.

"Okay, that's enough, where are the drugs?" Zorro said in a more aggressive tone.

Edwardo could hear the entire conversation between his father and Zorro. He also heard the squeaky door from the other cellar open. Although scared at that point, Guillermo summoned the courage to climb down the steps. He retrieved the green duffle bag containing eleven bricks and holding it up, he climbed back up the steps. Both men were still pointing their guns in Guillermo's direction. The bag contained seven bricks of cocaine and four bricks of heroin. Zorro asked him to slowly open the bag. Zorro could see the drugs from where he was standing. He told Guillermo to zip the bag back up and drop it on the floor. As he dropped the duffle bag, he said to Zorro, "You have always been a slimy snake, and I never liked you. You will burn in hell for this. What are you waiting for? Do what you came here to do, coward!" said Guillermo.

Two shots rang out from Zorro's pistol, one to Guillermo's chest, the other to his head. This made Edwardo jump, but somehow, he managed to stay quiet enough not to give away his position. Zorro told the man with him to pick up the bag, and they both fled the scene, leaving Guillermo lying in a pool of blood.

Edwardo waited until he could no longer hear any of the voices, then slowly emerged from his hiding place. He pushed the trapdoor upwards with all his strength until the metal storage rack rolled off to the side. He saw his father's body lying there facedown, there was blood everywhere. He knew his father was dead, and tears filled his eyes as he sat next to the body, trembling. He eventually gathered himself, wiped the tears from his face, got up, and called 911.

"Hello, 911, what's your emergency?"

"Hello. It's my dad, he's been shot."

"What is your name?"

"It's Edwardo, Edwardo Dominguez ... "

"Okay Edwardo, are you hurt?"

"No, I'm fine."

"Okay good, can you tell if your dad is still breathing or if he has a pulse?"

"No, he is dead. They shot him in the head and in the chest."

"I am so sorry to hear that. How many people were there, do you know if they are nearby?"

"There were two men, they are gone now."

"Okay, do me a favour—don't touch anything until the police arrive. Do you think you'll be able to do that?"

"Yes."

"I will send the police to you right away. Do you want me to stay on the line with you until the police get there?"

"No, that's fine, I need to call my mom now. Thank you."

"No problem at all, hang in there, the police are on the way. I will call back in five minutes to make sure that you are okay."

"Thank you."

Edwardo noticed there were drugs and cash in the cellar he had been hiding in. So, after his call to 911, he retrieved the drugs and cash and stashed them behind a dumpster at the back of the restaurant. The plan was to move them to his bedroom at some point that night, while no one was watching. Once he did this, he contacted his mother to let her know what had happened.

Chapter 14

Hard Evidence
Where: The Nations High Court, The United Nations of Europe and Americas, Washington, DC
When: 1010 hours, Wednesday, October 30, 2041
Currency: UNEA credits

The time had come for the prosecution team to present its evidence to the court. Since I was no longer in custody, I would be given the privilege of being physically present in the courtroom during discovery proceedings. I would get to see the judge face to face. There would be no need for the Vexa transmission this time, which is good because I am not a big fan of the technology. I find it a bit surreal and creepy.

During discovery proceedings, the judge would decide what would be accepted into evidence and what would be excluded. Joe would have the opportunity to argue against evidence he deemed unsuitable or irrelevant. Of course, he would have to support his argument with sufficient reason to justify the request for exclusion. Joe was good, but there was no way of guaranteeing a positive outcome. This was completely out of our hands. Previously, we were unsuccessful in our attempt to find out what evidence the prosecution had on me. There was no way of accessing the evidence room or database—we even threw money at the problem, to no avail. We couldn't find a single corrupt enforcer directly involved in, or close to, the case. There also wasn't a single enforcer we could find who would accept a bribe in exchange for access to the evidence room. We didn't know anyone who had access to the local evidence database. It was a local database in the sense that it wasn't connected to any network, not even the local secured court network. Having the required access would have helped in manipulating the trial, but we didn't have it, so we'd have to look for other ways to ensure things go our way.

At this point, all we could do is hope for the best. Joe's strategy is to argue against every single piece of evidence. For anything that can't be argued against, he will come up with as many questions as possible to raise doubt during the actual trial. At the end of the session, the trial date will be decided by the good judge.

"Your Honour, for the charges of record tampering and identity cultivation, the prosecution presents Exhibit A, data footprints containing an exchange of digital dialogue between two IP addresses. The first address traced back to a comms device belonging to Edom Group. The other IP address belongs to an organization that has been linked to numerous criminal activities in direct violation of Section 7–9(C) of the UNEA Cyber-Security Act. These footprints will not only prove that the defendant has direct involvement with the data cultivation syndicate that is responsible for the generation and facilitation of numerous false identities, it will also show that Mr. Dominguez is the mastermind behind the criminal organization in question." said the lead prosecutor.

As planned, Joe wasn't going to allow any piece of evidence go by without scrutiny, so the first objection was raised.

"Your Honour, the defence would like to request access to a copy of the said data footprint in order to validate its authenticity as well as help us to prepare for argument. Could we please be granted this request, Your Honour?" Joe asked.

"Mr. Abrams, I find it ironic and amusing that in your current position and with the charge in question, you are requesting to verify information presented by the very team that is prosecuting your client. This is indeed fascinating. Permission granted. Mr. Grant, please make the relevant information available to Mr. Abrams. In the meantime, I will accept Exhibit A into evidence. If I find reasonable cause that this piece of evidence is flawed in any way, I will reverse my decision. Mr. Abrams, you have until after recess to prove your case on this matter." replied the judge.

"Thank you, Your Honour," Joe said.

"Oh, don't mention it. Anything for you, Mr. Abrams," the judge replied sarcastically.

The judge was a piece of work, his sarcasm was

unmatched. The lead prosecutor, Michael Grant, was one of the Nation's most ruthless prosecutors. Considering everything I've noticed with this guy, he seemed to be just like everyone else working in the judicial system, like he had something to prove. His co-prosecutor was Tracey Vorderman. Joe mentioned that, like the lead prosecutor, she also had a merciless approach to questioning and had been known to make a few tough guys crack under pressure. So, this was what we were up against: a couple of anal-retentive individuals who made it their life's mission to bring down me down. We will need to work quickly on the data footprints. Joe will only have a few minutes to look it over and then rebut, if need be. He will need to spend time on reviewing other pieces of evidence as well, so we didn't have the luxury of wasting too much time on just one.

"Your Honour, for the charge of online racketeering, we present Exhibit A(1). We have documents signed by four confidential informants that will prove the defendant's involvement in online racketeering. The testimony of these individuals will show how Mr. Dominguez gave the orders to his men to disrupt the online presence of their small e-businesses. The documents detail how the businesses would have been sabotaged had regular payments not been made to the defendant's organization. The evidence will also reveal how the payments were made regularly to the defendant," said the lead prosecutor.

This is the part I hadn't been looking forward to. I initially thought we would be dealing with one witness, maybe two. But four…

"Your Honour, we would like to request access to the testimonies," Joe said.

"Nice try, Mr. Abrams. Giving you access to these documents will reveal the identities of the witnesses, which is not going to happen. Their testimony will be admitted into evidence with no option for review," replied the judge.

Joe knew he wasn't going to be given access to those digi-docs—even I knew that. Joe was quite the character. I think he asked the question just to get a reaction from the judge.

"Your Honour, for the charge of distribution of illegal narcotics, we present Exhibit B. This plastic medicine bottle is one of many that contains drugs that were seized from one of Edom Pharmaceuticals' warehouses. As you can see, the container is clearly labelled Oxyoraliphine. After some testing had been carried out in the NLEU's labs, it was discovered that the composition of this drug contained ingredients that are not listed on the container. This was the case for ninety-nine other containers.

The evidence will also reveal that some of the ingredients haven't been approved by the NFDA. We will prove that the unlisted ingredients have been omitted intentionally by Edom Pharmaceuticals to conceal the mind-altering capabilities of the drug. We will make the case that the defendant, being the president of Edom Group, had direct involvement in this," said the co-prosecutor.

I guess the co-prosecutor would be doing the questing for this charge during the trial. This is the charge that I had no worries about. Drugs played a massive role in the Nation's revenue, legal or otherwise. We had so many ways to beat this charge. What perplexes me is that my organization is actually active in illegal narcotic distribution, but not a single eyebrow had been raised about that. We've been pushing coke and heroin across the UNEA for years with hardly any problems, but now they're trying to nail me for missing an item on the list of ingredients for our semi-legal drugs.

"Mr. Abrams, you don't plan on reviewing this piece of evidence?" asked the judge sarcastically.

"No, Your Honour, at this point we have no reason to review it. We are already prepared for arguments on this issue," replied Joe.

"Oh, how nice. Very well, Exhibit B is now admitted into evidence," said the judge.

The reason Joe was so confident about the drug thing was that there were a few senior officials in the NFDA that had been paid off by shareholders of Pharmotek, the pharmaceutical company responsible for manufacturing Oxyoraliphine. Edom Group's involvement was only procuring in bulk and redistributing in the retail market. For us to go down meant that Pharmotek would be going down as well, and Pharmotek's shareholders weren't going to let that happen. Also, Edom Group had earned Pharmotek hundreds of millions. We were protected. I'm not even sure how things got this far—the enforcers behind this must have kept the investigation very discreet. The prosecution team agreeing to pursue the case was a silly move. I believe that even the judge knew that this charge wasn't going anywhere. I was confident that this charge wouldn't make it to trial.

"Your Honour, for the charge of distribution of illegal military-grade firearms, we would like to present Exhibits C(1) and C(2). We have the signed testimony of an individual, along with photo evidence, that proves the defendant, through Edom Group, has supplied illegal military-grade firearms to street gangs across the state of Florida and across several other regions within the UNEA," said the lead prosecutor.

There was no way of finding out for sure who had cooperated with the NLEU regarding the guns. It could have been our director of armoury or the senior manager. It could have been one of the gang leaders—it could have been almost anyone. This one was going to require a thorough investigation of our own.

"Mr. Abrams, this is pretty much the same as Exhibit A(1), so this witness's testimony will be admitted into evidence with no option to review. You can review the photographs if you wish," said the judge.

"Thank you, Your Honour. We are happy with the

photographs, and we ask permission to retain copies," replied Joe.

"As you wish. Mr. Grant, provide the defence with copies of the photographs," the judge said to the lead prosecutor.

"No problem, Your Honour., replied the lead prosecutor.

The pictures only showed me inspecting the firearms, they didn't show any witnesses. The prosecution team was feeling confident at this point, made obvious by their demeanour. The lead prosecutor and his co-counsel were delivering evidentiary blows all over the place. Michael and Tracy had this self-righteous vibe about them, what a perfect couple. They made me sick. The judge did as well, I just couldn't stand it. I wasn't going to take all this without doing something. I could have them all killed, but that would only draw more attention to me. It was during this hearing that I decided I was going to put round-the-clock surveillance on all three of them. Hopefully we would be able to dig up dirt on them. If we got lucky, they would be discredited, and that would at least prolong the case pending their replacements.

"Your Honour, for the charge of kidnapping, the prosecution presents Exhibit D. We have signed testimony from an individual which reveals that they were taken against their will, following an order from the defendant. The evidence will prove that the instruction to kidnap this individual came directly from

Mr. Dominguez," said the co-prosecutor.

Another one for the co-prosecutor. This was getting ridiculous. So far, six witnesses had been mentioned. Their identities will have to be revealed at some point, and once that happened, I would have them killed. Of course, it would be out of spite at this point, because they would have already given their testimony. However, it would give me satisfaction to know the low-life chirpers had been permanently taken care of.

"Your Honour, for the charge of conspiracy to assassinate a government official, we present Exhibit F. We have in our possession an audio file that will prove the conspiracy to assassinate the governor of Wisconsin. This audio recording contains a dialogue between the defendant and the governor's aide, conspiring to have the governor killed. The governor's aide Jonah Edwards has been arrested this morning with the same charge as the defendant," said the lead prosecutor.

This was not good. The charge that Joe and I were particularly worried about now has concrete evidence to support it. I'm not even sure how they have come up with a recording. Jonah couldn't have been in on it, since he'd been arrested as well. He must have been under surveillance. Enforcers must have used some sort of long-range recording device to capture our conversation. If I'm found guilty for this, I'll never get out of prison. We would need to come up with something fast.

"Your Honour, the defence would like to request a

copy of the audio file and time to review this evidence," Joe asked.

"Review it you may, Mr. Abrams, but you will not be getting a copy of the file. You will get half an hour in court today to review the recording," replied the judge

"Thank you, Your Honour," said Joe.

I'm not sure what Joe had in mind, but he didn't seem as worried as I expected him to be. Maybe he knew something I didn't.

"Your Honour, upon final review of Exhibit G, the prosecution has decided to drop the charge of murder in the first degree," said the lead prosecutor.

"What! You woke up and decided that the defendant was no longer guilty? You better have a good reason for this, Mr. Grant," the judge said raising his voice.

"Your Honour, may we approach the bench?" the lead prosecutor asked.

"What for? We are the only ones here, and the trial hasn't actually started yet. What the hell is this, amateur hour?" the judge replied angrily.

"Very well, Your Honour. During initial analysis, the fingerprints found on the murder weapon did match those of the defendant. However, upon further analysis, the crime lab has confirmed that the prints found on the murder weapon failed the indentation test. Simply put, the prints were too faint. Considering that a tight grip would have been required to successfully discharge a single round from the weapon, this grip would have generated a more prominent print. So, for this reason, we will have to drop the murder charge," the lead prosecutor said.

"Are you suggesting that the prints were planted?" asked the judge.

"Yes, Your Honour, it seems that way. The Nation's Internal Affairs Unit is questioning the officers that showed up to the crime scene. The officer who retrieved the weapon, from the crime scene, is also being questioned," replied the lead prosecutor.

"I cannot believe this; this is absolutely appalling," said the judge.

Not that I was worried about this charge in the first place, but I was glad to see it dropped. What was even better was that the flaw that had been found in the murder investigation could be used to our advantage during the trial. If push came to shove, we could claim corruption on the part of the NLEU and point to this incident to support our claim. It would be a bit of a reach, but it would definitely raise doubt in the minds of the jurors.

"Mr. Abrams, I take it no objections if we adjourn?" asked the judge.

"No, Your Honour," replied Joe.

"Of course, you don't. The court will now take a recess for one hour—court adjourned," the judge said.

Joe's mind must have been all over the place—I know mine was. It all sounded very bad, but after seeing and hearing all the evidence, I was formulating plans on what to do about the charges to beat the case legally.

"So Joe, what do you think?" I asked.

"Well, it does look bad. I have to be straight with you, Dom, some of the evidence is a bit unsettling. However, now that we have a list of all the evidence, I think we have a good chance of beating most of the charges. I will need time to go through it all, but don't worry, I will be sure to keep you in the loop as things progress. This only means I'll have to work harder than I ever did on any case, but beating this case is not impossible. I need to scan and forward these files to Fredric back at the office. We also need one of your IT guys in the head office to go over the data footprints to see if what the prosecutors are claiming is true. I know it probably is, but it wouldn't hurt to try," said Joe.

"I'll do you one better, forward them to Alex. He will forward the data to a new tech guru we recently, put on retainer—the kid is brilliant. He will be able to tell us everything we need to know about the data, and if we're lucky, he might be able to tell us how to resolve the problem," I said.

"Okay, I'll do that now. This is obviously going to go into evidence. We don't have enough time to prove its authenticity, and the judge knows that. The only confidence we have in this matter is that you would never leave this sort of footprint on office comms. You never carry out shady business online or on your mobile device. It's either the data is fake, or someone had access to your office comms and planted the footprint. Either way, we'll get to the bottom of it," said Joe.

We went back to court just after midday. Joe informed the court he had reviewed the file and that he was happy for it to be entered into evidence. The judge announced the trial date, and surprisingly, it wasn't for another three months. This would give Joe more than enough time to prepare for the case, and it gave me time to wrap up urgent business matters.

Chapter 15

You're the Man Now
Where: Carabella Cemetery, North Walnut Grove, Miami
When: 1430 hours, Friday, February 3, 2012
Currency: US dollar

A significant number of people showed up to Guillermo's funeral, and it made Anna happy to see so many people had cared about her late husband. She didn't realize the extent of the impact he had made within the local community. He formed close relationships with a few of the families and other businessmen, and they all respected him. After the burial, everyone went over to Anna and her children to offer their condolences, they all had nice things to say about Guillermo. Six unfamiliar men approached the family after everyone else had their opportunity to speak with them. One of the men took Anna's hand and introduced himself.

"Mrs. Dominguez, please accept my condolences. My name is Hector Gallegos, consider me a member of the family. I am here to assure you that your husband's murder is being taken seriously. We are doing everything we can to find out who did it so we can bring them to justice. Please accept this token gesture. This should cover the funeral costs," Hector said.

"I appreciate your kind gesture, Mr. Gallegos," Anna replied.

Hector Gallegos was the head of the drug dealers in North Walnut Grove, Pearl Gables, and White Palms. He was very much aware of how smoothly things ran at Guillermo's restaurant. There were never any complaints about him failing to distribute drugs to the respective dealers in the associated districts. No one ever accused Guillermo of shaving drugs off the consignments, and his restaurant was the safest front the cartel had in North Walnut Grove. It was family friendly and had an impressive customer base. It was in the cartel's best interest to protect their investment, and Hector wasn't going to stop until they found the killer and got rid of whoever it was. In his mind, this would give the family a sense of justice, as well as eliminate the traitor. A win-win. As far as the cartel was concerned, Guillermo was a stand-up guy, and they couldn't understand why anyone would kill him. Hector was sure that it was an inside job, but he didn't know who was responsible.

Edwardo hadn't said a word about Zorro Loco to the cops. There was a code everyone in his neighbourhood stood by—no snitching. He told the police that on the night of the murder, he had forgotten his backpack and went back to the restaurant to retrieve it. He said it was when he got back that he found his father dead on the kitchen floor. This obviously wasn't true; he knew that telling the truth might lead to other questions. When the police asked him if he had heard gunshots, he said that he heard shots from the living room at home, but that he didn't realize the shots had come from the restaurant. They didn't question Edwardo for too long, because they didn't think he had motive to kill his father. Edwardo did tell his mother and sister that he was at the restaurant, though. He explained that he was in one of the cellars when the shooting took place. However, he didn't mention anything to them about the money or drugs in the cellar.

"Mrs. Dominguez, is it okay if I speak to your son a moment? Don't worry, he'll be okay," Hector said.

"Sure, no problem," replied Anna.

It wasn't like Anna had a choice—she knew exactly who these people were and how they operated. She wasn't going to argue with them, it would only make matters worse. Hector asked Edwardo to walk with him.

"Hello, Edwardo. How are you holding up?" asked Hector.

"I'm all right," replied Edwardo.

"Do you know who I am?" Hector asked.

"Yes sir, you are the king's right hand," Edwardo replied.

That was what all the region heads were called. The king's right hand was the cartel overlord for all of the business in Florida. He lived somewhere in Miami, and only the other district heads knew who he was.

"How did you know that?" Hector asked.

"The way you carry yourself and the way that these men have set up a formation around you. These guys are here to protect you," Edwardo answered.

"Boy, you are as smart as they come. Son, your father, he was an Honourable man, and may God so help the person responsible for his death. Whoever did this will pay, I guarantee it. With that said, I have to be straight with you. Your father was a vital part of our business, and that business has to continue. Do you know how the business works?" said Hector.

"Yes sir, I do. My dad stored and distributed drugs for the cartel," Edwardo replied.

"Yes, that he did and did it excellently. From this point on, we will need someone to take his place. We do not allow women in this line of work, so we cannot approach your mother. You will have to take over. Normally, in situations like this we would take over the establishment. However, your dad, may his soul rest in peace, had developed a special relationship with the community and his customers. We don't want to mess with a good thing. Now, I know that you are still in school, and that is not a problem. We won't stop you from going to school, all we ask is that you make yourself available for the deliveries and pickups. Do you understand what I am asking here?" Hector said.

"Yes, I do. I am willing to take over my father's duties," said Edwardo.

"Okay, that's good. We will obviously extend the same payment arrangement we had with your father to you. You can use the money to look after the restaurant and your family. Also, we know that from now on the restaurant will need some security. We will put a couple of our guys on watch. They will always be close by," said Hector.

"Can I talk to you privately?" Edwardo asked.

"Of course—boys, fall back, but stay close," Hector instructed his security detail.

"Mr. Gallegos, I was there when my father was killed, and I know who did it," Edwardo said.

"Is that so? Wait a minute, one of the cops we have on our payroll told us you said that you weren't around when it happened," Hector said.

"I was there, I was hiding in one of the cellars underneath the kitchen. I heard everything. Zorro Loco and another guy came to the restaurant that night. My dad had a bad feeling, so he pretended like he was only going to get drinks for Zorro and his friend. When he came into the kitchen, he told me to hide in one of the cellars until the coast was clear. While I was hiding, Zorro walked my dad back to the kitchen, and that's when I heard everything. He told my dad to hand over all the drugs, and once he got them, he shot my dad. After that he and his friend ran off," Edwardo said.

"Zorro did this?" Hector asked, looking rather angry.

"Yes, he did. The reason I am telling you this in

private is because I want your permission to get revenge for my dad. I would like to kill him myself, and I didn't want the word getting to him," Edwardo said.

"Are you sure about this, kid? Running your dad's business is one thing, but killing a man, that is entirely different. Once you go there, there is no turning back," warned Hector.

"He took my father away from me, he has deprived my family of a father and husband. I am only seventeen years old, there were still a lot of things I could have done with my father. I would like to look Zorro in the eyes when it happens," Edwardo insisted.

"I have never heard a seventeen-year-old talk like this. You talk with so much confidence," Hector said.

"I watched my dad and learned how he carried himself, I also listened to how he spoke to people. Everything that I know about life, I learned from my dad. I could have learned a lot more had Zorro not done what he did," said Edwardo.

"Fair enough, Edwardo, you not only have my condolences, but you have my absolute respect as well. You have my blessing on taking out Zorro, but I will have to give you support. My men will have to be there with you when it goes down, do you have a problem with that?" Hector asked.

"No, sir, I do not," replied Edwardo.

"Good. Listen kid, I am truly impressed by you. This is going to be the beginning of a wonderful relationship. However, I must warn you. Don't ever cross me," Hector said.

"Like my father, I am Honourable. You will not regret your decision, Mr. Gallegos," said Edwardo.

"You're the man now, and I expect you to handle your business accordingly," Hector said.

"You have my word," Edwardo replied.

Edwardo knew that someone from the cartel would eventually show up to discuss the future of the restaurant. His father's death had a profound impact on him. There was a certain darkness that came over him, and his outlook on life had completely changed. The innocence had been stripped from him, replaced with anger and a thirst for Zorro's blood. Consequently, Hector's plan for him and the restaurant had no effect on his emotions. If anything, his desire to become wealthy made Hector's offer seem like the perfect opportunity. The advantage to the new arrangement was that Edwardo would have a security detail; a necessity that would have kept his father alive had it been implemented.

Edwardo would have to break the news to his mother about his new career. Anna had watched the pair from a distance, and she knew that nothing good was going to come from the conversation between her son and Mr. Gallegos. She could tell that Edwardo was about to be entangled with the cartel, the very same thing that got her husband killed. This bothered her, but she was more concerned about her family's safety than the notion of high morals. She had detached herself from the concept of righteousness the day she decided to step foot on the dodgy ship in Puerto Plata. She had convinced herself that God understood her predicament, and that her failings would be pardoned by him.

"Edwardo, what was that about?" Anna asked.

"Well, Mom, I'm sure you already know who those guys are. Mr. Gallegos said that someone would need to take over Dad's position, and that we didn't really have a choice in the matter. I know that Dad always talked about moving to Milwaukee, but these guys were never going to let that happen. The restaurant is the perfect front for their business. Mr. Gallegos wanted to deal with me directly, because the cartel does not do business with women. They need the restaurant to keep running the way it has since Dad started working for them," Edwardo explained.

"I knew it! Oh my God, what have we done, what have we done! We should have never come to this country; we shouldn't have exposed you to all this!" Anna said as tears rolled down her face.

"Mom, it's okay. I'm not completely clueless on everything that had been going on. Dad opened up to me about the cartel right before he was killed. My friends' parents are in the same business, and they talk about it all the time. I am not naive about these things. We are in an impossible situation here. But in due time I will get us out of it, I promise. Also, I have Mr. Gallegos's word that I will be allowed to complete my education during the time that I will be working for them,"

Edwardo explained.

"My dear son, how did you become so wise?" Anna said.

"Everyone keeps saying that. I don't think I'm all that wise, I just pay attention to everything going on around me, and I use what I learn to my advantage. I saw Dad do the same thing over and over again, I learned it from him," Edwardo said.

Edwardo lied about not having a choice regarding doing business with the cartel. He also left out a couple of the other crucial details. However, he told his mother whatever she needed to hear in order to put her mind at rest. His sister, Isabel, was so distraught she didn't have anything to say about anything. Guillermo's death affected her deeply. Edwardo knew the responsibility of looking after his family was now on him, and he felt he needed to remain strong. So, he buried his emotions and proceeded to do everything that needed to be done to keep his family and the restaurant going.

Edwardo hadn't told anyone about the money he had retrieved from the restaurant cellar the night his father was killed. Guillermo always kept a low profile and had never spent lavishly. However, judging by the amount of money Edwardo had recovered, it was apparent that Guillermo had managed to stash away a considerable amount of cash. One of the duffle bags from the cellar contained a hundred thousand dollars. The money formed part of Guillermo's retirement fund and Edwardo's college tuition. All the money combined, including the money in the safe and the properties, would have been more than enough money to retire from the cartel business. Edwardo also hadn't mentioned to anyone that the cellar contained the other half of the cartel's drugs. There were eight bricks of cocaine and six bricks of heroin. Including his own money that he had been saving, Edwardo was already well on his way to becoming very wealthy at a very young age. He wouldn't be able to deal the cartel's drugs in North Walnut Grove, but the plan was to have a discussion with his friends Christopher and Alexander to figure out how they were going to move the drugs.

Edwardo didn't want to be mediocre at anything. He was going to complete high school and attend university. His plan had been to study automotive engineering. However, with everything that had happened, he decided he was going to attain a degree in business and entrepreneurship while working with the cartel. This qualification would not only serve as the perfect cover for his future career with the cartel, it would provide him the skills required to be successful in the business.

Edwardo's plan was to build his own empire, but he knew it was going to take some time. The money and drugs in his possession were a good starting point, but he understood he would need to save for a rainy day. He also knew he would have to reinvest some of the money. The extra earnings from the cartel would be spent on the family, the restaurant, and his education. He had everything planned out.

Chapter 16

Record Tampering
Where: Edom Group, The United Nations of Europe and Americas, Milwaukee, Wisconsin
When: 1010 hours, Tuesday, November 5, 2041
Currency: UNEA credits

My main office as well as a number of Edom Group departments were situated on the thirty-second floor of the second-tallest building in downtown Milwaukee. I owned the entire floor. The owners of the other floors and I shared the cost of security management and building maintenance. Since I spent a lot of my time in the office, I made sure it was designed to my liking, embellishing it with the most comfortable and luxurious Italian furniture. The office was mostly made up of glass, and every inch had been shielded with the highest calibre of bullet-proofing that ProteriTek had to offer.

My interactive desk was situated towards the back of the office. This position provided a view of the city, and from here all the other skyscrapers could be seen. If I needed to change the view, I could do so from my desk by selecting any widget of my choice. There was also an option to select a widget by voice command.

However, I disabled the voice feature as well as the comms device connected to it. I didn't trust devices that had the ability to eavesdrop.

One of my favourite widgets is the Mellow-317. It projects onto the full-length window a waterfall, surrounded by greenery with a sunset in the distance. This was my widget of choice on days when things got a bit hectic. I was holding a meeting with Alex, Chris, and Joe this morning, and I had the feeling I would need to replace the view of the skyscrapers with the Mellow-317 by the end of the meeting. On the other side of the office was a conference table that seated ten people. It was sort of like a mini-conference room right in my office. This was reserved for my inner circle. Occasionally, I would hold meetings with VIPs here, but it would have to be necessary for that to happen.

My personal assistant, Brandon, had impeccable timing when it came to serving coffee, and by ten o'clock we were already on our second round. We had been scrambling, trying to figure out what we were going to do about all the evidence submitted to the court. Matthew Harrington, the tech guru, had dropped by the office to deliver some information about the data footprint found on my office comms device. Matt apologized for the delay, saying that it took a bit of time to decrypt and extract the metadata on the file. The main data was accessible, but the metadata had been encrypted.

The main data revealed an inbound message to my

office from a remote device. The metadata, on the other hand, allowed him to see the date and time the data exchange took place. The main message contained information about individuals who had paid sums of money in exchange for college degrees and data injection. The data injection involved the keying of academic credits and degree information into student academic records. These records were stored in databases across several universities. The sender, who is still unknown, sent a request for approval of the data injection. In response, a confirmation message was sent from my office comms with approval for the generation of the college degrees and for the data injection. Once he delivered his report, I sent Matt on his way.

There were a couple of things that didn't add up. The first was that the message on the file hadn't come from me. Secondly, everyone involved knew better than to send such explicit information over the sat network. We have been involved in the record cultivation and data-tampering business for years, but I haven't had any direct involvement. The legwork has always been handled by our low-level guys. We had everything set up so that any visible digital exchange looked like a legal business transaction. The way the operation worked was that people paid us to provide them with identification or qualification documents. Our people that worked in the relevant government or education bodies would then key the corresponding information into their databases. Airborne Net-Cloud, Edom

Group's domain hosting and cloud services, served as the front.

Our client list provided a way for us to keep track of who paid for what. For example, someone who needed a driver's license would register for a website that offered driving lessons. That person would then pay us to design the website. They would also pay an annual fee for hosting the domain for the website. On the surface it looked like a legit business arrangement, and we did build the website, albeit a crummy one. However, what was actually happening was that the customer paid a down payment for an illegal driver's license. The annual fee was ongoing payment to keep the driver's licence active.

It was a perfect setup. If an investigation ever took place, it would be expected that a domain-hosting company would charge annual fees in exchange for its services. My company does actually provide these services to customers on the legit side of the business, and it is indeed profitable. In order to launder the proceeds from the not-so-legit side, the prices of services are ridiculously inflated. We justify the exorbitant fees by delivering the best value to our legit customers. Airborne Net-Cloud offers the most robust services, and we have one of the best data-security services in the Nations. Efficiency and security are key factors for most customers, and these organizations were willing to pay more for better services.

We added special transaction codes on client

records which allowed us to differentiate between illegal and legal transactions. If we needed to track down any of our illegitimate customers for any reason, we had a way of doing so. For example, if we needed to get a list of customers with outstanding payments, we would simply query our database to return all outstanding client fees, then we could filter through the results using the special transaction codes for illegitimate customers. To the untrained eye, the transactions would appear legit.

Once the customer list was filtered, we could see the customers who owed us, and we would harass them until they paid. Those that refused to pay would ultimately suffer the consequences. We once had a customer who felt he didn't have to keep up his annual payment for services rendered. He had already made several payments to the organization, and as far as he was concerned, we were being greedy. We weren't completely irrational, and we empathized with the idiot's frustrations—the annual fees were indeed quite high.

However, there was something he failed to remember. He approached us back when he was an illegal immigrant and he didn't have a profile on any government database. He wanted to start a small business. Desperate to build an identity, he approached us requesting the premium package. This package included a birth certificate, driver's license, medical records, and a social security number. He also wanted the data injection to go with it. He ended up getting the premium-plus package. At the time, our contact tried to convince him to start low and opt for the more affordable basic package, which was a reasonably priced and would get him an ID and social security number, both with injected data. With this he would be able to build a full legal profile over a period of time.

However, the stupid guy wanted everything quickly and insisted on the premium-plus package—a decision he would later regret. After he cancelled his online payments, he was approached by our representative. He was advised that our doing nothing about his failure to pay would make us look bad. Not that there was a need, but an explanation was given to him stating that part of the regular payment was used to pay the inside people we had in the different organizations. It was these people who keyed the information into their databases. Our services wouldn't be available without them.

I'm not sure if the guy was extremely brave, or just plain stupid. He refused to reinstate his payments and told our representative to tell his employers to do their worst. I doubt very much that the guy knew much about our organization. I run one of the most violent crime syndicates in the world, torturing and killing anyone who crossed me. I did all this and still managed to make the Edom Group appear clean. If the idiot knew this, he would have kept up his payments and kept his mouth shut. We would have killed the guy, but then his stupid decision would have affected his wife and kids. Not to mention, a dead guy can't pay annual fees.

It was always best to handle situations like this with patience. So, we didn't kill him, but we made sure that he never used his right index and middle finger ever again. When I gave the order for him to be punished for his insubordination, he was brought to an abandoned warehouse where one of our street thugs sat him down, tied him to the chair, put two of his fingers in a vice, and crushed them. In the end, the two fingers had to be amputated.

Regarding the incriminating message, only a couple of things could have happened here. Either someone came into my office to reply to the message, or someone figured out a way to hack into my comms and sent the message from a remote location. My instincts were leading me towards the latter. It would have been extremely difficult to get past security unspotted. Also, getting past Brandon would have been even more difficult. Unless Brandon was in on it, I didn't see anyone gaining access to my office. Everyone agreed with me on this. I suggested we would need to get the IT department to provide the access logs for my comms device for the time period when the message was sent. If we provided the logs to Matt, he might be able to find something that would point us in the right direction.

Record-tampering came to me in almost an epiphany-like way back in 2025. I had been thinking about a story that my father once told me. He spoke about illegally travelling to Miami on a cargo ship. When they got there, he, my mother, and my sister didn't have legal documents to live or work in the country. It was my dad's cousin Raphael who introduced him to a crime-syndicate that specialized in document falsification.

My family eventually managed to get legal papers by way of amnesty from the government. This rarely happened, but every now and then amnesty was granted to people who had been living in the country illegally but had managed to stay out of legal trouble and been productive members of society. The fake documents of those days just weren't sufficient. You were only able to get an ID and social security number. If anyone dug deep enough, it would be discovered that the documents and their corresponding numbers were fake. The individuals who possessed such documents would serve jail time and eventually be deported. Hence, there was an opportunity in the market for illegally obtained documents with genuine corresponding data.

I came up with the idea of connecting with people who worked in organizations of interest: hospitals, schools, universities, the Nations DMV—you name it. It was all about meeting the people responsible for the databases. Once we established contact, we made them offers that were too good to turn down. We sent in our lower-level representatives to offer these individuals an opportunity to earn regular income in exchange for their services. We also provided a way to launder their extra income to avoid drawing unwanted attention. The services they provided involved altering databases by changing personal information or even generating new details from scratch. We have people everywhere and pay them handsomely. Record-tampering and identity cultivation is one of our more lucrative rackets. It also changed lives by giving people the opportunity to earn money as well as contribute to society. However, it does have a negative impact as well. Overpopulation and social-welfare budget shortfalls had become a serious problem. The immigration numbers spiked significantly, and as a result, migrants occupy the major cities and have access to benefits and services that was once available to genuine UNEA citizens. Employment for professionals had also become an issue, because there was a saturation of job applicants and not enough jobs to go around. People getting jobs they weren't qualified for was also a problem. For many businesses, this had led to a decline in productivity and in the quality of manufactured goods.

There are lines that we refuse to cross though. For instance, we would not facilitate the forging of data that would enable someone to become a doctor. Having unqualified individuals treating patients would inevitably end in disaster. Needless to say, of all the record-cultivation and tampering crimes, falsifying documents of medical practitioners carried one of the heaviest prison sentences.

As we were going through the evidence, Joe's personal comms went off. It was Fredric. After a couple of minutes of ah-ha, oh yeah, and I see, Joe disconnected the call and shared his conversation with the rest of us.

"Dom, Fredric had a suggestion regarding the data. We could inform the court that Edom Group's IT department runs routine system maintenance, and that in order to do this, they regularly access your comms device remotely. The fact that your comms device can be accessed remotely introduces some vulnerability. This bit of information could weaken the prosecution's evidence and raise doubt in the minds of the jury," Joe said.

"Hmm, that sounds like it might just work. You better watch out for your protégé, Joe, it looks like Fredric might be gunning for your job," I said.

"Ha-ha. I've got nothing to worry about, my job here is safe. If you ever fired me, both our wives would kill you," Joe replied.

"Ah, you make a good point. I guess I better keep you around then," I said.

"Absolutely," Joe said.

"Speaking of wives, Laura wasn't as oblivious to everything as I thought she was, you know. She had her suspicions," I said.

"Yeah, I can't say that I'm surprised. Our wives are smart women; we need to recognise that," Joe replied.

"Indeed. In the meantime, if we are able to find out

who sent the message, we will present our evidence to the court. Whoever has done this is tech-savvy. Alex, please tell Brandon to get the IT manager up here," I said.

"Sure thing, Dom," Joe responded.

The IT manager was given his instructions, and Alex and Chris were given instructions to find a patsy to take the fall for the message. An offer would be made to someone to take the fall in exchange for a significant amount of money to be released to their family and additional credits after they served their prison term. This was only a last resort—we would avoid anyone doing time if we found an alternative.

Chapter 17

Revenge
Where: Guillermo's Cabana, North Walnut Grove, Miami
When: 1600 hours, Thursday, February 9, 2012
Currency: US dollar

Guillermo's body hadn't been in the ground even a week when Hector Gallegos decided it was time to get the ball rolling on Zorro. He also wanted business to reopen over at Guillermo's Cabana. So, he sent a couple of henchmen to tell Edwardo to prepare. When they arrived at the restaurant, they found Edwardo sitting in the same spot his dad did when he was still alive. He had literally stepped into his father's position. Edwardo had been given permission by the school to take as much time off as he needed to mourn his father. He took a couple of days to catch up on homework.

As the men approached Edwardo, he looked up and said, "It's time, isn't it?"

One of the men replied, "Mr. Gallegos wants to deal with the problem today. We are going to pick up Zorro now. The instruction is to take him somewhere quiet and then you can finish the job. Are you ready?"

asked the man.

Edwardo didn't hesitate, he quickly put his books in his backpack and got up from his seat.

"Give me a couple of seconds, I have to tell my mom I'm leaving." As he went into the kitchen, he told his mother Mr. Gallegos wanted to have a meeting about the business. He told her that it shouldn't take too long.

Anna looked at her son, and he could see the sorrow in her eyes. She had never imagined this was how things would end up. She was looking forward to retirement with her husband; to her children being law-abiding citizens and to them having illustrious careers. Her son was now officially working for the cartel. She didn't know which was worse, losing her husband in a violent, drug-related shooting, or the induction of her only son into the drug trade. She thought the meeting would be about instructing Edwardo on how to conduct business going forward. As true as that might have been, she didn't know her son intended to commit murder. She gave Edwardo a hug and told him to be very careful. Anna tried to hold it together as she let go of Edwardo, but as soon as he left the kitchen, she burst into tears.

When they got outside, waiting was a convoy of two dark-tinted SUVs and an unmarked van. Edwardo was guided to the SUV in the middle of the convoy. The first destination was Zorro's house. The cartel had been keeping an eye on Zorro's front door from a car parked down the block from the house. If Zorro left the house, he would be followed, and the lookout would contact the convoy.

As the convoy got closer to its destination, one of the henchmen pulled out a small pistol and handed it to Edwardo. He put the firearm in a side compartment of his backpack. The man noticed Edwardo had put some gloves on and a beanie that covered his forehead down to his eyebrows. When they arrived, the car that had been parked near Zorro's house drove off in the opposite direction. From Edwardo's vehicle, they could see a man sitting on Zorro's porch. A few men stepped out of the other SUV and headed toward the house. Edwardo looked closer and saw that the man on the porch was the guy who showed up at the restaurant with Zorro on the night his father was murdered. Edwardo mentioned this to the man who sat next to him, so he sent the guy in the front passenger seat to make sure that both the guy on the porch and Zorro were brought to the van. He also instructed them that no women or children were to be harmed. The lead henchman was aware that Zorro had a wife and young children.

In less than two minutes, both men were tossed in the back of the unmarked van and sacks were put over their heads. The men had also seized duffle bags containing drugs and money from Zorro's house. It was the drugs that Zorro had taken from Guillermo on the night of the murder. Zorro had been bagging them for resale; the money had been collected from his lieutenant. Zorro would normally hand the cash over to the cartel once a week. This week the cartel collected early.

Twenty minutes later they drove into an abandoned dockyard. Edwardo could see another SUV parked outside a building. It was identical to the others from the convoy. As they got out of the vehicles, Zorro and the other man were dragged out of the van and led into the building. As they approached the entrance, Edwardo scanned the area for anything that seemed out of place or indicated they had been followed. There was nothing unusual that Edwardo could see, only abandoned cars, machinery, and rusty old shipping containers.

He had never been to this part of Miami. In fact, he didn't know where he was. For some reason, nothing about what was going to happen gave him great concern. He knew exactly what to do, and he knew that he was in good hands. The thought of killing his father's murderer didn't bother him—he didn't feel anything at all. As they stepped into the building, Edwardo saw six men standing at a distance. When they got closer, he saw Hector Gallegos and five bodyguards. This time their weapons were not concealed. Each of them had a pistol visible in their holster, and they were all also carrying submachine guns.

"Edwardo, my main man," said Hector.

"How's it going, Mr. Gallegos?" Edwardo replied.

"How's it going! It's your show, kid, it's your stage," said Hector.

When Zorro heard that Edwardo was there, he knew they had been picked up for what they did to

Guillermo. He knew that somehow the cartel had found out they were directly linked to the murder and the missing drugs. Zorro and the other man were still blindfolded, but they didn't need to see anything to figure out what was going to happen to them. Gallegos ordered the sacks to be removed from their heads. The two killers were face to face with their judge and executioner. Zorro had never been this terrified in his life, as the duffle bag containing the drugs and money was placed in the middle of the floor. Hector stood in front of the bag, Zorro kneeling next to it.

"So, what made you think this was okay?" Edwardo asked.

"Listen, I can explain…" Zorro tried to explain but was interrupted.

"Shut your mouth, you filthy animal, the question was rhetorical. You took an innocent man away from his family, leaving a fifteen-year-old to pick up the pieces. You have disrespected the cartel family, and you have caused damage to our image and integrity. This is not how we operate here, and I am going to make an example of you. People on the streets will know that no one crosses the cartel and gets away with it," Hector said.

"Mr. Gallegos, I am deeply sorry. I messed up, and I see that now. I was being greedy; this was all my plan. But I beg of you to please spare my nephew, he is his mother's only son. He only came to the restaurant because I made him do it. It was my fault," Zorro pleaded.

"Your nephew knew exactly what he was getting himself into! Today, you and your nephew will die, and everyone in the streets of Miami will hear of this. Edwardo, do what you came here to do. Aim for the heart," Hector said.

"You brought this on yourself. You have no sympathy from me: you have deprived my father of living out his dream of watching his children grow up and thrive. You have taken my father away from me, and now I will take you away from the people you love… and because your nephew took part in this, I will kill him as well." Edwardo said.

"Edwardo, wait, please…" Zorro tried to beg for his life.

Before Zorro could finish talking, Edwardo released four shots from the pistol, two shots each to the chests of Zorro and his nephew. The bodies lay motionless as blood oozed from them. Everyone briefly stood in shock. Because of how young he was, no one expected Edwardo to do it so quickly, with no emotion.

"Wow, that's impressive. You didn't even flinch," said Hector.

"I came prepared for this, Mr. Gallegos. Thanks for trusting me to take care of it," Edwardo replied.

"No problem, kid. Are you sure you're okay?" asked Hector.

"I'm fine," Edwardo answered.

"Wow. Okay, so you're the real deal," Hector said.

"I need a favour, though. I need to get rid of everything I'm wearing when we leave this place. I have brought some extra clothes and shoes to change into. I also brought a lighter and a can of lighter fluid. On our way back, I'll need to stop somewhere to burn everything. I would like to get rid of this gun myself as well. I plan on taking it apart and depositing the individual parts across Miami," Eddie said.

"You know how to dismantle a gun? Damn kid, what are you, some kind of professional hit man? Not to worry, we have a spot not too far from here. We will stop there on the way back. It's a bakery that we control. They have an incinerator; you can toss all your garb there. It's also hot enough to melt that piece you've got. We had the incinerator installed for this very reason. Is that thorough enough for you?" Hector asked.

"Yes, sir, thanks. Please give me a couple of minutes to get changed," said Edwardo.

"You see boys, this is what I'm talking about. A real pro!" Hector said with a smile on his face.

Edwardo wasn't taking any chances of having the two murders pinned on him. He would have to change clothes because of the gun powder residue. Along with the extra clothes, shoes, lighter, and lighter fluid, he had a trash bag. He made sure he was wearing gloves when he handled the trash bag. An over-the-top precaution but one that would put his mind at ease.

"I am truly impressed with you, kid. From this point on we will call you Soap, because you like to keep things clean, leaving no loose ends. You hear that everybody? From now on, we call him Soap. Kid, welcome to the family. No one touches you or your family, you have our full protection. You now have full control of your dad's restaurant, and to Honour your dad, we will offer you all the opportunities that are available to members of this family. Everyone, welcome Soap to the family!" Hector said.

Just like that, Edwardo was a bona fide member of the cartel. As long as he stayed in line, the cartel would not only allow him to operate his restaurant, they would also provide means for him to earn more if he wanted to. Most importantly, he now had cartel protection, an invaluable relationship to have with the crime family that dominated the most significant parts of Miami.

Edwardo got changed, and tossed his clothes, shoes, beanie, and gloves in the trash bag. He clenched the trash bag, guarding it as if his life depended on it, and it did. Once Edwardo had finished getting dressed, Hector ordered a couple of guys to clean up the mess. Then he signalled it was time to leave. All but one of the SUVs drove off in a convoy. Hector asked Edwardo to ride with him, as he had a few other things he wanted to discuss. When they got in the car, Edwardo sat in the back with his new boss, Hector.

"So young Soap, I have plans for you. You're brave, and even more important you are smart, you are very smart. I believe you can go far in this line of business; we need more people like you to take the family to greater heights. We need the next generation of cartel leaders to have the qualities you have displayed today. With the people we have started to partner with, we will need individuals with a certain level of panache and eloquence going forward. So, I will definitely need you to stay in school. I want you to attend college and get a degree. This is the direction we are taking with our senior members. You stick with me, and I will make you a very rich man. Are you ready for this, are you on board?" Hector asked.

"I am ready to learn everything you are willing to teach me, Mr. Gallegos. Believe it or not, after we spoke the last time, I decided I would get a degree in business and entrepreneurship," Edwardo said.

"Again, I'm impressed. I won't be going into details with you now, but consider this the start of your journey as my protégé," Hector said.

"Thank you, sir." replied Edwardo.

Edwardo's mind was racing. He never really thought that he'd one day become a gangster, let alone a leader in a crime syndicate. He had always wanted to be rich and successful, but those dreams were materializing a lot quicker than he'd expected. It didn't bother him much that he was becoming a criminal—any sense of good morals had been diminished by the death of his father. All he cared about now was financial success, and he was already on his way.

Chapter 18

Online Racketeering
Where: Edom Group, The United Nations of Europe and Americas, Milwaukee, Wisconsin
When: 1222 hours, Tuesday, November 5, 2041
Currency: UNEA credits

One of our other lucrative businesses was online racketeering, which generated a ton of credits for us. It was only a matter of time before online racketeering became law enforcement's main focus. It all originated from ransomware. The first recorded ransomware attack happened in 1989. However, the attacks didn't become prominent until the mid- to late 2000s, when hackers were consistently using stolen data as leverage. Reports show companies across the globe have paid billions and billions to ransomware attackers. Those figures are likely to remain consistent, because hackers will always find a way to bypass data security.

We took ransomware to new heights. We hired the best hackers in the Americas, got them whatever software and hardware they needed, and paid them very well. Their only job was to do what they did best—hack into systems and retrieve valuable data. The rest of it was left to our data analysis team. They were responsible for assessing the stolen data and figuring out how much the owners of the data would be willing to pay to stop the data from being sold, or worse—the press being informed that the data had been stolen from the victim's organization. Most owners would do whatever it took to stop this data from being sold or information about the theft leaked.

So, one of three things would normally happen. The custodian would pay our asking price, or they would refuse to pay the ransom and just accept the loss as collateral damage. The third option was one that a number of companies have started to utilize—fighting back. They started to realize the importance of cyber security and data protection. After suffering numerous attacks that led to loss of income and reputational damage, companies started to take matters into their own hands, combating hackers themselves.

The UNEA Cyber Security Enforcement has struggled to deal with the most advanced cyber criminals though, all due to inadequate resources. Hacking was becoming considerably more complex, and the individuals with the highest and most diverse range of skill sets were choosing to play on the wrong side of the law. Working with crime syndicates was the more lucrative option. Law enforcement was left with low-level computer geeks with mediocre hacking skills, and this just wasn't enough to efficiently deal with cyber criminals.

With our team, we were able to attack small to medium businesses. Whenever we did, the victims were provided with a few options: an opportunity to buy back their data, the chance to pay us not to sell or divulge information that would expose the vulnerabilities in their systems, or cooperate or suffer real-life consequences. Our ransomware activities went beyond the cyber world and spilled into the real world. When businesses refused to pay, we threatened to interrupt their online productivity. When we crashed their platforms and they still refused to pay, we physically paid them a visit at their places of business.

We have a customer that owns a chain of dry cleaners. The guy's business had continued to experience a significant amount of growth over the years. Since a few of his buildings were in our jurisdiction, we were due protection fees. His business operated online services, and these could be accessed via the sat network. The services included the ability for customers to select laundry or dry-cleaning service, alterations, pick-ups, drop-offs, and the like. When he refused to pay his protection fees, we got hold of his client list of around five thousand high-profile customers. Again, we asked for our fees, and this time we asked for a ransom for his data, but he still didn't budge. So eventually, we took down his sat-net services. When that happened, he simply changed all his domain information, restored a backup of his client data, and it was business as usual.

It was clear that the guy was as stubborn as a mule. He was of Irish descent, and was willing to deal with whatever we dished out. We even sent some of our foot soldiers to all the dry cleaners in the chain to ruffle a few feathers. A few windows were shattered and a few pieces of machinery were destroyed. Yet the guy wouldn't budge; he simply replaced whatever we broke and claimed it on his insurance. When everything else failed, we decided to take the drama to his home. He was clever though and managed to keep his residential information unlisted. In the end, we had to beat the information out of one of his store managers.

We ended up sending goons to his house. When they got there, they opened the front door and walked into the living room, where he'd been sitting with his wife and kids. Apparently, they didn't even have to force their way in, the front door was unlocked. . The head goon described how he sat in a leather chair next to the fireplace. The other six guys stood around the family with submachine guns and pistols in hand.

The head goon, still sat in the chair, leaned forward with his leather-gloved fingers interlocked, and started to explain the purpose of their visit.

"I'm guessing you already know why we are here. You see, my employer is a gentleman, very patient, and a reasonable person. You operate your businesses in our jurisdiction, and we have allowed you to thrive. For months now, we have given you the opportunity to pay your fees. However, you have shown us that you have no regard for the order of things. What you don't understand is that up until this moment we have been very lenient with you. It didn't have to come to this, you could have behaved like a professional and just paid what you owe. There are costs associated with owning businesses in the location where you operate, and that cost for you is fifteen percent every month. It was going to be twelve, but we have had to penalize you for all our trouble. I think it goes without saying that if we have another encounter, it will not be this civil. Are we on the same page here?" asked the head goon.

"Yes, we are, just don't hurt my family," the drycleaner responded nervously.

"Well, like I mentioned before, it didn't have to come to this. This was your fault. Your first payment from each location is due by 5 p.m. today. Inform your managers to have the funds ready and transferred to this account number with the reference *Airborne Net-Cloud services*. From this point on we are your content management service, every now and then we will provide you with advertising in exchange for your monthly payment. You know, we wouldn't want anyone getting the wrong idea. We run a reputable company, and we wouldn't want anyone thinking we were extorting you," said the head goon.

"Sure, no problem," said the drycleaner.

"Well, I guess we're done here. My associates and I will make our way out now. Thanks for your hospitality," the head goon said as they headed for the front door.

We called the head of the goons Henry the Turk. No idea why he was called that; he wasn't even Turkish. What was fascinating about this guy was that he was very calm, respectful and articulate. However, he was also meticulous, ruthless, and sinister. He was a no-nonsense type of guy, and we could always count on him to get the job done. There was an incident involving one of the foot soldiers who tried to get cocky when Henry asked a question about a job not being done the right way. The situation concluded with the foot soldier getting his throat slit. Without blinking, Henry killed him on the spot right in front of everyone. As though he hadn't just murdered a man in cold blood, he simply asked for the body to be disposed of. He then carried on speaking to some of the other goons as if nothing had happened. All this was to evoke fear, causing the men who had just witnessed this to think twice before uttering a disrespectful word.

Alex and Chris have had several meetings with Henry, and the report I always received was that he was efficient and never made mistakes. For this reason, we chose him to oversee our online racketeering business. We were always reassured that there would be no hiccups and the credits would keep flowing. We didn't extend our online racketeering business to existing Airborne Net-Cloud customers though. We are already making a decent amount from them from regular subscriptions for the identity data. We show them a bit of leniency on that front.

Now that four witnesses have come forward and are willing to testify, I would only be able to beat the racketeering charge by finding out who these witnesses are and looking for a way to get rid of them. We wouldn't be able to kill everyone on our racketeering list, but we could narrow groups down to individuals and then work our way through them.

"We have to deal with the witnesses for the racketeering ordeal, fellas. Joe, I think you're going to need to be all the way in on this. We won't be able to send you out of the room every time we plan an execution. The waters will only get murkier from this point on. Are you okay with that?" I asked.

"Yeah, that's fine. If we're going to beat this thing, I'll need to know every bit of detail. I'll be able to defend you better that way. I'm all the way in, Dom," Joe replied.

"Good. Chris, Alex, get the ball rolling on the witnesses, please. Have our people go through our client list. I want a list with all the names of people that have ever complained about payments, people who have missed payments, people who have been forced to make payments at some point, and people who have abruptly closed their businesses. Chris, you get all your directors for Europe to provide their list, and Alex get hold of the directors in the Americas to provide theirs," I said.

Since we couldn't kill everyone on our client list, the best we could do was gather the names on our naughty list and start taking out the business owners one by one. There was only going to be one of two outcomes here: either we got our chirpers, or the chirpers got scared enough to change their minds about testifying. Either way, I wasn't going to go down for this. No way.

I decided to end the meeting around 3:30 p.m. and moved on to other business. I asked Alex to have someone pick up Jason and bring him to one of our warehouses on the south side of Milwaukee. Jason always stopped for a few drinks at the bar near the Portland office. Being the director of that region was a high position within Edom Group, so we needed to be careful in how we executed his termination. He would receive a call from Alex about another Assembly meeting. Whenever this happened, the CSOs would normally block their IDs, so this wouldn't make Jason suspicious.

The calls were encrypted for an additional layer of anonymity. The connection would bounce off several satellites across the globe for the duration of the call, making it untraceable and eavesdrop-proof. With no way of identifying the last person who spoke to Jason, law enforcement wouldn't be able to name any of us as suspects in his murder. Alex would inform Jason that an emergency Assembly meeting had been called and all directors had been summoned. He would be informed that a car to take him to the airport would be waiting outside the bar. Jason knew hanging out at the bar wasn't a secret, so a car being sent to his exact location wouldn't raise any suspicions either. Upon arriving in Milwaukee, he would be taken to one of our warehouses where he would be held overnight.

I wanted to speak to Jason myself, to see his eyes when I asked him if he was the chirper. The thing is, he had to go either way, regardless of whether he was the chirper. Him speaking up the way he did during the Assembly meeting had sealed his fate. I didn't want anyone else getting too confident and thinking it was acceptable to speak-left. Whenever people spoke out of line or were saying something we didn't like, we referred to that as speaking-left. I was going to kill two birds…, getting rid of a greedy and disrespectful ingrate as well as terminating a potential snitch.

After Alex and Chris left the office, I walked to my desk and logged back into my desk comms. I pinged Brandon, asking him to bring me the bottle of Gładka Królewska. It was a bit early for vodka, but that's the kind of day it had been, and I needed to unwind. Brandon left the bottle, a half-filled glass of club soda, and a slice of lemon on the left corner of my desk. I poured the Gładka Królewska then loaded up the Mellow-317—I needed a view that would help me relax. I sat at my desk for half an hour, taking slow sips of my drink as I contemplated everything that needed to be done about the trial and the business.

Chapter 19

Business Plan
Where: Guillermo's Cabana; North Walnut Grove, Miami
When: 0730 hours, Friday, February 10, 2012
Currency: US dollar

Edwardo, mulling over his actions from the previous day, decided, that just like his father, he too was going to shield Anna and Isabel from the inner workings of his business with the cartel. There was no point compounding an already devastating situation in the loss of Guillermo. Edwardo's plan was to make sure Anna and Isabel were happy and sorted out financially. He planned on speaking to his friends Christopher and Alexander during school lunch break about the drugs he had inherited from the Guillermo and Zorro fallout. Edwardo and Anna woke up early to set up for the day's business at the restaurant. Afterward, he would head to school. It would be his first day back, and he knew a lot of his fellow students would have questions about his father's shooting. Edwardo had already made up his mind: he wasn't going to talk about the situation.

"Well, Mom, all sorted out now. I've taken the

meat from the freezer, all the potatoes, peppers, onions, and spinach have been washed. Is there anything else you would like me to do before I leave for school?" Edwardo asked.

"No, son, you're all done here. Hey, listen to me, you are a good boy and I love you so much," Anna said.

"I know, Mom…" Edwardo replied.

"No—listen. This thing with the cartel, you understand that as your parents we should have protected you from this. We shouldn't have gotten into this business. I love you, and as your mother, I will continue to worry about you for as long as I live. I want you to be very, very careful from now on. These people are dangerous, so you need to be smart. I am here to give you guidance whenever you need it, okay?" Anna said.

"Okay, Mom, but don't worry too much about it, I have a good feeling that everything will be fine. I'm worried about you, though. Are you going to be okay?" Edwardo asked.

"I miss your father so much, but I will be strong, we will get through this together as a family," Anna replied.

"How is Isabel? She hasn't really said much about it," Edwardo asked.

"Your father's death has been really difficult for her to deal with. I spoke to her this morning, though. She plans on going in to work at 11 a.m.," Anna said.

"She'll be okay?" Edwardo asked.

"Yes, I'm sure that she will be fine. We will always

remember your father, but we will all be okay eventually," Anna said.

"All right, Mom, say hi for me when Isabel wakes up. I have to go now, but I will come straight back after school," Edwardo said.

"Okay, you have a nice day, son. I love you."

"Love you, mom."

Anna was putting on a brave face. The truth was that she was hurting on the inside. Edwardo seemed to be dealing well with everything. The reality was, he had no option. He didn't have the luxury of dwelling too much on the pain he'd felt days after the murder. He needed to focus on taking care of the family and doing everything he could to keep the cartel happy. Hector Gallegos would be taking him under his wing, and so Edwardo was going to do everything he could to gain his trust.

As he stepped off the school bus with Christopher and Alexander, he saw it was just another school day. There were other students getting out of other school buses, some students being dropped off by their parents, and others chaining their bikes to the bike racks.

"Guys, I have something to talk to you about. It's really important. We will talk at lunch today, in our usual spot. The good thing is that no one sits near there, so no one will hear what I have to say," Edwardo said.

"Hey Dom, what' on your mind?" Alex asked.

"Don't worry Alex, we'll get to it when we get to it. I will explain everything at lunchtime," Edwardo replied.

All the kids in school called Edwardo "Eddie." They all thought his name was Edward. When his parents applied for his social security number shortly after his birth, his name had been misspelled, leaving off the last letter. His parents hadn't even noticed until years later when they applied for his state ID and noticed that it read *Edward.* At the time, they didn't want to address the issue, because they were still illegal immigrants. Complaining about the spelling of their son's name might have jeopardized their own residency status, so they just left things as they were. As if the Edwardo-Edward-Eddie fiasco wasn't confusing enough, Alex and Chris called him Dom, short for Dominguez.

Throughout the morning, students and teachers offered their condolences to Eddie. He responded politely but didn't say much else. The girls especially seemed to be very empathetic; they kept asking if there was anything they could do. The buzzer for the first period sounded, and the students dispersed to their classrooms. Eddie's first period was algebra, a subject he excelled in. He made As and Bs in all subjects—he understood the importance of a good education and made sure he kept his head in his books. This made Anna happy, because she knew some of the other kids from the neighbourhood did not have the same focus as her son.

At 12:30 p.m., another buzzer sounded, and fourth-period physics came to an end. Eddie got up and put his books in his backpack. This was the same backpack that had contained the spare clothes he changed into after taking out Zorro and his nephew. He had initially planned on getting rid of the bag, but he felt there was no need now. Everything else had been incinerated, and there was nothing linking the backpack to the murder. He headed towards the cafeteria, and as he approached, he saw Alex and Chris already standing near the entrance. He gave the boys a nod from a distance, and when he arrived, they all walked in.

In a matter of minutes, the old cafeteria was packed with students. The paint on the walls was a dull grey colour, and the wooden floor was light brown with the faintest trace of sheen. There were rows of tables which sat a maximum of six students each, resembling the tables found in the State Prison visitation rooms. It wouldn't have been a surprise to anyone had the tables actually came from the prisons. Like every other high school, there was a hierarchy, and a student's position within the hierarchy determined who they sat with and where. There were the rich cool kids, the poor kids, the nerds, the emos, the goths, and then there was Eddie's crew. They didn't fit into any of these groups—they did their own thing. They generally didn't interact with a lot of the other kids. There were a few other children from their neighbourhood, but Eddie only offered the occasional nod to them. Eddie was the natural leader of his crew, sharing his entrepreneurial skills with Alex and Chris, allowing them to earn money with him. They would help Eddie in selling jeans, caps, sneakers, and any other merchandise Eddie could get his hands on. Once the items were sold, he gave them a cut of the money. Eddie let them have a decent share of the profit, but he would never disclose who his suppliers were. He did this for two reasons: First, the guys that sold him merchandise sold it at a significantly discounted price, meaning they were probably stolen goods. This was a nonissue as far as Eddie was concerned, because he could always deny all knowledge of whether the goods had been stolen. In fact, his suppliers told him to do just that, play stupid. The second reason was that Eddie wanted to make a profit, and the only way to ensure this was to guarantee there was no competition. The fewer clientele his suppliers had, the better for him.

The boys grabbed their lunch and walked over to their usual spot next to the side door leading to the main courtyard. There were windows providing a view to the courtyard. Through the windows, other students could be seen eating, reading, rehearsing for plays, and so on. The boys always sat here, they never had to sit anywhere else; their table was always available. Perhaps it was because the table could only seat three people. The other three stools attached to it had broken off. As they sat down to eat, Eddie dove right into what he needed to tell them.

"So, where do I begin…look guys, a lot has happened over the last couple weeks since my dad died.

I will cut to the chase and tell you that you are now looking at a new custodian for the cartel. The youngest in North Walnut Grove and maybe the youngest ever," Eddie said.

"Yo, Dom, this is crazy! How did that even happen?" Chris asked.

"The boss made me an offer I couldn't refuse. He said the cartel would like to keep storing their drugs at the restaurant, and that they were happy to take over the entire operation. This meant they would take the restaurant from us. The other option they gave me was to be in charge of the restaurant and run it myself, but I would need to continue the work my dad did for them. Well, let's just say I chose to keep the restaurant," Eddie replied.

"Your mom okay with this?" Alex asked.

"She had no choice, Alex. If we hadn't agreed to do it, they would have taken the restaurant and given us very little for it. We couldn't afford for that to happen. Working in that restaurant is all that my mother knows. It is also part of the legacy my dad left behind. So, I had to agree to work for them," Eddie explained

"So, what now?" Chris asked.

"You sound worried, Chris—it's not all bad news. The head of the cartel likes how I handled myself when he talked to me. He basically told me I could run the restaurant and still go to school if I wanted. They have offered to provide me and my family with twenty-four-hour security. They were really pleased with the service that my dad provided. They are extending me the courtesy in his Honour," Eddie replied.

"Dom, this is nuts!" Chris said.

"They've already given me a nickname—you are not going to believe what they call me. They call me Soap," Eddie said.

"Dude, this is crazy! I feel like you have changed already, it's almost like you've become the man overnight," Chris said.

"Yeah, Chris is right, man. I'm definitely getting some kind of manned-up vibe from you right now. So, what does this mean for us, Dom, where do we fit in?" Alex asked.

"I'm glad you asked. Going forward, there will be opportunity for you guys to make a lot more money than what you are making now. I will have access to more money from the cartel, which will be split between me, my mom, and my sister. I will give you guys some of my share of the money. Here's the thing though, we will need to use some of the money to keep selling merch to students or anyone else, really. We can import our own stuff from China. By doing this we cut out the middleman. We can sell it like we always have, but we can also sell stuff online. We need to be able to justify how we are making so much money if the cops start snooping around. The guys that I am buying goods from now are still getting a slice of the pie, and we need to cut them off. We will start small and then gradually do bigger imports over time, and we'll have to be low-key for a while," Eddie said.

"Dude, how do you even know how to do this stuff?" Chris asked.

"I do my research. Now, I have something even bigger than that to talk to you guys about," Eddie said.

"What! There's something even bigger than what you've just told us?! I don't think I can handle this," Chris said.

"Ha-ha. Chris, our lives are about to change, man. Trust me on this, we will have everything that we ever wanted. I have access to some drugs, eight bricks of cocaine and six bricks of heroin. It's important that the cartel not find out about this, so you can't tell anyone. My father's cousin Raphael has connections in Fynnwood, and with his help we'll be able to move the drugs. Once he has agreed to help us, I will need you guys to work with us to sell the drugs. Once all the drugs have been sold, I will give you twenty-five percent each on the total profit. All I ask for is your loyalty and that you always have my back. Are we good on that?" Eddie asked.

"Wow, definitely bro, we've got your back," Chris said

"Hey, you know that we'd do anything for you, bro," Alex said.

"Good to hear. So, after selling the dope, the only money that we will be making for a while will be what we get from the cartel and money from selling merch. Guys, this only works if we agree to do this together, and we can't talk to anyone else about it. If the wrong people find out, we can end up in prison or even worse, we could be killed by anyone looking to rip us off. Word could also get back to the cartel about the drugs, and they'll kill us. So, we have to keep this low-key. Are we all in agreement?" Eddie asked.

"Are you kidding, Dom? Me and Chris are in, all the way in! You're in, right, Chris?" Alex asked.

"Umm, let me think about it… of course man, why would I pass this up? Look Dom, we've always talked about getting rich. I am all the way in," Chris said.

"Okay, cool. I'll go into more detail later. Remember, do not tell a single person about this! We'll talk some more this evening. Let's meet up at the restaurant around 6:30p.m.," Eddie said.

After all the whispering, it was now official, Eddie had successfully convinced his friends to join him in the business. He needed people he could trust to watch his back at all times and Alex and Chris were perfect for that. Eddie had no intention of telling the guys exactly how he managed to get his hands on the drugs, but he was sure they had an idea. The next thing to do was get in touch with Raphael and have the conversation with him.

Chapter 20

Jason's Departure
Where: Edom Group warehouse, The United Nations of Europe and Americas, Milwaukee, Wisconsin
When: 1935 hours, Wednesday, November 6, 2041
Currency: UNEA credits

Alex and Chris picked me up from the house around 7:30, and we headed for the warehouse on the south side of Milwaukee where Jason was being held. By now he would have figured out why he was being detained. He would have known his predicament was a result of his big mouth. I never understood that about people—they show their hand when they don't know what the opposition has in their deck. If Jason had kept his mouth shut, this would have never happened. He would have remained in a well-paid job, spending most evenings at his favourite bar. Instead, he put me in a very awkward position.

As we approached the industrial area where the warehouse was located, Alex informed me that the Turk had already arrived. He would oversee the disposal of Jason's body once I was done questioning him. The SUV came to a halt, and after the security team from the other vehicle scanned the area, they gave the signal that it was safe for us to step out of our vehicle. Alex jumped out of the front seat, and Chris hopped out from the rear driver's side. The chauffer opened my door on the rear passenger side, and as I emerged, I did a quick scan as well. It was already dark, but it looked like the coast was clear. We'd owned this warehouse for a few years now, but we didn't use the building for anything important. It was where we stored old machinery, office supplies, and endless rolls of fibre-optic cable. The building could do with a bit of refurbishment; fresh paint and new windows would make it look less abandoned.

As we walked in, I saw the Henry the Turk standing next to Jason, who was sat in a wooden chair, looking terrified. The Turk's guys were with him, and as expected they were all armed. As I got closer, the Turk gave me the usual respectful nod.

"Hello Henry, how've you been?" I said.

"I've been okay, boss," the Turk responded.

"Family okay?" I asked.

"Yes sir, everyone is doing well," he responded.

The Turk was a man of few words—at least when dealing with me he was. There was something about him that commanded everyone's respect; he had a certain presence. He was quite the professional as well. We never had to spell out an order; he always knew what needed to be done and just did it.

"So, Jason, it really breaks my heart that it has come to this. What were you thinking?" I said.

"Mr. Dominguez, I was out of line, I get that now. Please show mercy," said Jason.

The Turk, whose fists were wrapped in premium Italian leather, landed two heavy blows on Jason, one on his jaw, and the other split his right cheek. This is exactly what I meant: the guy's timing was impeccable. He knew exactly when and how to execute. He hit him with just enough force not to knock him out, but enough to let him know this situation was serious, and no one wanted to hear his whimpering.

"Now, we know that you've been talking to enforcers. Why did you start chirping? We gave you everything a man could ask for. Not many people your age are in the position we placed you in. What did you tell the enforcers?" I said.

"Mr. Dominguez, I swear to you on my life, I haven't spoken to anyone. It's like you said, I'm in a very good position, and I earn too much with you. I have way too much to lose," Jason pleaded.

Blood had started to trickle down his cheek, and I couldn't tell yet if he was lying. The Turk landed another couple of blows, and Jason almost fell out of his chair. There were no cuts from these strikes, but I could tell the punches hurt. Jason was tougher than I had thought—he was no longer begging.

"You are not getting out of here, alive, I think you know that. If you tell me the truth, not only will I spare your family, I will make sure they are well looked after. You have to tell me the truth, though. What did you say to the enforcers?" I asked.

"Like I said before, I haven't spoken to anyone about anything, Mr. Dominguez. You are making a mistake," Jason said.

Before he finished talking, the Turk punched him a couple more times. I could see we weren't getting anywhere with Jason—he wasn't going to confess. I have interrogated a few people in my time, and something told me Jason was telling the truth. I still had to get rid of him though, so I gave the Turk the nod. The Turk drew a muzzled, nickel-plated pistol from the holster under his jacket and shot Jason in the head. What a waste—he had so much potential. The Turk would make sure the body was untraceable. Jason would be sawn into bits and placed in several trash bags. The bags would be distributed to three separate locations, liquified with acid, and incinerated. It doesn't get any more thorough than that.

We got back in the SUV and headed downtown. We would be making a stop at the Big Fish to go over everything that needed to happen before we headed to Nasarawa, and so I could get an update on any developments relating to the trial.

"Guys, we're heading for the Big Fish. We can grab a drink or two and go over the list we discussed yesterday. I take it all is in order?" I said.

"Yes Dom, I have the list for the Americas. I had a glance, and I think we've got something to work with," Alex said.

"Same here Dom, we should be able to make some moves with the list from Europe," said Chris.

"Excellent. Someone, please get Joe on the comms and ask him to meet us at the Big Fish. We'll need his input," I said.

We pulled up to the Big Fish about 8:45, and as soon as our vehicle came to a stop, one of the valets opened my door. As I stepped out of the SUV, I could see it was a busy night. I saw a number of high-profile customers through the restaurant windows as we approached the entrance. There were businessmen from all over the city, a few crooked politicians too. There were a couple of doctors from Milwaukee Memorial. I made it my business to know the people who frequented my restaurants.

The doorman held the door open for us, and as we made our way to our table, I got polite nods from everyone who noticed me enter the building. My permanently reserved table was towards the back of the restaurant. So, as I walked past, I shook a few hands and exchanged a bit of small talk with people who mattered. Just before we arrived at my table, a couple of waiters hurried over and started placing bottles, glasses, and a bucket of ice on the table. The place always reminded me of the day I met Laura. I remembered seeing her for the first time. It was as if time froze, everything else in my peripheral vision had collapsed, and all I could see was Laura at her table. Boy, did Cupid hit hard that night. Shortly after we sat and poured our drinks, Joe arrived and took his seat.

"Hey Joe, glad you could make it. Guys, I take it this area has been swept?" I asked

"Indeed Dom, it was done before we got here. It's okay to talk freely," Alex said

"Good. We need to go over our lists. Joe, hopefully you'll be able to flag any legal ramifications based on our plan of execution. If there are issues, I would like you to talk us through the best options. Alex, let's go through your list first," I said.

"The list isn't that long, Dom, I have only three people. Fidel Guzman from Guzman's Fabrics. He has never complained about payments, however he missed last month's fee, citing slow business. We looked into his books and found that, although business has slowed down a bit, he could have managed to squeeze out at least half of what he owes us," Alex said.

"You mean Antonio Guzman's kid, he took over the family business in North Walnut Grove?" I asked.

"Yeah, about ten years ago," Alex replied.

"Wow. I knew his dad. He was an Honourable man. That business has been around for years and years. He was a front for the cartel before I became the boss. He decided he no longer wanted to store our drugs, something about a guilty conscience. In the end, the cartel made him pay for protection. Oh well, Fidel has to go. Joe, what are we looking at here?" I asked.

"I had Fredric look into everyone on both lists, and I've scanned the summary. As far as Guzman is concerned, there is always a possibility he could be involved in your indictment. The good thing is he doesn't have any local political affiliations or influence in the community. He doesn't have any association with the local church. There won't be any significant eyebrows raised if he goes missing, so making a move on him should be okay," Joe said.

"Good. Alex, see to it that Guzman is taken care of," I said.

"Consider it done. Next on the list is store owner Karpal Singh. This guy has complained about protection payments ever since he opened his business. He always says he doesn't need the net-cloud services we provide, says all his clients do business with him offline. For this reason, he thinks he should only pay half of what we ask. We've monitored things, and the business is doing okay, he hasn't really done anything that would indicate he is chirping. However, I don't think we should risk it. We should probably take care of him too," Alex said.

"Joe, what do you think?" I asked.

"This is a tricky one, Dom. We pulled a file on him, and Singh has an affiliation with the local Sikh temple. Members of his temple might kick up a fuss with the local authorities. These Sikhs look out for each other, and I don't think they would rest until Singh's death was accounted for," Joe said.

"Thanks Joe, we will make a move on him anyway. We'll make it look like he died of natural causes. It will be expensive, but it'll be worth it. Alex, please get the Pharmacist on the case," I said.

"Gotcha, Dom," Alex replied.

The Pharmacist was no pharmacist. He was an assassin who specialized in taking out his victims with self-concocted pharmaceutical cocktails. He had a knack for producing injections that would kill his victims and make it look like they died of natural causes. His MO was to get his victims in an isolated situation and administer the injection. The Pharmacist regularly switched his formula to ensure that law enforcement never connected the dots when they looked at an autopsy. The fact he was ex-military guaranteed that he was efficient and covert. Our Pharmacist came at a cost, but he would be worth every credit.

"Now, who's the last person on your list?" I asked.

"This client has only been with us two months, Dom. Right off the bat, she missed her first payment by a week, but get this—when she did pay, she also paid with interest. Her New York coffee shop does okay, but I think the shop runs a massive overhead, which affects the bottom line. Her name is Joanna Alvarado, and I don't know what to suggest with her," Alex said.

"Put one of the foot soldiers on her—they are to monitor her every move. If she is found anywhere near a police station or courthouse, or interacting with any form of law enforcement, take her out. Also, get Matthew Harrington to track all her comms," I said.

"No problem, Dom," replied Alex.

It's tricky with female victims. Whenever the press runs a story on young female victims, the story tends to generate more attention than other stories. This results in more sympathy from the public, which in turn could lead to an outcry for justice to be served. We needed to tread carefully with this one if we planned on killing her. It would be a PR nightmare, bringing unnecessary heat our way. We wouldn't get the Pharmacist in on this one. Two of our clients dying of natural causes would be suspicious.

"So, Chris, what do you have for Europe?" I asked.

"Only two on the list for Europe, Dom. I expected the numbers to be higher than they are. I guess our tactics are effective for the most part, seeing as most customers tend not to offend us," Chris replied.

"Hmm, I guess so," I said.

"The first on my list, Muhamad Mahmood. This guy runs a butcher shop in North London, we've had reports that he's been complaining about his fees. Whenever our foot soldiers turn up to collect, it has been noted he can be a bit rude. He coughs up the credits but talks-left while doing it. On one occasion, we were informed that he damaged one of our payment scanners during a routine visit to his shop. He dropped the scanner, but claimed it was a mistake. We added the cost of the scanner to his fees, of course. Speaking of scanners, I recommend we upgrade them across the Americas and Europe. The guys are finding that the scanners can be quite slow, and sometimes payments don't go through for ten to fifteen seconds. As you know, time is credits, so the more time we can save dealing with just one customer the better. As far as our friend Mahmood, my recommendation is we get rid of him," said Chris.

"I think I agree, Chris. Joe?"

"No one would miss Mahmood. His business is not on the up-and-up anyway. The word according to reliable resources is that the business is a front. He is involved in some small-time scams, nothing of great significance to your organization though. There are reports that no one in the area gets along with him. He is constantly involved in arguments with suppliers, other merchants, and the local government. I think you'll be doing everyone a favour by removing him from the equation," Joe said.

"Then it is settled. Chris, take care of it," I said.

"Done," said Chris.

By the time we ran through the list, only one person would be allowed to live. After we had finished our drinks, we left the restaurant and all headed home.

Chapter 21

Business Plan Part Two
Where: Guillermo's Cabana, North Walnut Grove, Miami
When: 1830 hours, Friday, February 10, 2012
Currency: US dollar

Eddie had been helping Anna in the kitchen and when finished, he sat in the usual spot and waited for his friends. Anna didn't mind having the boys around, she knew that being in the restaurant meant they were out of harm's way. Eddie knew his crew would be arriving any moment, so he cleared the table, ridding it of books and paper. He asked Anna if they could all have dinner at the restaurant, and she agreed. She didn't mind feeding the boys every now and then. She didn't know Alex and Chris that well, but she knew their parents and she didn't think much of them. Making them dinner gave her the opportunity to get to know the boys a bit better. As far as she was concerned, this evening would be no different from all the other Friday or Saturday evenings when the boys came to the restaurant to hang out with her son. She knew they mostly talked about movies, music, and clothes. Sometimes the boys talked about girls, but it was never in a disrespectful way.

The boys turned up on time, which was a good sign, this proved to Eddie that they were serious about business.

"Hey guys, what's up?" Eddie said.

"Hey, Dom. I hope your mom made some of her rice pottage, I am starving, dude," said Alex.

"Man, you're always hungry, Alex."

"Ha-ha, yeah man. Do you even eat at home?" said Chris.

"Come on, dude, I'm still growing, ," Alex said, laughing.

"Yo, Dom, this is so weird man. This used to be your dad's corner, now we're sitting here with you. It's an Honour, bro," said Chris.

"I know, man. It's cool though, my mom doesn't mind either. I think she's just happy I'm here at the restaurant and I'm okay. Especially after everything that went down with my dad, you know?" Eddie said.

"Yeah, I hear you, man," said Chris.

Anna had finished making dinner, so she shouted for Eddie to come to the kitchen to grab the tray. Isabel had the day off, so she was at the restaurant that evening helping Anna. Eddie brought the tray of food and put it on the table, then he went back to the kitchen for orange sodas. With the food and drinks now served, he sat down with the boys—it was time to talk business.

"Yo, Dom, um, there are a couple of guys at one of the tables out front drinking coffee. I've never seen them here before, are they new customers or something?" said Alex.

"Nah, Remember I was telling you the cartel would send protection? Well, that's them, they are the muscle. They're here to make sure no one gives my family any trouble," Eddie said.

"Dude, that is so cool!" said Alex.

"Yeah, I guess so man," said Eddie.

"You guess so? Man, this guy is always trying to play it cool," Chris said.

"Ha-ha, play it cool? Chris, I'm as cool as ice, and you know this!" Eddie said.

"Yeah, I hear you, man. But anyway, let's continue our talk from this morning," said Alex.

"Yes, our talk. So, I spoke to my dad's cousin Raphael. I told him there was an opportunity to make some good money, and I convinced him it will be worth his time. He knows it wasn't something we could talk about on the phone, so he'll be joining us soon. When he gets here, we will go over everything," Eddie said.

"Do you think he'll be on board with all this?" asked Alex.

"I am one hundred percent sure that he'll be on board. Raphael is not like my dad. I've watched how he moves, and I know he is connected with some guys that don't play according to the rules. Raphael is a player, I know he is—his clothes, his shoes, his jewellery, his car. All this points to him being a player in the drug game or something else illegal," Eddie said.

"Okay man, I hope you're right," said Alex.

The boys had almost finished eating when the restaurant door opened. It was Raphael. He saw the boys and headed for their table. Raphael was draped in jewellery. Around his neck were two necklaces, one herringbone and the other Cuban link. He wore a gold watch, a gold bracelet, and two gold rings on the index and middle finger of each hand. He was wearing a white silk shirt and linen trousers with a pair of alligator skin shoes. He didn't remove his gold sunglasses when he sat down with the boys.

"So Edwardo, how have you been since the funeral? I was a bit worried when I saw you that day, you looked a bit lost," said Raphael.

"I'm fine, Uncle Raphael, I'm doing much better now," said Eddie.

"Good, good… and Anna and Isabel?" asked Raphael.

"They are doing much better. Actually, they are in the kitchen. Do you want me to let them know you are here?" Eddie asked.

"Nah, let's get to it. Why am I here, Edwardo?" asked Raphael.

"Okay, you remember my friends Alex and Chris?" Eddie said.

"Yes, I've seen you hanging with them outside the restaurant. I also saw them at the funeral," Raphael replied.

"Well, I trust these guys, and I need them to be

involved in this," Eddie said.

"Okay, fair enough," Raphael said.

"I've come into some drugs. I have eight bricks of cocaine and six bricks of heroin, and I want you to help us move it," Eddie said.

"Where did you get the drugs?" asked Raphael.

"I think it's best if you didn't know. Let's just say I found them," Eddie replied.

"The drugs belonged to Guillermo, didn't they? I knew it, I knew my cousin was a gangster," Raphael laughed knowingly.

"Well..." Eddie said.

"Okay, you don't want to tell me where the drugs come from. I can respect that. Now, what's in it for me?" Raphael asked.

"Seeing as there are four of us, I think it's only fair we split the profit four ways. Does that sound fair to you?" Eddie asked.

"Hey, it sounds more than fair to me. I haven't invested any money here, so it's all profit," Raphael replied.

"Oh, hi mom. Look, Uncle Raphael is here," Eddie interrupted, not wanting Anna to hear what they were talking about.

Anna loved Raphael, she knew he was involved in some shady dealings, but she loved him all the same. As far as she was concerned, he was there for her family when they first emigrated to the United States. He also made sure they obtained identity documents—a gesture she would never forget.

"Raphael, how's it going, what are you doing here?" asked Anna excitedly.

"What, a man can't drop in to check on family?" Raphael said, with a big smile.

"Don't be silly, come over here and give me a hug, you. How are Angelina and the kids?" Anna asked

"Everyone is okay. Hey, you all should come over for dinner soon," Raphael said.

"Of course, of course. Don't worry, we will do that very soon. So, would you like something to eat or drink?" Anna asked.

"No thanks Anna, I'll be leaving shortly so don't bother," Raphael replied.

"Okay, no problem. Well, I came out to check on the boys, but I can see they are in good hands. I need to go back to the kitchen, but we will see you soon. Send my love to Angelina and the kids," Anna said.

"I will, thank you," replied Raphael.

Anna knew something was up, she knew that Raphael had some business with Eddie, but she wasn't going to get involved. She had no worries because she trusted Raphael. Anna knew he wouldn't do anything that would get Eddie hurt, even if Raphael had ulterior motives.

A couple of customers turned up, so Isabel emerged from the kitchen and took their order. On her way back to the kitchen, she said a quick hello to Raphael, then went to sort out the customers' order. It didn't get too busy at the restaurant that evening, so the guys were able to carry on talking, but lowered their voices. The last thing they needed was word getting out about the new venture. Raphael was excited—a significant amount of money was coming his way, and all he had to do was make the necessary arrangements to sell the drugs.

"So, Edwardo, I have a plan that will guarantee we move the drugs over six weeks. It has to be at least six weeks because we have to move slowly, so we don't draw too much attention. The cartel is active in my neighbourhood, and I don't want to step on their toes. But we should be able to do it completely under the radar over six weeks without them finding out," Raphael said.

"That makes sense. I was thinking we should sell nickel and dime bags to make a bigger profit. This means we'll need as much help as possible, that's why we need Alex and Chris. If they help, we should be able to move the stuff quicker," Eddie said.

"Nickels and dimes—ha-ha—what do you know about nickels and dimes, Edwardo?" said Raphael.

"Come on. Uncle Raphael, I live in North Walnut Grove and I have eyes and ears. I see and hear things. This stuff is hard to miss in our neighbourhood," replied Eddie.

"Yeah, I guess so, man. Yeah, Alex and Chris will definitely help make the stuff move a lot quicker. But I think we need to keep all options open. If we can sell wholesale, then we should; it doesn't all have to be nickels and dimes for us to make a decent profit. Tell me something though, does anyone else know about this?" Raphael asked.

"Nope, just us. The people here now are the only people that I can trust," Eddie said.

"Good, so when do you want to start?" Raphael asked.

"I don't know, we can start as soon as you're ready, I guess. How about next week?" Eddie said.

"Next week might work. We need to figure out the best way to get the drugs to my place in Fynnwood. There are too many eyes on the restaurant and on your house right now. I don't want people here to see me helping you move the package. Sin Nombre controls North Walnut Grove and most of Fynnwood. We need to be careful every step of the way. We'll only be able to sell in Alicante Grove, that area doesn't belong to Sin Nombre. The dealers there can buy from whoever they want. You guys will need to be in Alicante Grove every Saturday for six weeks. How do you boys plan on selling this idea to your parents?" Raphael asked.

"I might not be able to be there every Saturday. Something might come up at the restaurant that my mom or Isabel won't be able to deal with," Eddie said.

"Yeah, that's something else I wanted to ask, what does it feel like taking over for your dad? You know, now that you're the man and all," Raphael asked.

"You know about that?" Eddie said.

"Come on Edwardo, this is me you're talking to. I can put two and two together: the drugs that we're pretending didn't belong to your father, two goons at the table outside, your family still running the restaurant, you being the only male in the family and sitting right here at this table with your own Assembly. This used to be your dad's table," Raphael said.

"Assembly?" Eddie asked.

"Yeah, Assembly. Back home, our country's government has a House of Assembly. They were responsible for making the laws of the country, so the members pretty much ran the country. This is your assembly, and you are the head. You decide what happens here," Raphael said.

"I guess you are right. As far as the family business, I was put in a situation to make a decision, and I chose what I felt was best for the family, you know," Eddie said.

"Hey, you're my little cousin who is no longer little. I can't judge you; you did what you had to do. I'm impressed by the decision you have made on behalf of your family. I respect the way you have stepped up. I appreciate that you recognise the age gap between us and call me uncle. The respect does not go unnoticed," Raphael said.

"Thanks, Uncle Raphael, that means a lot to me. So, guys, I hope you'll be able to hold down the fort in Fynnwood whenever I can't make it. Uncle Raphael will be counting on you to play your part," Eddie said.

"I don't have a problem with it, Eddie, I'll work things out with my parents. How about you, Alex?" Chris said.

"I'm in, no problem. Chris and I are all the way in, Uncle Raphael," replied Alex.

"Good. I will come up with a plan to get the drugs to Fynnwood, Uncle Raphael. Leave that to me," said Eddie.

"Are you sure?" Raphael asked.

"Yes. No one will suspect kids our age of having that much weight. We have a better chance of getting it to Fynnwood without your involvement," Eddie said.

"Good, it is settled then. Just let me know when you are ready. I'll be leaving now, say goodbye to Anna and Isabel for me," Raphael said.

"No problem, I'll do that," Eddie replied.

"Hey guys, be very careful. I'm sure I don't have to tell you how dangerous this is," Raphael said.

"We'll be careful, Uncle Raphael," Eddie replied.

Eddie already had a plan. He was going to repackage the heroin and cocaine, because it still had the Sin Nombre brand on it. To transport the drugs to Fynnwood, he had devised a plan to buy three travel cases to put the drugs in and cover it with clothing. Then he was going to hire an airport taxi to pick them up along with the bags. The cover story would be that they needed to fly to Houston for a school debate. They would tell the taxi driver they needed to pick up their team coach in Fynnwood on their way to the airport.

Anyone curious enough would see that there was something odd about kids needing to pick up an adult and not the other way around. However, Eddie knew the taxi driver wouldn't be interested in whatever was going on. Most taxi drivers only wanted to get from point A to point B as quickly as possible, so they could get to their next passenger.

Upon arrival at Raphael's, Eddie would pretend to call the team coach from the taxi to tell him they had arrived and were waiting outside. After a couple of seconds, Eddie would pretend there had been a mix-up, saying another taxi had been booked by the coach by mistake and the taxi would arrive in fifteen minutes. The boys would opt to take that taxi instead. Eddie would pay the full fare so as not to upset the driver and attract even more attention to the situation. He had thought about everything in case they were pulled over by the police. He even looked up flight times to make sure they coincided with the journey time to Fynnwood and then to the airport. If the cops asked for plane tickets, they would say that they had been reserved and ready for collection at the airport. Eddie was thorough.

Chapter 22

Distribution of Narcotics and Firearms
Where: Edom Group, The United Nations of Europe and Americas, Milwaukee, Wisconsin
When: 1030 hours, Thursday, November 7, 2041
Currency: UNEA credits

The previous day had been a really long one, and we were completely shattered. We decided this morning's meeting would not be as early as the previous day's. We pulled up to the main entrance of Edom Group around 10:30 am. The door opened, and I stepped out of the vehicle and headed towards the massive glass doors. There was the usual activity in the lobby: employees who worked in the building were scanning their way through the security barriers using their comms devices. I had a separate entrance to the offices. To the far left of the lobby near the security desk was a narrow entrance with a glass barrier. We headed to the private entrance and as we got close, the security staff gave me a nod as they opened the barrier from their desk. There was a private elevator that went straight to my office lobby, bypassing the other floors.

Two of the guys from my security team got in the

elevator with me, and the other two remained in the lobby downstairs. Although there were other offices on the thirty-second floor, there was no way of getting to my wing without using the private elevator or the emergency shoot. The shoot had only one entrance, from the top floor, and an exit to the basement parking lot. Both were secured by magnetically bolted doors that could only be controlled from the security desk and from my personal and office comms. These were designed to quickly get me out of the building during a fire or any kind of attack. The convoy would be on standby in these sort of emergency situations and would be able to quickly transport me to a safe location.

When the elevator door opened, I could see Brandon scrolling through eMessages on his interactive desk. The desk faced the elevator, and he was the first point of contact for the VIPs who were allowed on my wing. Brandon only used his virtual privacy screen for confidential messages. The disadvantage to this was that anytime he activated privacy mode, a dark tint would cover the glass screen from behind, and this restricted his view to the elevator. He didn't like using this mode, because he wanted to be prepared for whoever was coming from the elevator. He knew it would more than likely be me and the VIPs, but he liked to be prepared.

From the reverse view of his eMessages, I saw it was the usual stuff: building maintenance, suppliers, company updates, etc. Underneath his desk, attached to customised compartments, was a laser-sighted .45mm

Aggressiv, a German-manufactured handgun. The compartment also contained its counterpart, the Aggressiv AI submachine gun with programmable DNA-heat-seeking bullets. The submachine gun is impressive; it uses a combination of DNA and heat to locate its target. It also had a "fire-at-will" mode. With this, Brandon was capable of incapacitating anyone who managed to bypass all the security measures that have been put in place. This was highly unlikely to happen though. It would take a great deal of effort to make it past the lobby downstairs, through the narrow glass barrier, and up the private elevator. Even if somehow, someone was able to bypass security, and Brandon, there were still the two giant, auto-tint bulletproof glass doors shielding my office from intruders. The doors could easily absorb the impact from a pistol or assault rifle of any kind. In this building, I was almost one hundred percent safe.

As I approached Brandon's desk, I saw that Alex, Chris, and Joe were already there with coffee in hand. Brandon and I exchanged greetings, and he informed me that I had a direct message on my comms. This must have been important, because only a few people had my desk-comms address tag. Brandon had no access to my direct messages; he could only see that a message had been left. He asked if I would like auto-tint activated, and I said yes. He said coffee had been served—he must have seen me from his screen the moment I entered the downstairs lobby. He had access to security cameras in the building—another security measure that would ensure the building was safe enough for me to roam.

As I walked in, I took my coat off and hung it on the coat rack near the entrance. I said hello to the guys, walked over to my desk and brought the message up on my comms. It was an encrypted message from an unknown comms device. The message read, *Eddie, the narcotics charge is a nonissue. Don't worry about it, the charges will be dropped before you know it. Regards, Renegade.* The message was from one of my contacts at the NFDA, Commissioner of Food and Drugs, Charles Rickman. Those of us at the very top of our respective organizations used code names when exchanging messages with one another and didn't want to incriminate ourselves. This was excellent news. If only I had more men like Rickman in other branches of government—I would be untouchable.

There were many revolutionary drugs and supplements that hadn't been approved by the NFDA for various reasons. Some of these drugs had already been approved in regions outside of the Nations. However, due to red tape and propaganda by other parties, the NFDA as a collective was unable to give approval for these products. One reason was that there had been issues with drug trials. There was always some animal-rights activist group that would protest drug trials on animals, which meant human trials couldn't begin. All this even though animal and human trials had been successfully completed in other regions.

Another issue was the Nations Revenue Service was suggesting an unreasonable thirty-five percent tax for a number of products that did pass trials. Pharmaceutical companies would have to agree to the proposed level of taxation before the drugs could be made available to the public. There was also turmoil within the NFDA where not all officials agreed on various policies relating to the drugs.

For some stakeholders it was just too much of a hassle trying to go the legal route. With all the barriers and misaligned stars, there were still individuals in various branches of government who were willing to bend the law in order to facilitate selling these drugs by any means necessary. This is why the production and distribution of illegal drugs and supplements was at an all-time high. As long as these key government officials had been compensated, the drugs were allowed to find their way to the black market and most times even to retail. This of course depended on individual circumstances. The products couldn't be traced back to any particular company, and any investigation would lead to several suspicious candidates, leaving too large a pool of suspects and insufficient proof to charge or convict anyone.

"Good morning, all," I said.

"How's it going, Dom, sleep okay?" Chris asked.

"Yeah, thanks, Chris. After I got home, I went straight to bed," I replied.

"So, you're all refreshed and ready to go then," Joe

asked.

"Well, I wouldn't go that far. But it has to be done, so let's do it. We have a bit of good news. I can't go into details, but all you need to know is I have confirmation that the narcotics charge will eventually be dropped. Joe, we just need you to figure out a way to drag out the issue until the charges go away," I said.

"That's great news. To be honest this one wasn't going the distance; there are just way too many officials on the take for this to have stuck. This is really good. It means that we can focus on the other charges," Joe said.

"What's next on the agenda, Joe?" I asked.

"The firearms charge. I am a bit worried about this one. I have a feeling that an undercover enforcer might be involved," said Joe.

"You think?" I asked.

"Yeah," Joe replied.

"Let's have a look at that photo again," I said.

Joe passed the photo to me.

"It was a new shipment of assault rifles, and I wanted to see the merchandise for myself, that's how they ended up getting me in the shot. Wait, the angle of this photo… I know who did this. Alex, the driver from that day, the guy that was going to drive the guns across state. The angle in this picture could only have been taken from where he was standing, he must have been wearing a body micro-camera of some sort. The camera must have been offline, and if it was that would explain why our signal sniffer didn't pick it up. How long had he been with us? Is he even still around?" I asked.

"I'll make a call, leave that with me," Alex said.

"In the meantime, the evidence is already out there. What can we do about it, Joe?" I asked.

"At the end of the day, it's only a picture. Look at the expression on your face and the pointing gesture, it doesn't appear that you were happy with what you were looking at. We can put a spin on it. The story would be that during routine quality inspection, you were expecting to see a particular product in Edom Group's armoury line, only to discover the illegal firearms instead. You instructed the driver to notify the NLEU and turn in the weapons to them. We'll also claim you initiated an internal investigation to find whoever was responsible and hand them over to authorities." Joe said.

"You think that will work?" I asked.

"There is a good chance that it will. I mean, it is standard practice for company presidents to sometimes inspect their inventory." Joe replied.

"Could you please quantify this 'good chance' you are suggesting?" I asked.

"I'd say an eighty-five percent chance of beating the charge. It's down to me to convince the jury." Joe replied.

"I guess that's not too bad, all things considered," I said.

"I just got off comms with our guys. The driver vanished a while ago." said Alex.

"And no one thought to raise this? We should be

better than this. We've always been careful with the people we employ. How did we not know this guy was an undercover enforcer—Chris, Alex?" I asked.

"We run all the necessary checks before taking people on. The enforcers can be resourceful, they can create profiles for their undercovers, similar to how we cultivate identities. I'm sure when we ran all the checks, the driver's profile passed." Alex replied.

"Fair enough. Spread copies of the guys picture around, I want him dead. If he's not around to testify, we'll have an even better chance to beat the case," I said.

It felt great to find out the narcotics charge would eventually be dropped. The firearms charge was still a problem—a major one. The guns in question were Russian engineered submachine guns and long-range assault rifles. This kind of weaponry was only available to the Russian army. There was no weapons trade agreement between Russia and the UNEA; there was no agreement with Ukraine either. This provided an opportunity for us, and we were able to broker a deal with the Russians that allowed us to buy their weapons at a price that still hit a reasonable profit margin. We had been smuggling Russian weapons into the Nations for years without a single incident—until this fiasco.

This was one of sixty or seventy shipments since we brokered the deal. I was present on the day of delivery, because I wanted to check out the new upgrade to the weapons. The new weapons were equipped with improved trigger stability, upgraded laser-tracking and a new target-lock system. There was also the holo-display which indicated the number of rounds contained in a magazine at any given time. Other upgrades included a heat warning indicator, an oil level indicator, a cooling system, and a faster and more accurate fingerprint reader. Synthetic oil would be periodically dispersed from an attached cartridge, allowing the oil to be distributed to chambers within the weapon, reducing jams by ninety-nine percent. Another cartridge contained a bio-gel that when heated by gunfire would convert into a cooling fluid dispersed throughout the weapon. The display that showed the bullet count also displayed the heat, gel, and oil levels. Weapons had evolved over the years.

These Russian weapons had become a problem in the streets across the Nations and were prevalent in drug-related gang wars. It had become a major issue for law enforcement because a few enforcers had died of gunshot wounds from these very weapons. The main reason why the Nations never had a weapons deal with Russia was down to the fact that the UNEA manufactured its own weapons. The Nations manufacturers did not want the competition. They had travel agreements and other charters in place, but Russia and the Nations weren't allies.

We had been discussing the case for a while and I was starting to get a bit hungry and needed a break.

"Okay, I am famished. Anyone else hungry? I think we should order something for delivery from the Big

Fish, but I'm easy, I don't mind if we order from somewhere else," I said.

"Hey, how about Sergio's? I'm in the mood for spaghetti and meatballs." Alex said.

"Ha-ha! Of course you are, Alex, some things never change." I replied.

"Hey, I'm no good to anyone when I don't eat. It slows me down, you know." Alex said.

"Ha-ha. Okay, Sergio's it is," I said.

We decided to take a break and continue our meeting after lunch. Brandon called Sergio's and placed our orders. Sergio was a good friend, and his restaurant was one of the most popular in downtown Milwaukee. Like me, his parents migrated to America many years ago, and they went into the restaurant business. Sergio Russo Jr. inherited the restaurant after learning how to run the business working with his parents. The restaurant had been successful when his parents were still in charge. Now, after opening the second restaurant downtown, it had become a staple in the area.

The plan was to go over the kidnapping charge after lunch; it would be interesting to see what the guys had been able to come up with. Kidnapping was a very serious offense and could get me life in prison. There was no question about it, the kidnapping charge and the conspiracy charge was where most of the money was going to be spent.

Chapter 23

The Road to Fynnwood
Where: Guillermo's Cabana, North Walnut Grove, Miami
When: 0200 hours, Saturday, February 18, 2012
Currency: US dollar

It had been over a week since Eddie's Assembly had their meeting with Raphael. Eddie needed to get the product ready, so he woke up around two o'clock Saturday morning to repackage the drugs. He knew his mother and sister would be fast asleep at this time. He retrieved the drugs from the secret compartment in the wall of his bedroom closet. This was also where he stashed his cash. He re-bagged the heroin and cocaine then put them into the individual travel cases he had bought. He put a brick of cocaine in one suitcase and a brick of heroin in another. The plan was to take two bricks per trip. Travelling with all fourteen bricks would have been too risky. He then filled the suitcases with his own clothes and some of the merchandise he sold at school.

He had informed the boys of his plan for transporting the drugs to Raphael's. He told them to prepare for this and emphasised that they needed to all be on the same page. They would be dressed in their school uniforms and have their backpacks and books with them. They needed to look like they were attending a school event. Eddie told the boys that if they were pulled over by the police and the plan fell apart, they would blame the driver. The story would be that the driver coerced them into posing as passengers and threatened to hurt their families if they didn't cooperate. It was genius.

Eddie told his mom the lie about the school event. He told her he had joined the debate team and that Saturdays was when practice took place. With this, he had a cover story for the next six weeks. After the six weeks, he would tell his mom that he was no longer a member of the debate club. Raphael got the call from Eddie the previous day to give him the green light. So, Raphael made all necessary arrangements from his end. Eddie set his alarm for 6:30 a.m., giving him an hour to get ready before the taxi arrived.

Eddie's mom would already be at the restaurant by the time he woke up. Saturday was the restaurant's busiest day, so Anna liked to get in early to prepare the food. Some Fridays, Isabel worked nights and would get home at 5 a.m. the following morning, so she would be fast asleep. On the Saturdays that she had off, she would sometimes wake up early to help Anna at the restaurant. Either way, no one would be around to see Eddie and his friend getting into a taxi with three suitcases.

Eddie was done packing the suitcases, so he put them back in his closet and went back to bed. As he was laid in bed, he thought about the amount of money he and his friends were about to make. It was almost fourteen kilograms of cocaine and heroin with a street value around $1,500,000. This worked out at around $375,000 split between his uncle and his friends. None of them had ever received that amount of money in their lives, and in six weeks or so it was going to become a reality. He kept rehearsing the trip to Fynnwood in his head, going over every detail and mulling over the problems that could occur on their way to Raphael's.

Eddie was awoken a few hours later by his alarm clock. As he was about to get out of bed, there was a knock on his bedroom door.

"Come in," Eddie said.

It was Isabel.

"Hi, Edwardo," said Isabel.

"Oh, how's it going, sis?" Eddie replied, surprised to see Isabel and hoping she would be going to bed soon.

"Hey bro, just checking on you. I heard your alarm go off. How are you doing? We've not really had the chance to talk," Isabel said.

"Umm yeah, I'm okay I guess," Eddie replied.

"Are you sure, Edwardo? You've got to be still hurting about Dad, I know I am," Isabel said.

"I mean, of course I'm still hurting, but I know I have to be strong—Dad would have wanted that. Right?" Eddie said.

"I guess you're right. I just miss him so much, you know? He was always there for us; I feel like there is so much we've missed out on," Isabel said.

"I know, I feel the same way. This doesn't do much for our pain, but I hear that the cartel got to the person that did it. I hear that the guy is dead," Eddie said.

"You are right, that doesn't get rid of the pain. Edwardo, I don't like the idea of your involvement with these people, it doesn't sit well with me at all," Isabel said.

"I hear you, sis, but what do you expect me to do? This wasn't my burden to carry, I inherited it. I didn't see that we had too much of a choice. We were about to lose the restaurant. What would we have done after that, who is to say the cartel wouldn't have just killed us if we had chosen not to cooperate?" Eddie said.

"You make a good point, but I don't like it all the same. I mean, you're still in high school for crying out loud. You are still a kid," Isabel said.

"And I understand how you feel, Isabel, I completely respect your feelings on the matter. Unfortunately, we need to make the best of the situation we find ourselves in. I'll be careful, don't worry," Eddie said

"Anyway, I got back from work about an hour ago and I'm tired, I'm going to bed. See you later, little bro," Isabel said.

"See you later, sis," Eddie replied.

Eddie rushed for the shower and got ready for the

trip to Fynnwood. He received a couple of text messages from Alex and Chris, saying they were on their way. Eddie waited for the boys in the living room, leaving the suitcases in his closet until the taxi pulled up. When the boys arrived, there were dressed up with their uniforms neatly ironed, as instructed by Eddie.

"Hey guys, we all set?" Eddie asked.

"Yes, Dom. I have been looking forward to this, man. Chris, you've been looking forward to this as well, haven't you?" Alex said.

"Of course, our lives are about to change, I'm pumped," said Chris.

"I'm glad you guys are pumped about this, but we gotta keep our voices down, I don't want to wake Isabel," Eddie said.

At exactly 7:30, Eddie received a text message alerting him that his taxi had arrived and was waiting outside. He peeked out the window and saw the red MPV. He didn't like the fact that the taxi was red. He remembered his dad telling him that red cars attracted police attention. The cars that Eddie saw being pulled over by the police were mostly red or some other bright colour. There wasn't time to cancel the taxi and book a different one, and there was no guarantee that the next one wouldn't be red as well. For all he knew, this was the taxi company's colour. Eddie could see that there were a couple of cartel goons across the street, watching their house. This was part of the agreement—Hector Gallegos kept his end of the bargain.

Eddie grabbed the suitcases and gave one each to Alex and Chris. There were only two bricks, so he put one in the suitcase that went to Chris, and he put the other in Alex's suitcase. As they were heading for the taxi, Eddie glanced at the cartel goons and gave them a nod. From time to time, the goons offered to provide Eddie with security away from the house, depending on where he was going. They never followed him to school or church, because turf wars or any other cartel-related incidents never extended to such places.

"Hey Soap, you need off-site support, my friend?" asked one of the goons.

"Nah, don't worry, Chiquito, it's just a school thing. I'll be all right," Eddie replied.

"Okay, see you later," said Chiquito.

"Cool, see you later," Eddie replied.

The driver got out of the vehicle and opened the trunk. He grabbed the suitcases from the boys and placed them inside. Once the boys had gotten in the car and fastened their seatbelts, the driver drove off. Eddie told the driver about their school event and that they needed to make a stop in Fynnwood to pick up their coach. The driver nodded and keyed the destination into the navigation system. They were almost halfway to Fynnwood, the boys trying their best to act natural. They talked about clothes, sneakers, and the fictional debates. The driver didn't say a word the entire time, he just drove. Every now and then he reached for the thermos in the console cup holder near the dashboard. It was really strong coffee, the smell made its way into the back seat. Alex made a comment to the guys that the coffee smelled nice, and they started a conversation about coffee. The driver didn't respond, he just kept driving.

They were getting close to Fynnwood when they heard a couple of bleeps from a car behind them—the sound of a Miami PD siren. The driver pulled over, and the boys went silent, tension engulfing the back of the car. Although Eddie had gone over this scenario with his Assembly, the police confrontation still came as a shock. The officer didn't get out of his car for almost four minutes. The driver and the boys stayed put as well. When the policeman finally stepped out of his vehicle, he put his left hand on his sidearm. He walked up to the taxi, headed for the driver's side. As he approached, he looked towards the back seat and saw the boys there.

"License and registration, please," said the police officer.

"No problem. I will need to reach in the glove-box, okay?" said the cab driver.

"Yes, do that slowly, please, and keep your left hand where I can see it," said the police officer.

"Could you please tell me why I was pulled over?" asked the cab driver.

"You slowed down a couple times, and your right brake light didn't come on. Where are you headed?" asked the police officer.

"These kids have a school event to attend, we are

making a stop to pick up their coach in Fynnwood. After that, I'm taking them to the airport to catch their flight," replied the cab driver.

"Are you carrying any weapons in this car?" asked the police officer.

"Absolutely not, officer, I hate guns," replied the cab driver.

"How about you guys, are you carrying any guns or drugs?" asked the police officer.

All three boys said "no" to the officer's question. The officer stood and stared at the boys for what seemed like an eternity. Eventually he walked back to his unit to run checks on the driver's documentation, remaining in the car for at least ten minutes. The policeman returned with the driver's particulars then asked the boys for their IDs. They handed their IDs to the officer, and again he returned to his vehicle. The boys remained quiet. Finally, the policeman returned to the taxi still holding the boys' IDs.

"So, what is this school event you boys are travelling to?" asked the officer.

This was Eddie's plan, so he felt responsible for answering the officer's question. He already had his plan laid out if the officer decided to search the car. He was going to make the taxi driver take the fall, and the poor guy didn't even have a clue about what was going on. Eddie was a bit less nervous than the other two.

"We are representing our school in this year's annual debate competition. We plan on bringing the trophy home this year," said Eddie.

"Is that so? This coach of yours, what's his name?" the police officer asked.

"Alfredo Guzman, sir," Eddie replied.

"Do you have a contact number for him?" asked the police officer.

"Sure, it's 305-209-9801," Eddie said.

"Okay, I'm gonna check this out. You all sit tight," said the officer.

The boys were now even more nervous. They couldn't talk amongst themselves without exposing the fact that they were nervous. There wasn't much they could do without looking suspicious. Five minutes later, the officer walked back to the car and stared at the boys for a few seconds.

"Everything checks out, you are all free to go," said the police officer.

He handed their IDs back to them, and the taxi driver drove off. The boys were so relieved, they all looked at each other, seeing the relief in each other's faces. Eddie had previously spoken to Raphael asking him to verify that he was Alfredo Guzman and corroborate the story.

Moments later, they pulled up to Raphael's. Since the plan had been disrupted by the police officer, the original plan—to make a phony call saying that another taxi had been booked—had to change. If that story was true, the second taxi would have already arrived and left by the time the boys arrived. Thinking fast, Eddie pretended to make a call indicating that Mr. Guzman would drive them all to the airport instead.

"Sorry, sir, Mr. Guzman decided he'll just drive his car to the airport instead. He will use the parking service there. But here's the full payment anyway. Thank you, sir," Eddie said.

The driver got out of the car and retrieved the boys' luggage. As the taxi departed, the boys grabbed the suitcases and headed for Raphael's door.

Chapter 24

Kidnapping
Where: Edom Group, The United Nations of Europe and Americas, Milwaukee, Wisconsin
When: 1330 hours, Thursday, November 7, 2041
Currency: UNEA credits

The lunch from Sergio's went down quite well. Everyone must have been starving, because there was no food left by the time we were finished. We needed to go over the rest of the charges and take action where we could.

"So, Joe, what's next?" I asked.

"The kidnapping charge," Joe responded.

"Yeah, that one. Here's the problem with that one, having kidnapped so many people over the years, it would be difficult to figure out who chirped," I said.

"What we can do is get on the secure comms to our people on both sides of the Nations. We'll need to rely on our guys' memory seeing as we don't keep a record of kidnappees," Alex laughed. We'll try to narrow down who we didn't get rid of after they were kidnapped and then get rid of them. That is if they haven't already gone into witness protection," Alex continued.

"Good idea, Alex—can you and Chris get started with that right away? Compile the list and proceed accordingly, " I said.

"We're on it." Chris replied.

Like I did with Jason Byrne, I had given several orders in the past for people to be picked up and questioned for whatever we suspected they were involved in. We hadn't killed everyone we had abducted, so it was obvious that one of the people we released was chirping. I never thought any of those people would be brave enough to cooperate with the enforcers. As we decided for the other charges, we would narrow down our list of offenders and start wiping them out.

I recall an incident with a guy we snatched up for being rude to Laura. We decided to celebrate our tenth anniversary by having dinner at the Big Fish. This was the perfect location, because it was where Laura and I first met. Since I owned the place, the staff would go the extra mile to make everything perfect. On this night, we went in through the rear entrance. We said hello to the chef and everyone working in the kitchen. Laura walked over to the big pot of bubbling tomato sauce. The chef saw she was intrigued, so he offered her a taste by handing her the wooden spoon he'd been stirring the sauce with. She had a taste and complimented the chef, telling him he made the best sauce in all of Milwaukee.

After entering the restaurant from the kitchen, we sat at our table and made our way through our starter.

Laura stood and said she needed to visit the restroom. As she took a few steps, a guy at the bar suddenly rose from his barstool and somehow managed to bump into Laura. She apologized to the guy. Instead of responding with poise, he started yelling at her. The guy clearly didn't know who he'd yelled at, otherwise he wouldn't have done it. We get people from all walks of life at the restaurant. Most were wealthy people with class, but sometimes we got wannabe gangsters who behaved as if they owned the joint.

Laura didn't think much of it, she just apologized again and kept walking towards the bathroom. When she was out of sight, I nodded at one of my security guys, and they knew exactly what needed to be done. The security guys, one on his right and the other to his left, grabbed the punk by both arms, took him outside, and put him in their car. One of the guys came back and asked me what I wanted them to do with the guy. I told them to rough him up a bit and let him go. Word got back that the guy was the son of a retired Milwaukee Miners player whose father also frequented the Big Fish. I didn't care who his daddy was—he should have taught his kid some manners. He was one of a few people we'd released after we snatched them. He, along with anyone else on Alex and Chris's list, was going to die. If any of those guys were in protective custody, we were going to make sure their testimony would never be heard.

"Joe, what's the legal strategy in a scenario where

a victim testifies?" I asked.

"Well, it depends on whether the victim heard you give specific orders to have them kidnapped," replied Joe.

"I don't think so, no. I'm too careful," I said.

"If a victim testifies, we can discredit them. We will find all the dirt on them and use it in court. That's in the unlikely event we can't find out who it was," said Joe.

"I won't let it get to that. We'll have to nip it in the bud before it goes to court. We can't take any chances," I said.

Moments after Alex and Chris got in touch with their contacts, we had a list of names to work from. The guys had narrowed it down to four individuals, one in Europe and three in the Americas. Thinking about it now, it was a bit disconcerting to know that we had kidnapped so many people over the years, and we could account for releasing only four. Oh well, we do what we need to do. Sacrifices have to be made in business, and if people needed to die in order to maintain the status quo, then so be it. I had come too far—I created an empire— and jeopardizing this for the lives of a few would be senseless. The companies that I have built have contributed significantly to the Nation's economy. Which raises the question of why anyone would want to bring me down. I, Alex, and Chris had amassed a significant amount of wealth over the years and become accustomed to a particular lifestyle. Even though we were all wealthy, we still had individual financial goals that we were still trying to achieve.

"So, as far as the four people on the list, I'm not even going to ask how our people remember who's done what. If our people are documenting this stuff, they better make sure the information is encrypted. Anyway, I want those people taken care of. We can assume that if anyone on that list is missing, they have gone into protective custody. What this means is that we will have to take them out on their way to the courthouse," I said.

It turned out that the baseball player's son who had disrespected Laura at the Big Fish had died in a car accident. Reports stated he was driving too fast in a sports car bought for him as a birthday present by his dad. He lost control of the car, spun, crashed into a lamp post, and the car burst into flames. Ah well, it's quite sad, and I can only imagine how devastated his family must be. However, that's another person we don't have to account for, so we're down to three potential witnesses. That fact the kid's father was a high-profile individual would have made it a tricky situation anyway. There would have been serious pressure on law enforcement to bring his murderer to justice, but luckily, we no longer have to worry about that.

It was settled: we were going to get rid of all potential threats for a better chance of beating my case. I wanted to move onto other business, and Joe didn't need to be around for the next discussion. We had an opportunity to make a trip to Nasarawa to go over the logistics that would make the erratanite deal happen.

"Joe, I think I have enough information for the trial, and I am happy for you to carry on with the rest of the research. I will be taking a trip to the AU in a couple of days. You'll be able to reach me on the comms. I'm sure you have things to do, so you're free to go now. The guys and I are going to be here for a while going over travel logistics and other business matters," I said.

"Sure Dom, I'll head to the office to see what else Fredric has been able to come up with," Joe replied.

"Okay, see you later. Call me if you need anything."

We planned on flying Saturday morning from MKE with a stopover in Brussels to refuel the jet. From Brussels, we would touch down at Dahiru's private airfield in Nasarawa. Dahiru would be at the airfield to welcome us, and with both of our security teams in place, we would be able to mitigate any problems that might arise. In the AU, Nigeria had become one of the safest places to travel to, however, there was news of robberies and kidnappings every now and then. I needed to make sure all company-related digi-docs I needed for my trip had been sorted out and sent to my inbox. I buzzed Brandon, asking him to come into my office.

"Everything sorted for the trip to Nasarawa?" I asked.

"Yes, Mr. Dominguez, I spoke to the staff at the house, so your luggage has been sorted out. You might already be aware that the visas for you, Mr. Lewis, and Mr. Abbadelli are still showing as 'Active' on your digipassports. The same goes for the security personnel. The visas are still valid from your last visit. Limos have been arranged to pick up all three of you from your individual homes at 8:45 a.m., and then arriving at the hangar in time for the flight. The pilots and flight personnel will be on board two hours before you arrive, making sure everything is ready for the flight. All the staff have been informed this trip is top-secret and none of the flight info should be disclosed. I have ordered a bottle of Vieux Vignoble for Mr. Wali, which will be ready for you to present to him upon your arrival in Nasarawa," Brandon said.

"That's great, thank you. Get Matt Harrington on comms and tell him to come to the office as a matter of urgency," I said.

"Okay, will do," Brandon replied.

"That'll be all for now, Brandon, thank you. So, guys, you both ready?" I asked

"What, for the AU? Of course, Dom. Great weather, good food… what else can a man ask for? We should definitely squeeze time in for a bit of R and R, right?" Chris said.

"Of course, all work and no play, right Chris?"

"Definitely. But, hey Alex, you gotta take it easy on the local booze when we get there. That stuff is lethal," Chris said.

"Hey, I learned my lesson last time okay, I had a hangover for months!" Alex said.

"Ha-ha, that'll teach you." Chris said.

"On a more serious note... Dom, we made Jason disappear, and his body won't be found. Do we need to worry about his wife making trouble about him being missing? I have a feeling he might have talked to his wife about our business. Do we need to worry?" Alex said.

"Nah, it's okay, let's leave her be, she has suffered enough," I replied.

"Okay, I just don't want things to take a turn for the worse. Am I being paranoid?" Alex asked.

"Just a bit," Chris said.

"Why do you say that, Chris?" asked Alex.

"If Jason's wife knows who we are, then she knows the score—she won't say a word. Also, she's entitled to Jason's severance package; she wouldn't do anything to jeopardize that," Chris replied.

"Okay guys, let's discuss Jason's wife at another time; for now, we need to get Dahiru on the comms. We need to let him know we'll be heading to Nasarawa in a couple of days, it'll give him enough time to prepare," I said.

We finalized everything with Dahiru. Matt Harrington turned up, and I asked him to do the extra checks on the tracking bracelet. He ran diagnostics on the device to make sure everything was okay in terms of configuration and connectivity. For the final touch, he programmed the bracelet with pre-set readings that would make it look as though I had never left the UNEA.

Chapter 25

Welcome to Fynnwood
Where: Raphael's residence, Fynnwood, Miami
When: 0900 hours, Saturday, February 18, 2012
Currency: US dollar

The boys rang Raphael's doorbell. He opened the door, again dressed extravagantly and draped in jewellery. As he let the boys in and turned around to head for the living room, Edwardo could see the bulge from what appeared to be a pistol tucked into Raphael's belt.

"You always packing, Uncle Raphael?" Eddie asked.

"Oh, you can tell?" replied Raphael.

"Ha-ha, yeah, the silk shirt doesn't hide it very well," Eddie said.

"Yeah, I need to remember that. But seriously though, I'll keep this piece on me for the next six weeks. Selling drugs to low-lives requires you to stay tooled up, because you never know when someone will decide to test you," Raphael said.

"Yeah, I know that too well," said Eddie.

"Sorry Edwardo, I didn't mean to..." Raphael realising he might have struck a nerve, but Eddie cuts him off.

"Nah, it's cool, I'm okay now. My dad is gone, and there is nothing anyone can do about that. Do I feel like he would be alive today if he had a gun with him that night, or if he had security to protect him? Of course, but what's done is done. We have to move on," Eddie said.

"Your dad would be proud if he could see how you've handled everything so far. Anyway, welcome to Fynnwood! Today, we'll have to pack guns, move weight and we deal with a few undesirables. But by the time we're done, we'll have enough money to venture into other businesses and eventually I can say goodbye to this hellhole," said Raphael excitedly.

"Indeed, uncle. Where is Aunty Angelina?" asked Eddie.

"She's taken the kids out shopping, and they'll be going to the movies after that," said Raphael.

"Is she okay with all this?" asked Eddie.

"She doesn't have much of a choice, Edwardo. She likes to go shopping, for herself and for the kids. I think she knows that money don't grow on trees, she knows I'm a hustler. I was a hustler when she met me, I'm a hustler now," Raphael replied.

"Fair enough. Are you able to make sure she doesn't mention what we are doing here to my mom?" Eddie said.

"Wives who come from where we come from generally don't ask their husbands about business. They also don't talk to other wives about their husbands," Raphael said.

"I see," Eddie replied.

"So, trust me when I say this: your mom isn't going to find out about what we're doing here. Besides, we'll be out of here before Angelina and the kids get back and they won't see a thing," Raphael laughed.

"Ha-ha! Okay. Now, where do we start?" Eddie asked.

"I have arranged for a few low-level dealers I trust to buy the heroin from us at fifty percent above the wholesale price. They'll still make a reasonable profit from their investment. We'll move the cocaine ourselves out of a motel in Alicante Grove. I already have a few customers lined up, and since this is not Sin Nombre territory, we'll have no problem selling there. These guys aren't your average junkies. Some of them are professionals. There'll also be some gofers buying coke for their D-list celebrities. We're definitely going to be able to sell everything you have within six weeks," Raphael said.

"So, what role do we play in all this, Uncle Raphael?" Eddie asked.

"You guys will bag up the coke in twenty- and fifty-dollar baggies. I will deal directly with the customers and the money, and you guys will take turns being the look-out at the window of the room. Next time we do this, it will be best if you guys go to the motel directly. I also need to figure out a new way to move the drugs from your house to Alicante Grove. I don't like what happened with the cop and the taxi this time, so we'll look for a different way," Raphael said.

"Okay, I agree. Things did get really tense this morning," Eddie replied.

"Oh, there is one thing that I forgot to mention. We will need some muscle while we're doing what we're doing in Alicante Grove. Drugs deals tend to go wrong; it's the nature of the business. We can't trust anyone completely, so we'll need a couple of guys with guns for security. The daily rate for the two guys I have is two hundred dollars each. There's also the fee for paying the receptionists on duty to allow us to operate without calling the cops, another hundred per day. The payment for all this will come from each of us, so that's about $166 each. Everyone okay with that?" Raphael asked.

"We're okay with it, Uncle Raphael," said Eddie.

"Good, because we don't have a choice anyway. We need the security plain and simple. The two guys will be meeting us at the motel," said Raphael.

"No problem, we're all on the same page." Eddie said.

"Okay, even with the muscle I'll be carrying a pistol while we're there. Any of you know how to handle a gun?" Raphael asked.

"I do—you have a spare one for me?" Eddie said.

"You do?" asked Raphael.

"Yes, Uncle Raphael," Eddie replied.

"Wow kid, I don't even wanna know. I'll be giving you the piece when we get there. Okay let's go, we'll take my car. Oh, if we have even the slightest hunch that we are about to be raided by the cops, we flush everything down the toilet, got it?" Raphael said.

"Absolutely!" Eddie replied.

"Good," said Raphael.

The guys loaded up the trunk of Raphael's car and headed for the motel in Alicante Grove. They decided to stick to the school debate story in case they ran into the police again. Luckily for them, the backup story wasn't required. They eventually pulled up to the One in a Bed Motel, a rundown cesspool in the most corrupt part of Alicante Grove. The massive florescent sign was very old and missing several lightbulbs. In the surrounding neighbourhoods, all they could see were rusty old cars. Almost all the homes looked dingy, with overflowing trash cans and old furniture out front.

After Raphael parked, he asked the boys to remain in the car while he paid for the room. He stepped out of the car and scanned the area, but things were quiet at that time of day. There were a few hookers hanging around looking for clients. They looked at Raphael, but something about him let them know that he wasn't to be approached. The girls looked like they were on drugs. Raphael knew the area well—they wouldn't have any problem moving cocaine here. What he wasn't sure about was how much raw coke would sell or how fast. Crack was mostly the drug of choice for users in the area. However, most drug heads would generally make do with whatever they could get their hands on, even if it meant buying a more expensive baggie of raw cocaine. Raphael and the boys would not have problems with the police, because every receptionist working during their hours of operation would be paid off. The hookers knew better than to call the cops, because that meant putting their own lives in danger. Besides, they needed the convenience of being able to buy drugs without having to travel too far. There would be a tiny bit of competition in the area. Nothing too substantial though, because the guys that dealt drugs there were small timers and generally didn't have enough product to move.

Raphael paid the receptionist, and she gave him the key to room 406. He had the boys put the suitcases in the room. The guys who were going to provide security had arrived earlier, parked in a white pickup. Raphael signalled them over, and they had a conversation about securing the room. One of the guys would remain outside the room door, while the other guy kept an eye on the wider area of the motel.

After getting the suitcases into the room, the boys unpacked the drugs and started to bag them. Raphael had already spoken to his contacts to get the word out on the streets to let people know they had high-quality cocaine for sale. While the boys were busy packaging the product, he handed a pistol to Eddie as promised. Eddie tucked the gun behind his back, under his shirt just like his uncle did.

It had been a couple of hours since they had bagged the drugs, but there was not a single customer in sight.

"So, is it just me or does it feel like we're not going to sell anything today?" Eddie asked.

"It might seem that way, Edwardo, but trust me—this business is different from the restaurant business. People don't use drugs at a particular time of day. There are a lot of things to consider when dealing with drug heads. Some of them sleep through most of the morning from being up all night. Some of them might be scoping out the motel as we speak to make sure that our setup is for real and not a sting. There is also the fact that there will be people who will not buy from us. Even though we have very good product and we're only a stone's throw from drug-heads that live in the area. So, patience Edwardo, patience," Raphael said.

Soon after he said that, there was a knock on the door. It was the security guy posted outside the door. He brought in the first customer, who told Raphael he'd been told to come there if he needed anything. The guy was a crackhead and mentioned that word on the street was that he could get pure white from the motel. Edwardo had his hand behind his back, ready to pull the gun out if Raphael felt it was necessary. The security guy patted down their customer but didn't find anything. Raphael gave Chris the nod, and he got out two twenty-dollar bags and handed them to the customer. It was done—their first sale.

The boys were now officially drug dealers, and their confidence grew. Shortly after that, customers were pouring in. People were turning up every ten minutes, buying as much as two hundred dollars of drugs in one deal. At one point, someone turned up with some jewellery and watches, wanting to trade them for cocaine. Raphael sent them away. He figured the jewellery was stolen, and if it was, then selling the jewellery for cash would cause problems.

Raphael's contact turned up to buy the heroin. Again, the security guy patted him down to check for a wire and weapons but found nothing. The security guy also checked the bag the guy brought with him but found it only contained money. Raphael's contact expressed his disappointment with the search, but Raphael stated that it was just business. He said that it wasn't only his call—everyone there wanted to feel safe, and he agreed that everyone who came to the room would be searched.

Raphael nodded at Alex, who carried the brick of heroin to the table. The heroin, along with the remaining baggies of cocaine, were hidden underneath the floorboards in the bathroom and the floorboards were then covered by a bath mat. Raphael's contact tested the drugs and saw they were high quality. He pulled out the cash and handed it to Raphael, who decided he was going to inspect and count the cash. It was $42,000—they had only sold a quarter of that amount in cocaine in the hours they had been there. Raphael knew that moving the cocaine would take longer, but he was sure they would be able to sell everything in one day. Raphael told his contact that another brick of heroin would be ready the following Saturday.

The cocaine was gone by 4:30 that afternoon, and it was time to close up shop. Raphael had been stashing the money in a plastic bag inside the mattress. He retrieved the money, and the boys watched as he counted it. They each ended up with $13,125, the most any of them had ever made for a day's work—not even Raphael had made that amount in a single day. Eddie and the boys put their cash in their backpacks. They paid the security guys, and the boys refunded Raphael for the motel room. Eddie handed the gun back to Raphael, and they all got back into the car, heading for North Walnut Grove.

Chapter 26

The AU
Where: Dahiru's private airfield, The African Union, Nasarawa, Nigeria
When: 1635 hours, Saturday, November 9, 2041
Currency: AU credits

The African Union comprised all the countries in Africa, excluding the Democratic Republic of Congo. All the other African countries agreed to a new treaty shortly after the UNEA formed their union. The leaders of the DRC had their own plans and didn't want anything to do with the rest of Africa. Congo's corrupt leaders, as well as the people close to them, had been running the country as they saw fit, stripping the land of its natural resources. They shared the spoils among themselves, while the rest of the country suffered in poverty.

The rest of Africa had seen enough corruption, poverty, hunger, and general instability, and they were ready for a change. The collective pooled its resources and generated enough revenue to pay off its loan from the World Bank just four years after forming the union. My friend Dahiru was already a successful businessman, but it was during the transition to the new union that he amassed much of the wealth he has today.

We landed at Dahiru's airfield, and after circling the runway, we headed to his private hangar. He had four other hangars he leased to VIP friends and clients; these hangars came with the bare minimum in terms of comfort. His own hangar included a lounge with a bar and grill, bathroom, pool table, music, and so on. He had four or five people running the place twenty-four/seven. The staff at the hangar lounge was made up of three ladies and a couple of guys. Nasarawa's population was about seventy percent Muslim, so the staff were all dressed in Islamic attire.

As we stepped out of the jet, we were greeted by a scorching heatwave. Fortunately, this had only affected me for a couple of seconds before my suit's cooling system kicked into overdrive. All my suits were equipped with a thermal-control system that consisted of electro-thermal conductive gels and nano-fibre-optic wires. A chemical reaction was triggered whenever the gels were charged by an electrical current. The temperature emitted from the gels was based on a couple of factors: the external temperature and the combination of an integrated thermometer as well as my own body temperature. The source of the electrical current were the buttons that were cleverly wire-stitched to my suit. The suit also had a thermometer, again powered by the buttons.

Built-in body armour was also included. This not

only stopped bullets from piercing my flesh, it also protected the thermal gel packs underneath. The suit's master craftsmanship was courtesy of Bellucci & Co. Bespoke Suits. I was the only customer who good old Mr. Bellucci agreed to craft all the tech for. Anyone could purchase a bespoke suit from him, but if they wanted to get the integrated thermal and armour systems, they would need to get it done elsewhere. Alex and Chris had this tech in their suits as well, but they used a different tailor.

I saw that Dahiru and his security staff had been waiting for us, as promised. His guys were all armed with assault rifles and submachine guns supplied by Proteritek. We exported the weapons from Russia to his private security company as a gift. My security team had their own weapons, so neither of us had to worry about our safety during my visit. As I approached Dahiru and his men, one of the air hostesses handed me the gift-wrapped bottle of Vieux Vignoble.

"Hey Mr. Dahiru Wali, how's it going, my main man?" I said.

"Assalamu alaykum, my good friend, long time no see. Welcome back to the AU," Dahiru replied.

"Always a pleasure coming here, it's like home away from home. Here, I brought you something," I said.

"Heeey, Vieux Vignoble, you know you didn't have to do this," Dahiru said.

"Come on, it's my pleasure," I replied.

"Chris, Alex, you guys made the trip," Dahiru said.

"We wouldn't miss this for the world, Dahiru, and you know how much Alex loves it here," Chris said.

"Ha-ha, I do. I think Alex likes it a bit too much, eh?" Dahiru said.

"Come on, Dahiru, take it easy on me, I still have flashbacks from the last trip. What was in that drink anyway?" Alex said.

"Ha-ha, you're a funny guy, Alex," Dahiru said.

"Come, come, guys, our transportation is ready. How about you guys ride with me?" Dahiru said.

"Yup, let's go," I replied.

Trips to the AU have always been fascinating to me—Nasarawa specifically. The lifestyle, the customs, and just the general demeanour of the people who live here: very different to life in the West. The people were down to earth and respectful, but there was also a sense of pride, and they expected the respect they gave to be reciprocated.

Our convoy of driverless vehicles manouvered along a busy freeway from the airfield into the town centre. The AU had implemented driverless-car zones in the regions where this was a necessity, mostly the busiest parts. Nasarawa was one of the more prosperous regions, therefore driverless-car zones made up seventy-five percent of the smaller streets and freeways. The drive from Dahiru's airfield provided the opportunity to admire the scenery, and it was fascinating. The strange thing about our journey was that the town centre was ridiculously busy, but this didn't seem to affect the flow of traffic.

Everything had been organized in such a way that allowed people, automobiles, and motorcycles to move freely. Driverless vehicles and networked roads were only just starting to catch on in the UNEA. The problem with most Western countries was that there was existing infrastructure that was obsolete and needed to be demolished before new infrastructure could be put into place. Things like underground electric, telephone, and old network cabling needed to be removed and replaced with new infrastructure. For the most part, the world had adopted wireless systems. However, there was still a requirement for underground cabling and equipment for all the systems to work together. Changing the old systems was quite expensive. This is why the West was still playing catch-up to the technological advancement achieved by regions that were once considered developing countries. Most regions in the AU previously lacked the finances to implement old technology when they were still relevant. So, implementing the new infrastructure was feasible and easy to execute since the cost of removing old tech wasn't an issue. Nigeria had become an innovator in commerce and technology. The Nigerian oil boom was a thing of the past due to the mass adoption of cleaner energy sources. Most AU countries now utilized solar, wind, and nuclear energy to generate electricity.

Gone were the days when it was perceived as a

third-world. The AU was fully developed, with opportunities for continuous growth. Nasarawa had developed so much that it had modern architecture and one of the most advanced comms infrastructures in the world. Glass buildings had been erected all around the town centre, and the buildings were powered by the material they were built of. The AU had figured out how to optimize solar energy, enabling them to harness the same amount of energy as before. The difference now was that they were able to maximize the energy output by two hundred percent using advanced solar amplifiers. There were holographic billboards advertising goods and services from AU corporations. It was all a sight to see.

"Eddie, you love it here, don't you? It's always the same every time you visit Nasarawa, you spend most of the ride looking out of the window," Dahiru said.

"I can't help it, Dahiru, it's a beautiful place," I replied.

"Have you ever thought about buying a place out here? Perhaps you could bring the family here every summer," Dahiru asked.

"Yeah, it's definitely worth considering," I replied.

"So, sorry that you've had to fly out here to complete our business. We could have done everything over the comms, however, AU laws on international business are quite strict. The government requires international businesses to be represented by the most senior individuals should those organizations wish to carry out business in the AU. Erratanite export is an area of great interest to the AU, because it generates a significant amount of revenue. So, one can understand why the government would want to make sure that everything from the regulatory side of things is handled with the utmost vigilance. But don't worry, everyone involved knows about your case and the travel situation. So, don't worry about the news about your visit getting out, everything we do will be confidential. We will be using secret entrances and exits everywhere we go as an extra precaution," Dahiru said.

Even if word got out, no one would be able to prove it. The tracking bracelet had been rigged and I was also wearing a camera signal scrambler if anyone decide to try to capture any photos or video footage.

"Hey, I understand. I don't mind travelling here anyway; it provides me with an opportunity to catch up with you while I relax a bit. So, what is the process?" I asked.

"We're heading to the AU Bureau of Foreign Investments first. They will need to scan your biometric details into their systems. No fingerprints, just facial and eye scans. They'll also need your physical and digital signatures saved to the system. Are you okay with this?" Dahiru asked.

"Of course, whatever it takes," I replied.

"After that we'll head over to AU Customs. They'll need you to complete the export forms and pay the relevant fees. Once all of that has been sorted out, we'll head to my office and go through all the documents and sign the contract between our companies. Does that sound good to you?" Dahiru said.

"Absolutely. But hey, seeing as we're here till Monday morning, I imagine you've made plans for us to see what the weekend in Nasarawa has to offer. What do you have lined up for us, Dahiru? You know Alex has been looking forward to this, and we can't let him down," I laughed.

"Disappoint Alex? Oh no, no, no, I would never do a thing like that to Alex," Dahiru chuckled. We'll be having lunch once we're done at the Bureau of Foreign Investments and the customs office. After that, we'll head to my place. This will give us the opportunity to freshen up and relax a bit. Later, we'll head downtown to the Fadar Sarki Casino for some dinner and a bit of fun. How does that sound, Alex?" Dahiru asked.

"Ha-ha, you guys are never going to let me forget that night, are you? I'm easy, I go wherever you guys go," Alex said.

"Then it is settled," replied Dahiru.

Later that night, we had dinner at the casino restaurant and afterwards we headed to the roulette tables. As we made our way past the entrance, the concierge greeted us and walked us to the private VIP section of the casino. This area had blackjack, poker, and roulette tables. The concierge asked one of the waiters to take our drink orders and the drinks arrived shortly after. I was violating the terms of my bail by being here, so I couldn't help but wonder if anyone present recognized me. I decided to keep a low profile. I checked my tracking bracelet again and everything looked okay.

After a few rounds at the roulette table, we decided to head to the jazz lounge on the second floor of the casino. When we got there, everything seemed okay. There were a few people there, who appeared to be high rollers taking a break from gambling. The performers were onstage playing traditional saxophone, drums, and guitars. This was perfect, hearing music generated by actual people using real instruments. Digital instruments were dominant in music today, and traditional instruments had fallen by the wayside.

We were all having a good time and chatting among ourselves, when a commotion suddenly kicked off at the other end of the VIP section. A man had been shouting at another man for what I could only imagine was money related. The shouting was becoming louder, and at this point the musicians had stopped playing, and some of the people in the room started leaving. One of the individuals had a group of men with him, and the other man was by himself. The man that was by himself got up from his seat, and the other man started to shove him backwards in our direction. Our security teams, mine as well as Dahiru's, were on alert and stood at the response position in case our safety became compromised. As the men were getting closer to where we were sitting, I noticed they all had military-style boots on, including the man that was getting shoved. This was a setup—people generally didn't wear boots with suits unless they were on some sort of mission.

Before I could tell my men to draw their weapons, the other men drew theirs and faced our direction. A couple of Dahiru's men as well as mine saw everything unravel. Our guys opened fire, and so did the men who we now knew had been sent there to take us out. A couple of the security guys pushed us out of the way, Dahiru and I fell to the ground and ducked behind the bar as the entire room became riddled with bullets. There was glass shattering all around us, and the bullets were leaving holes in the furniture and the wall behind us. Some of our guys had been hit, but luckily, they all had on body armour.

By the time the shooting stopped, the assailants were on the ground, lying dead in their own blood. Dahiru and I had been hit as well, but I was wearing full body armour. Dahiru had been hit in the arm. For some reason he wasn't wearing armour at all. The security details rushed us to our separate vehicles, and we drove off.

This was too much heat, and I wasn't supposed to be in the AU anyway. There was a real potential of going back to prison should the authorities find out that I was in the AU. I decided we were going to leave the country immediately. Alex and Chris called everyone from my flight crew, telling them that we were leaving sooner than expected and asking them to meet us at the airfield.

I called Dahiru's comms to find out how he was doing, and he said the injury wasn't too serious. He was being taken to the hospital to get stitched up, and he said he would get in touch with me once he got to the bottom of everything. I explained to him that we had to leave immediately, because I couldn't risk being questioned by AU law enforcement or the media. By the time we arrived at the airfield, the entire crew was waiting on board the jet. Within a matter of minutes, we all boarded the plane and were up in the air, heading back to the UNEA.

Chapter 27

All Part of Alicante Grove
Where: Outside the Dominguez residence, North Walnut Grove, Miami
When: 1715 hours, Saturday, February 18, 2012
Currency: US dollar

When they got back to North Walnut Grove that evening, Raphael wanted to go over a few things with the boys before they got out of the car. He wanted to switch things up a bit, because he felt the operation left them a bit vulnerable security-wise. He thought it would be a good idea to be better prepared in case of unforeseen events.

"Guys, today was a good day, but I think we can do better. The first thing I want to suggest is that we need more muscle, at least a couple of extra guys covering security. One on lookout, one patrolling the area, and two at the door. Alex, Chris, you two will need to have guns as well, and don't worry, I will get the guns. Also, we will no longer allow customers to come in the room, not even the guy buying the heroin. We will serve our customers by using our lookout, who will give us hand signals to indicate what the customers want, and we'll figure out a way to get the drugs to the customers without them coming to the room. We'll probably have to use one of the guys from the door. How does that sound?" Raphael asked.

"I completely agree, Uncle. In fact, I was thinking exactly the same thing. It felt like we were sitting ducks out there. I have an idea on how to get the drugs to the customers," Eddie said.

"Oh, you do now, do you?" Raphael asked.

"Yeah. You know how at the bank drive-through, the tellers send money to customers through the tubes from inside the bank? Eddie said.

"Yes…" Raphael replied.

"Well, we can get some tubes like the ones from the banks. Tubes that can be clipped together to form one long tube. We can feed the tube through the bathroom wall. We'll set up the tube at a height high enough that no one would notice it. With the tube at that height, the customers will not know that the drugs had been dropped from the tube directly above them. I saw a small air vent in the bathroom, and I'm sure all the rooms will have the same thing. All we have to do is unscrew and remove the air vent, and then feed the pipe through the hole the vent was in. Even if anyone notices it, it will just look like a drainpipe from the second floor. This would have been much easier if the bathrooms had windows. Anyway, we can get the lookout to tell the customers to collect the drugs from the back of the motel, which is where all the bathroom walls are facing." Eddie said.

"Kid, this is crazy, you watch way too much television," Raphael laughed. But that's actually a good idea. I know these tubes you're talking about; I'll go to the hardware store this evening on my way home… wait, I need to take this call. *Yes, yes… that's not a problem, we'll make that happen, see you tomorrow.* It's the guy who bought the kilo of heroin. He wants two more kilos tomorrow, and he also wants a kilo of cocaine," Raphael said.

"Wow, that's a lot, Uncle Raphael. Can we trust that guy not to rip us off?" Eddie asked.

"It's fine, don't worry about it. That's the reason we're getting more muscle and all of us will have guns. The guy won't be meeting us at the motel tomorrow. I will tell him where to meet us at the last minute. Make sure it's two bricks of heroin and an extra brick of cocaine tomorrow. We'll bag the nickel, dime, and twenty bags of coke when we get to the motel. Just like we did today. Tomorrow morning I'll be picking you up, using my friend's ice-cream van—the police won't suspect a thing." Raphael said.

"No problem, Uncle Raphael, I will tell the cartel guys who watch my house that I'm going to hanging out with you. They won't suspect anything either. To make it even less suspicious, Alex and Chris will have to meet us down the street, where the cartel won't see us. I will put all the drugs in my backpack and wait for you to pick me up," Eddie said.

"Sounds like a good plan, see you guys in the morning," Raphael said.

***

The following morning, they arrived at the motel at Alicante Grove around 11a.m. Raphael had made all the arrangements the previous night. The four guys to cover security were already there waiting. The guy that was going to buy the two kilos of heroin and the brick of cocaine would be meeting Raphael's crew later that day. Raphael was going to pick a neutral spot where it would be difficult for his contact to double-cross them. Raphael reached underneath the driver's seat of the ice-cream truck and pulled out a brown canvas sack; in the sack were four handguns. He pulled out two revolvers from the sack, turned around, and handed them to Alex and Chris in the back seat. He handed a semiautomatic pistol to Edwardo, and the other semi he tucked under his shirt behind him.

"You guys wait here while I go speak to the receptionist to make arrangements for the day. You should know that we will be paying the receptionist slightly more money than we did yesterday, because we'll change rooms a few times today. The receptionist is going to want more for this. There's also the fact that we've hired more muscle. These are all costs we can live with though. Our safety is worth it, do we all agree?" Raphael said.

"Absolutely! Alex, Chris, you guys have a problem with this?" Eddie asked.

"Nah man, I'm good. Alex?" Chris asked.

"Yeah, I'm good too. No complaints from me, man," replied Alex.

"Good, I'm glad that we are all on the same page. I'll be back in a couple of minutes, and we can unload the tubes," said Raphael.

Raphael spoke to the receptionist and made the arrangements. The receptionist promised to keep an eye on the surveillance cameras and inform Raphael of any suspicious activity. The receptionist also left four rooms empty, situated in strategic parts of the motel. This was ideal, because now the hookers wouldn't know which room the guys were in. More girls were hanging around, having gotten word that cocaine was available.

They unloaded the ice-cream truck, and everyone carried the tubes up the stairs to the second floor. Edwardo unscrewed the vent in the bathroom as planned and put one of the tubes in to make sure it fit. He connected all the tubes together.

The final piece was a corner piece with a bend in it. This was the part that would stick out of the wall on the inside to allow them to drop the baggies in.

Raphael gave the signal to one of the security guys outside the door, who walked to the part of the second floor where he could be seen by the look-out near the small parking lot. Shortly after the signal had been given, a signal was sent back by the lookout: six fingers up and then two fingers after that. This meant six twenty-dollar baggies, amounting to $120. This would be delivered to the room by the lookout. Transactions like this continued until around 2:30p.m. before sales started to slow down. They had almost run out of product at this point.

Then Eddie noticed that all the hookers had disappeared. He could see someone taking out the trash from other rooms on the same floor. The man doing this didn't seem like your average cleaner, because he was well dressed, with nicely groomed hair, so Eddie asked Raphael if it was worth checking the guy out. Raphael approached the receptionist to find out more about the guy and how long the man had been working at the motel. It turned out that the cleaner had been working there for years and he had always dressed the same way. Eddie calmed down when Raphael brought the news back, and everyone carried on as they had been.

By 5p.m. the drugs were all gone, and Raphael split up the profit with the boys after deducting the fee for the motel receptionist and security. The boys still had the two bricks of heroin and a brick of cocaine in their backpacks. Eddie went to the bathroom to replace the air vent. He retracted and dismantled the tubes, and everyone helped him carry them back to the van. Before driving off, Raphael placed a call to his contact. Speaking in code, he told his contact to meet them at a nearby parking lot in fifteen minutes. The parking lot was three minutes from where Raphael and his team were. He told the security guys as well as Eddie and his guys to be on high alert, saying that this was not your average drug deal. They had around three kilograms of product, and he knew too well things could easily go wrong.

The plan was for Raphael and his team to arrive at the meeting point early to check out the location. However, just as they were about to pull out of the parking lot of the motel, three SUVs pulled up in front of the car belonging to Raphael's security team, with Raphael's ice-cream van behind them. The security team's driver had a submachine gun in his lap, so he reached for it and as armed men stepped out of the SUVs, he started shooting. The driver hit the first and second guy from the first SUV, and then the other three guys pointed their weapons out the windows and started shooting at the other two SUVs. Raphael didn't have a good view of what was going on and neither did the boys. Raphael hollered at the boys to have their weapons ready. Eddie didn't appear to be shaken by all the shooting. Alex and Chris looked shocked but maintained their composure, guns ready.

After ten seconds of gunfire between the two crews, the shooting stopped. Raphael reversed the ice-cream truck to get a better view of the other vehicles. As he reversed, he could see dead bodies—the men from two of the SUVs on the ground, and the drivers had also been shot dead. The third SUV had fled the scene. Raphael stepped out of the ice-cream truck. Still clutching his pistol, he ran over to the car belonging to his security team. The front of the car was covered with bullets holes and had started to catch fire. All but one of the guys had died in the shooting. The only guy remaining was still ducking behind the front passenger side of the car, grazed from a bullet. Raphael helped him up and told him the car was about to blow up and that they had to leave right away. They jumped into the ice-cream van and drove off. After driving about fifty yards from the motel, they heard the explosion. An explosion meant the cops wouldn't have any DNA to link the car to anyone—they had caught a break. The car had been assembled with parts from four other vehicles, serial numbers scratched out—untraceable. The mood was sombre.

Raphael dropped the boys off and told Eddie he'd be in touch. Raphael's contact called to find out what was going on—he'd been waiting at the agreed location for thirty minutes. Raphael initially suspected that it was his contact who had set the entire thing up, but it turned out that his contact had nothing to do with it. Raphael thought to himself that perhaps one of the streetwalkers had something to do with it. His contact was still very interested in the product and convinced Raphael to go ahead with the deal. He even agreed to meet with Raphael alone to hand him the cash, trusting that Raphael would deliver the drugs. He told Raphael he would help him find the person who ordered the hit, and they would make that person pay.

Raphael contacted Eddie, asking him to get the product ready. Raphael turned up in his own car to collect the drugs, and shortly after he completed the deal with his contact, he came back to deliver Eddie his share of the money.

Chapter 28

Home Sweet Home
Where: AU Airspace, The African Union, Nigeria
When: 1635 hours, Saturday, November 9, 2041
Currency: AU credits

"Chris, please get Dahiru on the comms."
"Sure, Dom."

At this point, all sorts of thoughts were running through my mind. The shootout had me a bit rattled, enough that I was even more paranoid than usual for my safety and the safety of my guys. I started to wonder if the guys from the casino had been sent by Devin Carlsdale Jr., word on the street, was he'd been looking to expand. I also started to question whether it might have been the Russians; perhaps they felt I would cooperate with the enforcers about the weapons operation. It was difficult to tell where all this had come from. After a few minutes, Chris finally got hold of Dahiru on the comms.

"Hey Dahiru, what the hell happened out there?"

"So sorry for that, Eddie. This is my territory, and it was my job to keep you safe. Don't worry, we have found out where this came from."

"Wow, that was fast!"

"It was the Christians, and it was me they were after."

"Christians—really? You've got to be kidding me, and what if I got killed, I would have been, what, collateral damage?!"

"So sorry, Eddie, I'll make it up to you."

"It's okay man, at least we're both alive right?"

"Indeed, my friend, indeed."

"So, regarding the erratanite, I'll be getting the first shipment next month?"

"Yes, twenty tons this month, then another twenty in January. I can probably get you a better deal if you decide to sign another contract that runs through the rest of 2042."

"Yeah, that shouldn't be a problem, who else would I go to in the AU?"

"Well, I just thought that after what happened tonight you would want to keep your distance."

"Come on Dahiru, don't be ridiculous. Why would I let something like what happened tonight end our friendship or doing business together? I would never react that way."

What Dahiru suggested wasn't far from the truth. I was thinking about severing ties after tonight's ordeal. However, I still needed his business. With the hit my business has taken, I needed to keep the revenue flowing, and Dahiru was my way of doing that. Something told me that Dahiru knew this as well; he was a very intelligent man. My old man once told me that true friends in business were rare; people in business are always trying to find a way to maximize their profit and further their own agenda.

"Well, my good friend, I really need to get some rest now. I hope to speak to you soon, and I hope we get a favourable outcome from the trial. Let me know if there is anything I can do to help."

"That's very kind of you, Dahiru, hope you have a speedy recovery. Speak to you soon."

As far as I was concerned, this was far from over. No one jeopardizes my life and gets away with it. I planned on getting to the bottom of this. I'm not convinced this job was carried out by some Bible-reading, church-going Christians, who for the most part do not have a history of extreme terrorism. Granted, there had been a few rogue Christian extremists, but that was quite rare. The guys who attacked us were pros: their attire and formation reeked of ex-military. Alex asked one of the flight crew to bring us our usual drinks, feeling that we all needed it, and he was right.

"Guys, that was way too close. We could have died out there," I said.

"I know, Dom, those guys meant business," said Alex.

"I took one to the suit as well," said Chris.

"Sheesh, you too?" I said.

"Yeah. How about you Alex?" Chris asked.

"Nah man, they missed me," said Alex.

"Alex, you're the luckiest man I know, how did you manage not to get a single scratch on you?" I asked

"It's the lucky linen handkerchief, Dom."

"Oh great, not the damn handkerchief again," said Chris.

"What? Chris, I'm telling you, every time I have this thing on me, and bad things happen around me, I'm never affected," said Alex.

"Yeah, maybe we need to get a couple of lucky handkerchiefs of our own," I said.

"Ha-ha, please don't encourage him, Dom," said Chris.

"On a more serious note, I want you guys to look into this. We need to find out who did this and shut it down right away. Also, whatever you do, Dahiru must not know that we are looking into the matter. We can never be sure he didn't set this whole thing up, although I'm not sure how it would be in his best interests," I said.

"Yeah, no problem, Dom. I completely agree with you, we shouldn't let this go unpunished. Someone's gotta suffer the consequences," said Chris.

"Okay, I'm turning in, I need some sleep," I said.

We arrived back in Milwaukee safe and sound the following morning. I went straight home, and as I walked in; I could hear Laura's voice from the kitchen. I could hear the kids voices as well, and they sounded like they were in good spirits. It felt great coming home to the family after what happened in Nasarawa. If those gunmen had their way, I would have been back home in a coffin.

"Hello, everyone," I said.

"Dad!" Jonny said, sounding really happy to see me.

"Hi, Jonny," I said.

"Dad, you're home! We weren't expecting you home till tomorrow," Carlie said.

"Hi Carlie, umm, I can go back if you want," I said jokingly.

"What? Okay, now you're just being silly, Dad. I've missed you, have you been okay?" Carlie asked.

"Yeah, I'm fine, you don't have to worry about me," I said.

"Glad to hear that," Carlie replied.

My mom and Laura were there as well, everyone was dressed nice.

"Mom, you're here as well. You look great," I said.

"It's Sunday, Edwardo, we're going to church this morning. I don't suppose you would like to join us?" my mom said.

"No, Mom, thanks for asking though. Hi, Laura," I said.

"Hi, babe, did you have a good trip?" Laura asked.

"Yeah, it was quite productive," I said.

"Yeah?" She said.

"Yeah. I got all the documentation sorted out, so we're good to go," I replied.

"That's good to hear. Would you like to join us for breakfast?" Laura asked.

"Of course! What are we having?" I replied.

"The chef whipped up some eggs, sausage, waffles, pancakes, bacon, hash browns, and toast. There is fruit, cereal, and granola. There's also fresh coffee if you want some," Laura said.

"I'm going to go freshen up first, then I'll come back downstairs for the coffee," I said.

"You didn't shower on the plane?" Laura asked.

"I did, but I'd like to freshen up again and get out of this suit," I replied.

"Okay, no problem," Laura said.

"You going to church as well?" I asked.

"Nope. I'd like to catch up with my husband, if that's okay with you," Laura replied.

"Of course, you know I would never object to that," I said.

"You better not," Laura said jokingly.

"We're leaving now, Dad. We'll catch up later, right?" Carlie asked.

"Yes, Carlie, see you later. Take good care of Grandma. See you when you get back, Jonny," I said.

"See you, dad," Jonny replied.

It was really nice seeing everyone in such a good mood, at least it appeared that way. If I didn't know any better, I'd say that the situation with the trial was still bothering Laura, and she was just putting on a cheerful face for the children. Mom looked her usual self, poker-faced. Over the years she'd learned not to let her emotions get the best of her. When we lost Pops she really struggled emotionally, but over the years she had come to terms with his death. When I was done freshening up, I changed and went downstairs to spend time Laura.

"How are things at work, Laura?" I asked.

"Everything is great. We have two big clients. They'll bring in an extra sixty million credits each per annum for the next five years," Laura replied.

"That's excellent news, Laura, you signed them?" I asked.

"Yup," Laura replied.

"Really pleased for you, honey."

"Thank you. Coffee?"

"Absolutely, thanks."

"So, everything going well with trial preparations?" Laura asked.

"Yeah, so far so good. You know Joe, he's always got something up his sleeves," I said.

"Yeah, he is good."

"He's confident that we don't really have anything to worry about at this point. He believes we'll beat this case."

"That's really good to hear, I can relax a bit now. I'd be lying if I said I'm not worried about this."

"Well, all we can do is hope for the best. At least the murder charge has been thrown out."

"Yeah, that was in the news. I'm really happy about that, it was one of the things I was worried about."

"Well, you can put your mind at ease now."

"We should all take a vacation together soon, we should bring your mom as well."

"That's actually a great idea. It'll have to be somewhere within the Nations though, I already took a risk going to the AU this weekend."

"I did ask you if going was a good idea."

"I know, I know. I won't risk it again. If the trial is prolonged and there is an urgent need to travel, I'll ask Joe to get permission from the judge."

Laura and I spent the rest of the morning catching up on family matters and discussing how to move forward. I reassured her that everything would work out just fine and that things would be back to normal, eventually. Laura's main concern was how the charges and the trial would affect the kids long-term—she didn't want kids picking on Jonny or Carlie. I assured her that the kids would be okay. Jonny is a tough kid and he has thick skin. He doesn't really care what people say about him. The school kids have parents who are just as shady as I am, so I knew that none of this mess would affect him. Carlie was the sensitive one, but she seemed to be doing okay. Nevertheless, people knew not to mess with my kids. They knew that was the one thing that would lead to trouble. There'd always been stories about my mob ties, but they had always been just that, stories. With my trial being such a public affair, it would only reinforce what people suspected about me.

The kids got back from church later that afternoon, and my mom decided to pop in before heading back to her annex. Mom loved it when the kids went to church with her. Going with the kids gave her the opportunity to show off how great her grandkids are—her pride and joy.

"Hey Dad, I'm going to be heading back to Connecticut in a couple of hours, I have lectures tomorrow afternoon. Is it okay if I take the jet?" Carlie asked.

"Sure, no problem. Get Brandon to get the flight crew together," I said.

"Excellent! Thanks, Dad," Carlie said.

"Hi Mom, how was church?" I asked my mom.

"It was good. Father Thaddeus asked about you again," my mom replied.

"He did?" I asked.

"Yes, he did. With everything that is going on, it wouldn't hurt to go see him for prayers, you know. It would also help rebuild your image," my mom said,

"Mom might have a point here, honey. A few press photos with him would be a good look for you," Laura said.

"Not you as well, Laura. Fine, I'll go see Father Thaddeus," I said, reluctantly.

"Good," my mom said.

I hadn't been to church in a while. I just had no interest in the rhetoric. It was the same stuff every time: love your neighbour, repent, have faith, Jesus loves you. The same stuff over and over, but I will make the time to go see him just to make everyone happy.

"Okay, if I'm no longer needed here, I'll be heading to the study. Hey, Jonny, you got a minute, kiddo?" I said.

"Of course, Dad," Jonny replied.

"So, how are things with you, school okay?" I asked.

"Yeah Dad, I mean the kids have been asking a lot of questions but nothing malicious really," Jonny replied.

"Oh, I'm really glad to hear that. I know kids can be mean at times, I just wasn't sure if you were being picked on because of everything that has happened," I said.

"Nah, nothing like that, Dad. In fact, a lot of the kids that I hadn't even been friends with all want to hang out with me now. I've got kids wanting to buy me lunch, some of the younger kids wanting to carry my school bag and stuff. It's all a bit weird, to be honest," Jonny said giggling.

"Ha-ha, it's called respect, son. I never wanted things about my business to come out this way. Now that it has, and people know you are my son, they want to get close to you. They probably think that an affiliation with you is cool," I said.

"Oh, I see," said Jonny.

"Don't misunderstand what I'm saying here, though. I never wanted you to have this type of attention. There is nothing cool about the allegations I am facing," I said.

"Did you do all that stuff that they are accusing you of?" Jonny asked.

"I'm gonna pour myself a drink. Have you tried alcohol yet?" I asked.

"Ummm..." Jonny hesitated.

"You don't have to lie to me, Jonny," I said.

"Okay, yes I have, but I've never been drunk or anything like that. A few of my friends go out and get drunk and stuff, but that's not my style," Jonny said.

"Fair enough. Well, I would like for us to have our first official drink together. I'm a vodka-and-club-soda guy. Here's a glass. Try some and let me know what you think," I said.

"Arrrgh, it's a bit strong," Jonny said.

"Ha-ha, I know. Now here's the thing, I have been involved in things that I am not proud of. Some of my business dealings haven't been on the up and up. Growing up where I did and in the times that I did, I was exposed to a lot of bad stuff. As a result, I've had to be involved in shady dealings with shady people. However, I have cleaned up my businesses to a point where they are ninety percent legit. The plan is to get all the businesses I own clean and legit over the next five to eight years. So that by the time you and your sister come to inherit all of it, it will be completely clean," I said.

"I understand Dad, you did what you had to do. Nothing will ever change the fact that I love and respect you," Jonny said.

"Son, that is the best thing I have heard in a long time. Come here, you," I said.

Jonny was a smart kid, and the conversation we had made me a bit emotional. Kids are very forgiving. One will gain their trust and respect as long as you're honest with them and don't treat them like idiots. From that moment on, I decided I was never going to hide things from the kids.

Chapter 29

Success
Where: Dominguez residence, North Walnut Grove, Miami
When: 0730 hours, Thursday, June 7, 2012
Currency: US dollar

It was graduation day, and Eddie was excited that high school was finally over. He would be moving on to college, where he would have more flexibility in what and when he wanted to study. Anna was very proud of her son. Despite all the trauma Eddie had experienced, he still maintained good grades. He also helped her in the restaurant most days after school, which was a difficult task. Most kids only needed to worry about homework, but Eddie was juggling many things at his young age. Anna couldn't be prouder.

It had been a few months since the drug-dealing escapade, and Eddie and his friends had made a significant amount of money. So much that Raphael opened his own restaurant and stopped dealing drugs altogether. He still dabbled in petty scams here and there, but nothing major enough to land him years in prison. Eddie, Alex, and Chris saved the majority of their money. Eddie was becoming a money-making machine. He was earning money from restaurant profits; he still had the money he found in his father's stash; and there was the regular income from the cartel operations.

Eddie and Anna agreed it would be a good idea to carry out some major upgrades to the restaurant, so it was given a complete face-lift. Everything from floor to ceiling had either been replaced or refurbished. However, Eddie left instructions that the store room was not to be touched. With this, the restaurant started pulling in even more customers than it had before. Due to the increase in customers, Eddie and Anna agreed to hire a couple of people to help Anna with the workload. This made even more sense because Eddie was going to be enrolled in college after the summer break. Trying to juggle the restaurant business as well as the cartel business would be a stretch, to say the least. As far as Anna was concerned, Eddie no longer being able to help at the restaurant was a good thing. For her it felt great knowing her son was going to be enrolled in college, and the restaurant was gaining its first employees. Eddie had managed to attain a level of financial success his father hadn't reached. As much as Anna hated being involved with the cartel, she couldn't deny that if it wasn't for their involvement, they wouldn't have been able to achieve everything they had.

Eddie felt a sense of accomplishment: At his young age he was basically in charge of his family's income and safety; he was an outstanding student; and a businessman well on his way to becoming a millionaire. He was always cautious about how he spent his money. He made sure he wasn't flashy, didn't draw attention to himself and have law enforcement poking around.

Eddie and his Assembly, Alex and Chris, all purchased outfits for the graduation party. The boys were draped in Italian suits, shoes, and accessories. Their pact to refrain from making extravagant purchases was broken for this special occasion. The boys were comfortable with making a splash, because other parents would be spending extra to make sure their children looked great for the graduation ceremony and party. The party would be held in the school's gym later that evening, and the boys had hired a limousine to take them to the party and drop them home afterwards. The minimal-spending pact would be reinstated after graduation until they were able to prove that the purchase of any luxurious goods was done using legitimate funds.

"Good morning, Mom," Eddie said.

"There he is, look at you. You have grown so much," Anna said.

"Awww, come on, Mom, don't get emotional on me."

"Don't get emotional! Boy, it's my job to get emotional. Listen, I need to give you something."

"Oh. What is it, Mom?"

"Here, open the box."

"Oh Mom, you didn't have to do this."

"Edwardo, just open the box."

"Okay, okay…oh, is it, it's Dad's watch. Wow!"

"He would have loved for you to have it. Look at the inscription underneath."

"To Edwardo, a good son."

"You look upset, don't be. Your father is looking down from heaven, and I know he is smiling at you right now. He was proud of you, Edwardo, he really was."

"Thank you, Mom, this is the best gift ever."

"Just be careful, an expensive watch like that is eye-catching. I'm even having second thoughts about you wearing it today."

"Don't worry, Mom, you know I'm protected. We all are. I'll see you later, okay?"

When Eddie stepped out of the house, there were three SUVs parked out front. A man from the SUV in the middle emerged from the front passenger side and opened the back door. Eddie saw Hector Gallegos in the back seat, so walked over and hopped in.

"Good morning, Mr. Gallegos," Eddie said.

"Hey, young Soap, my man. Congratulations on your graduation," Hector said.

"How did you know?" Eddie asked.

"Come on, I have kids too. Us parents have to be aware of the things happening in school," replied Hector.

"That makes sense," Eddie said.

"I got you a little graduation present," said Hector.

"Wow, there's about twenty thousand dollars in

here!" Eddie said.

"We look after our own," said Hector.

"Thank you so much, Mr. Gallegos," Eddie said.

"I think it's time you knew my real name. It's Manuel Guzman."

"Huh, but you look more like a 'Hector Gallegos,'" said Eddie.

"Ha-ha-ha, I like that. Most people don't know the names of senior cartel members, street-level guys don't even know who we are. That's how we're able to stay under the radar and operate the way we do. I told your mother my name was Hector Gallegos, because I wasn't sure what kind of encounter I was going to have, with your family. Now that you are a my protégé, it's only fair that you know my name. I am taking you places, Edwardo, you just have to follow my instructions, and I promise that you will thrive in this business," Manuel said.

"I am ready to do whatever you tell me to do," Eddie replied.

"Good. Listen, we have some serious business to discuss. Have you ever heard of the Carlsdale family?" Manuel said.

"Yes, before my dad died, he told me they might cause trouble for Sin Nombre," Eddie replied.

"That's right, we've had full control of our territories for the last fifteen years. Other families have been trying to get our territories, but we've not allowed them. The Carlsdales were close, but we've been able to fend them off. As you probably know, the head of that family, Devin, recently escaped custody, and word on the street is he is planning a strike to try to take over a number of territories. Since his incarceration, his business has taken a hit, and he's looking to make up for previous losses. The truth is that we don't know how long he'll be on the run before he gets caught, if he ever gets caught. All I know is that we have to take him out. He is a problem for us, and he has always been a problem. Being out of prison just gives him a clearer mind and an opportunity to mobilize his people against us. We think he will attempt to start a war with Sin Nombre, and we're ready for him. We have many more soldiers than we did when he tried to attack us in the past. This time we won't wait for him to attack, we will strike first. I know there will be some backlash for this, so for this reason we will be shutting down some of our key operations for a couple of weeks. This includes the restaurant," Said Manuel.

"Oh, the restaurant?" Asked Eddie.

"Yes. Guillermo's Cabana, along with a few other businesses, are our main storage facilities. Your restaurant has a good reputation and is one of the cleanest businesses we use. If things go wrong and raids were carried out by law enforcement, your restaurant wouldn't even be on the cops' radar. We have to provide extra protection for you and your family for the next few weeks. Once everything dies down, you'll be able to reopen for business. Make sure you pass this information to your mother," said Manuel.

"Yes sir, Mr. Gallegos, I mean Mr. Guzman. I will tell her as soon as you leave. We will put a sign up saying that we are closed for refurbishment," Eddie said.

"Very smart," said Manuel.

"I take it you want this done right away?" Eddie asked.

"Yes," Manuel responded.

"Okay, I'll take care of it as soon as you leave," said Eddie.

"Good. Something else I wanted to talk to you about is other opportunities within the cartel. Now, what are you plans after you graduate?" Manuel asked.

"I will attend college here in Miami after the summer break. I want to get a degree in business, so I can be a better businessman for the cartel," replied Eddie.

"Kid, I knew I liked you the moment that I saw you. That is a very good idea. You have foresight and you already think like a boss. Stick with me and I will make you a boss before you know it. Now, the reason I asked about your next plan was that since we terminated Zorro Loco, we've not been able to fill his position. I was thinking maybe you would like to take his place. Do you think you could handle that?" Manuel said.

"It depends on how much time I have to put in, I will still need time for studies," Eddie replied.

"Yes, I am aware of that. Basically, all you have to

do is distribute product to the street dealers in Zorro's old neighbourhood and make rounds to collect money from sales once a week. All the money you collect will be delivered directly to me. So, it's basically this new job as well as carrying on with the current arrangement at the restaurant. Can you make that happen? Of course, you would receive the same amount that Zorro received when he was doing the job," Manuel said.

"If that's all that I have to do, I don't think there will be any problem," Eddie said.

"Music to my ears. Now, because you are my protégé, you will be assigned a couple of extra security guys who will follow you everywhere to keep you safe. The guys who currently watch your house and the restaurant will still be there as well," said Manuel.

"Thank you, Mr. Guzman," Eddie said.

"Don't worry about it, young Soap, we look after our own. However, I have one warning for you: It goes without saying you should never ever rat on this family, there is nothing worse than that. Also, if you ever steal from Sin Nombre or betray us in any way, you and your entire family will die. Is that clear?" Manuel asked.

"Very clear, sir," Eddie replied.

"Good. Now off you go, I'll be in touch. Happy graduation," Manuel said.

"Thanks, Mr. Guzman," Eddie replied.

Eddie went back inside and told Anna about shutting down the restaurant, but he didn't tell her that he had just gotten in even deeper with the cartel by accepting Zorro Loco's old position. He felt this wasn't something she needed to know, because all she would do was worry about him all the time. Anna didn't hesitate about closing the restaurant.

Eddie and his Assembly showed up at school that morning in style. They were the best-dressed students, and this gave them a sense of pride. The boys had garnered the respect of everyone in the school over the last few months—the students could tell something was different about them. It wasn't the fact they were now selling merchandise at the highest rate ever, but because they were able to get their hands on cherished, high-quality, hard-to-come-by items that weren't available at retail. The boys had maximized their inventory and were importing clothing, sneakers, and electronics directly from China. All their stuff was bought at wholesale prices and then resold for a 100 to 150 percent profit.

What was more perplexing was that although the boys weren't overly flashy, they weren't dressed shabbily, either. They just had an extra bounce in their step, and they were very confident, and this resonated with the other students. Later that evening, the boys showed up to the school in a brand-new white limousine. In the limo were Eddie's security guys, who kept an eye on the doors as the kids went into the school building. The party ended around 10:30 that evening, and some kids decided to go out clubbing, but Eddie and the boys went home.

Chapter 30

Business as Usual
Where: Edom Group, The United Nations of Europe and Americas, Milwaukee, Wisconsin
When: 0935 hours, Monday, November 11, 2041
Currency: UNEA credits

Monday morning, the CSOs and I met at the office to go over business matters, and Joe was present to go over other trial preparations. There were a few things I wanted to go over business-wise. In terms of the first shipment of erratanite, we needed to draw up a business strategy that mapped out product design, production, testing, marketing, and distribution. As far as trial preparation, we still needed to come up with a plan to deal with the conspiracy charge.

"So, after all the drama in the AU, I can gladly say that the erratanite deal has been finalized, and we will get our shipment soon. As it stands, we know that we can use erratanite in a new line of body armour and perhaps in vehicular armoury as well. The light-weight nature of erratanite makes it the perfect solution, not to mention that it is not currently on the market. This puts us in a perfect position, we will be the first company to roll this out, and we can charge premium prices for all products. So, I need you guys to liaise with your teams to start researching other solutions where erratanite can be implemented and to create an initial draft for design and implementation. Joe, I need you to get someone to look at the legal side of things to see if there are any other regulatory or safety issues we may not have considered," I said.

"Alex and I will brief the directors in the armoury department on both sides of the Nations. As soon as we get the first draft in place, we'll bring that back to you for sign-off," Chris said.

"As far as I'm concerned, the only issue I think might come up is pricing. There are already a few products out there that are almost capable of doing what erratanite can do. How do we convince people to buy our product if we're charging more?" Alex asked.

"Simple, Alex, marketing. This stuff will pretty much sell itself once people know what they are getting. We know it won't be street-level goons who will be buying this stuff. It'll be high-profile individuals, private security firms, and wholesale armoury distributors. So, where are we with the conspiracy charge, Joe?" I asked.

"I've gone over this one over and over again, but I haven't been able to come up with anything yet. They've got a recording and they've got a witness, and I don't have a legal strategy for now. With that said, if something was to happen to the audio file and Jonah

Balenciaga was to mysteriously go missing, it would be very advantageous. Seriously though, Fredric and I haven't stopped working on it, we will keep trying to find a way," Joe said.

"Nah, you might have a point there. While you look into the legal side of dealing with this, the CSOs and I will see what we can do regarding the file and Balenciaga," I said.

I could always count on Joe to be straight with me. The audio file is probably out of reach and might have been copied across a few secured storage devices. This wouldn't stop us from trying to find someone who has access to all copies of the file. Jonah Balenciaga had disappeared immediately after he posted bail, so killing him is proving a bit difficult. People were saying he'd been staying out of the public eye in an effort to avoid the media and paparazzi. However, it would have been obvious to anyone with a brain that Jonah would be fully aware that his life was in danger and my men would be coming after him. There was also the possibility that he'd struck a deal with the enforcers and turned Nation's evidence. The fact that the evidence was so strong meant that Jonah's options were limited: it was either prison, death, or chirping. The more I thought about it, the more I leaned towards the notion that he might be in witness protection.

"Does anyone have a line on Jonah yet?" I asked.

"Not yet, Dom," said Alex.

"Well, what are we waiting for? Please get a move

on this, guys. Do I need to remind you of what's at stake here?" I said raising my voice.

"We are on it, Dom," said Chris.

"Please get hold of the tech kid, see if there's anything he can do about that audio file," I said.

"No worries, Dom, I'll sort that out," said Alex.

Wisconsin Governor Dave Easterman was as shady as they come. He and his colleagues were blocking several contract applications from Edom Group. I recently made a proposal to take over some of the abandoned inner-city buildings for development. My plan was to refurbish the old buildings and rent them out as apartments and offices. Other applications included restaurant and alcohol licenses, but these were declined as well. He was hell-bent on making sure that none of my innovation plans would see the light of day. All it took was one call from Easterman, and his friends would shut down proposals I made to their offices as well. This was frustrating to say the least, and this was why I had initially plotted to kill him. I later decided to hold off on killing Easterman. It would bring a lot of heat on me, so a more subtle approach was required.

Prior to my decision, I held a meeting with Jonah, and offered him a huge number of credits to provide intel on his boss. In exchange for the credits, he provided me with the governor's daily itinerary for an entire month. This included the governor's exact whereabouts at any given moment.

It was during this meeting that I let Jonah know I

was going to kill his boss. For some reason he didn't seem to care: he just wanted his credits. I told him that confidentiality was of the utmost importance and that being a friend of ours could prove profitable for him in the future. I made him aware the alternative would be killing him and wiping out his family if word ever got out that I was plotting to kill the governor. For this reason, I wasn't convinced that Jonah was aware of the recording—he had too much to lose. However, now that the prosecution had evidence of our conversation, I wouldn't be surprised to find that Jonah had struck a deal with the enforcers in exchange for his freedom in witness protection. It did seem the coward was willing to jeopardize his family's lives to spare his own, because his family was still very much around, despite knowing what we would do to them.

"Dom, still no word on Jonah. However, Matt said that the last signal trace from Jonah's comms was at his family house shortly after he posted bail. Apparently, he had been speaking to a colleague for three minutes and five seconds. We don't know what the call was about, but Matt is currently trying to retrieve that call from a secured database," Alex said.

"That's good. Look, since we haven't heard from Jonah, send our guys in to take one of the children," I said.

Around 12:30 we decided to take a break. I needed some fresh air, so I suggested that we should head to Sergio's for lunch. Brandon called Sergio's to let them know we were on our way.

When we arrived at Sergio's, a table had been set for us. As we walked towards our table, people who were having lunch paused and either gave me a nod or stood up to say hello. I shook as many hands as I could before sitting down, and we spent our time there discussing sports and politics. As we were talking among ourselves, I couldn't help but think that it would be advantageous to get a few more politicians in our corner. None of the stuff I was presently going through would have happened if I was connected to a few more politicians. One of our immediate agendas would be to reach out to politicians across the Nations and figure out a way to win them over.

"Dom, the thing we spoke about just before coming here..." Chris said.

"Yeah..." I replied

"It's done," Chris said.

"Good. Someone needs to have the conversation with the kid to see if they know where our friend is," I whispered.

"I've already sent someone," said Alex.

"Well done, Alex. Okay then, let's head back to the office and wrap things up. Joe, I guess you can go now. Unless there is something else you need to share, of course," I said.

"Nope, I'm going to head back to my office to do some more work on the case. See you later Dom. Alex, Chris..." Joe said.

"See you, Joe," Alex said.

"Yeah, see you, bud," said Chris.

The people in the restaurant posed a risk, and I wasn't sure Sergio's was a hundred percent bug free, so we went back to the office where we could speak freely. When we got back, I made my intention for Jonah's kid very clear. I didn't know Jonah's wife or kids; I didn't know if the person we took was male or female. What I did know was that if he or she didn't know where their dad was, our foot soldiers would spread the word. If Jonah still refused to make himself available, we would kill the kid within twenty-four hours. If after killing the first kid Jonah still didn't come out of hiding, we would kill the rest of his family. I didn't want things to go down this route, and I normally wouldn't involve women or children in Assembly business. It was a tough decision, but one I had to make, all the same. We couldn't show weakness, we had to let people know what happened to those who crossed us.

"I just don't understand people, you know. Jonah knew the score, why would he put his family through this?" I said.

"Some people are just selfish; they only care about themselves. People like this, they are cut from a different cloth from us. No Honour, no integrity," Chris said.

"That's right, Chris. Honour is just an empty word now, and it seems integrity has also become non-existent. Seriously though, we have to make sure the conspiracy charge goes away," I said.

"Don't worry, the foot soldiers have been dispatched," Alex said.

"So, cocaine. How are we doing numbers-wise?" I asked.

"Not bad, the numbers are good. People are gradually going back to the old-school stuff now instead of synthetics," Alex said.

"That's good news, I guess. Things will probably change if we're able to successfully complete Matt Harrington's Project Neon. We should probably start thinking about how to kick off the project. We can probably use the proceeds from the coke," I said.

"Sounds like a good idea, Dom," Chris said.

"Are we sure we'll be able to cover the cost?" Alex asked.

"Alex, what is up with you, what's up with the negativity?" I said, raising my voice for the second time in one day.

"Hey, I'm just saying..." replied Alex.

"Yeah, okay. I'm done here, I'm going home, guys," I said.

After I got home, I spent the entire evening thinking about the decision I made on Jonah's kid. This really bothered me. I felt like I had become desensitized to a lot of the things that had happened over the years. Things couldn't carry on like this. The following day, I would be giving the order to spare the kid's life.

I had been thinking about moving my dad's coffin

to Milwaukee from Miami. I wanted to have him buried at the far end of our estate near the plot of land by the river. The logistics of moving a corpse from one state to another was quite complicated, but it was worth doing. It meant that I would no longer need to do trips to Miami just to visit his gravesite. This would also mean a lot to my mom, who hadn't been to the gravesite in a couple of years.

Something else that had been on my mind was Project Neon. It had been a while since our discussion with Matt, it was time to get that show on the road. Even if we opted not to use cocaine funds, Edom Group still had enough legal funds to at least kick off the project. I wasn't sure what Alex's problem was about this; it was simply a case of giving the order for things to get started. It's probably nothing though. With everything that has been going on, he might genuinely just be worried about the amount of funds available at the moment. I'll have a one-to-one conversation with him at some point, just to see where his head is at.

To be continued ...

Printed in Great Britain
by Amazon